Steel

Armageddon

By
Jorgen Flood

Tank Battles, Love and Survival in WW II and the Cold War

Published by Jorgen Flood at CreateSpace

COVER PAGE BY

Arne Ragnar Johannesen

MAIN CHAPTERS:

Matilda

Churchill

Panzer III

King Tiger

Fiat M 13/40

IS-2

JagdPanzer IV

Centurion

T-34/85

T-54

STEEL ARMAGEDDON
*
AUSTRIA, APRIL 1945
*

Guderian's Duck, what a name for a tank. Whoever came up with that one had to have a pretty sick sense of humor. Carl-Fredrik Johnsen (Carl to his friends) was peering through the telescope of his Jagdpanzer IV "Lang", towards the Russian lines. Well, at least it was a hell of an angry duck, he chuckled, laughing quietly at the thought of an angry duck attacking a tank. He suddenly became aware that the rest of the crew was eying him strangely, wondering if he had finally lost it.

"Ha,hrm" he cleared his throat to hide the smear on his face. At least this killer duck had the excellent L-70 long barreled 75 mm gun, able to smash any Russian, or Allied, tank that ventured into its path. Previous models had the L-48, same caliber but less powerful. The only disadvantage with the heavier L-70 was it made the tank a bit front heavy and unwieldy, but its power more than made up for that inconvenience. The popular name of Guderian's Duck was unofficial, but had caught on. Guderian was of course the brilliant and respected German Panzer General, popularly called 'schneller Heinz', while the origin of the "duck" name was more obscure. It was probably the low silhouette and somewhat wobbly movement that gave the vehicle its unofficial name.

"Carl, can you see the enemy?" Fritz asked. He was the loader. Inside the tank they were on a first name basis. Outside they used officer titles.

"No, not yet", he answered, "but, I am sure they are right around the corner. Check that you have AP (Armor Piercing) and not HE (High Explosive)" he said, rather unnecessarily. Fritz was far too experienced to make that kind of mistake, and now he looked a bit annoyed at being asked to double check his work.

Fritz had, yet hated, the ultimate German name, but he was a nice guy, quiet and reliable. They all knew the Soviet nickname for any German soldier was Fritz, and often teased him it was all due to his looks. He took it well, but the jokes were a bit worn by now. In fact Carl's full crew of three were great guys. They had been together for two years, a very long time for any tank crew in this war.

Their current vehicle was named "Mutti 6", indicating it was the 6th. vehicle Carl had commanded. The first two had been Panzer Mk. III models, then various versions of the Panzer Mk. IV. Their current Jagdpanzer IV was essentially a Mk. IV without a turret, which allowed a bigger gun and a lower silhouette. It also facilitated a reduction in crew size from five to four. Unfortunately the lack of a turret meant it could not fight offensively. That was not a major concern at this stage of the war. The Jagd (Hunting) name indicated that it was meant for hunting enemy tanks. Every time they had traded tanks for one reason or another, they had hoped for a Panzer VI (Tiger) or Panzer V (Panter) but were disappointed when they received another version of the Mk. IV. It was a good tank though, in fact the only German tank that was produced throughout the war. At a disadvantage against the new Russian T-34/85's, it could still hold its own against most enemy vehicles, even now in 1945. Besides, it was extremely reliable, an advantage the more flashy Panter and Tiger tanks did not share.

He looked at the rest of his, by now admittedly pretty shabby looking, crew. Gone were the days of fancy uniforms. Peter, the driver, was slightly older than the others, close to 30, with a good sense of humor. Hans, the wireless operator, was in his early twenties (like the rest of the crew) but a bit gloomy. Once you got used to it, it was OK though.

They were part of the 6th Panzer Army under General Sepp Dietrich. With remnants of the Waffen SS Viking division they were trying to stop Ivan before he reached Vienna and the rest of Austria. A hopeless task, but then they all knew the war was lost. The joke among the troops was that they were called the

6. Panzer Army because they only had six panzers left. Oh yes, there were a few fanatics who still believed in a victorious Germany, wonder weapons that would turn the allied fortunes upside down, but most knew it was all over. In fact Carl had known it since the Wehrmacht lost the battle of Kursk two years ago, the last large scale German offensive. After Kursk they always encountered endless streams of Russian tanks and soldiers, backed up by an ever growing air arm. You did not have to be a General to realize it was too late for Germany, all you needed was a little common sense, and a less fanatical outlook on life. In addition to the problems in the east, they also heard from other soldiers about the ever increasing number of defeats in the West, where the allied air forces were wearing down the Luftwaffe and chasing it from the sky. Every time somebody had been on R&R back home, they returned full of stories about German cities being reduced to ruins, one after the other. With low voices they told how many friends and relatives had been killed, and so on. The last bit of bad news was that Italy had been knocked out of the fight while Finland had switched sides.

Despite this knowledge they continued to follow orders. Defections and desertions were becoming more commonplace, and most soldiers were tempted to "leave" at various times. However, with fanatical SS bands roaming the countryside behind them, and the vengeful Russkis in front of them, defections were decidedly a risky business. Both groups were ready to shoot or hang any lone soldier or perceived deserter at sight. Most soldiers therefore found it best to hang on. Besides, where should they go? The whole world seemed to be united against Germany and the soldiers fighting for her at this stage, even previous allies. Interrupting his own thoughts before he became completely lost in memories, he took a minute to scan the sky for hostile aircraft. Luckily there were none. The Red Air Force, though powerful, was not such an omnipresent force as the air forces of the western allies. The saying among the harassed Wehrmacht infantry was that a silver aircraft was American, a blue aircraft was English and an invisible aircraft was German. He smiled to himself, and yet they said the Germans did not appreciate humor.

Carl knew the end would be terrible, the hatred towards the Germans in general, and the SS in particular, meant no mercy could be expected, from the Russians or anybody else. The western allies had added to this feeling among the German populace with their 'Unconditional Surrender' demand. Carl had also seen the incredible brutality displayed by some SS units, and not only in the East. It was inconceivable to him that they acted that way, it only created enemies everywhere. In fact the Germans had initially been received as liberators in many parts of Ukraine and White Russia, but before long the blood thirsty 'SS Sonderkommandos' with their crazy racial policies and general terror tactics, had turned the population away from Hitler and back to Stalin. Thus, despite all the horrors Stalin had unleashed upon his own population with deportations and executions, by allotment no less, it was soon forgotten in a universal hatred of the foreign invaders, the Nazi's. Carl had a strong suspicion that the revenge and following treatment of the German soldiers would be handed out without regard to how guilty or innocent the individual was with regard to those crimes. He had also heard the rumors of the extermination camps. If that was true, and it probably was he decided, all hell would break loose. It was one of those things you heard about, but found it best to ignore, better not to know.

Finally, there was another thing, the victors wrote the history. Soviet atrocities would certainly be excused or glossed over as revenge or justified retribution, even though many of them, not least the mass murder of 25,000 Polish officers in the Katyn forest, had taken place before Russia and Germany were at war. The indiscriminate bombing of civilians was another tragic part of this war. For some reason it was deemed terror bombing when the Germans did it, but other names such as carpet bombing or strategic bombing was used when the allies did the same. German soldiers and officers often listened to the BBC in secret, which interestingly enough was considered by many the most reliable radio station, and he had noticed those subtle changes in describing what was essentially the same activity.

Oh what the hell, he thought, at least I know from the BBC that I have to stay away from the US and Norway. He was very aware that the vast majority of Norwegians sympathized with the Allies, and after the war all the fence-sitters would certainly come forward claiming they were "good" Norwegians, whatever that meant. The problem with the fence sitters was that they had to show themselves super patriotic once the danger was over. That invariably meant being harsher on the losing side than those who had participated would be. His parents would be OK, after all they lived in the US. In their last letter they told him his younger brother had been called up for the US Air Force. The funny thing was that if he had known, or suspected, that the US would enter the war against Germany, he would not have volunteered for service against the Soviets. He had made a mess of his future, which became very obvious the moment he heard about Pearl Harbor and the grand alliance against Germany and Japan. The new alliance made him realize he was in a way fighting against his own brother. By then it was too late to change direction, which meant he had to live with his decision for many years. Unlike most of his comrades, his knowledge of the size and industrial potential of the US meant he had always known that Germany could not win a war against the US, Great Britain and the Soviet Union, particularly not fighting all three at the same time. Thus, he had long ago decided he would have to stay in central Europe after the war, if he survived the fighting that was, but the question was where?

'What was that?' Suddenly he became aware of movement, and the present returned with a jolt. He could see something through the periscope, but was not certain what, or rather who it was. It seemed like shadows moving back and forth. The periscope was a damned nuisance, always fogging up, but he did not dare to open the hatch. He had seen too many tank commanders, including one of his own, cut down by snipers or shrapnel.

"Kanone Bereicht?" (gun ready) he called out.

"Jawohl" came the answer.

There it was, the shadows finally materialized through the fogged up scope. The emerging shape was unmistakable, a heavy tank, but which one, he had not seen it before. He looked at his recognition sketches, supplied by HQ, and there it was. One of the new IS-2's, a 45 ton behemoth with a huge, but slow firing, 122 mm gun. The abbreviated name IS was a tribute to Josef Stalin. It was closely followed by 2 T-34's, both of them the older T34/76 model and an American built Sherman. The Russians had received thousand of tanks from the Western allies. Then came the infantry, spread out like a fan behind them. The tank formation was optimized for field of fire, flank protection and ease of maneuver. Ivan had come a long way over the years, and now they were as skilful as any in tank warfare, particularly the elite Red Guard units. One aspect still surprised the Germans though, Russian infantry was usually riding on the tanks, a very dangerous proposition.

"It is an IS-2, let's take it out." Carl said.

The urge to fire right away was almost unstoppable, but he forced himself to wait till he had the perfect shot. The Russkis had not detected him, and the way they were moving presented him with beautiful side silhouettes. A big advantage since even his L-70, one of the best tank guns of the war, could not be trusted to crack the frontal armor of an IS-2 if the angle of the shot was off. Thus he wanted to be certain of a kill on his first try. Too bad he was alone in this position, or they could have taken out the whole column. Five Seconds later he let the L-70 roar, the muzzle flash pointing directly at the IS-2. It was a beautiful shot, hitting the turret side, penetrating, then causing a tremendous internal explosion. Red and yellow flames were shooting out in every direction, almost like a fresco painting. The turret spiraled upwards almost like a ballerina. The shot had set off the tanks internal ammunition.

"Bulls eye." he screamed excitedly, the adrenaline pumping.

"New target."

It was almost too late, a T-34 was turning its turret towards them. Carl fired the next shot, but the second he pulled the trigger he realized he had rushed it and missed.

"Verdammt", he yelled. Now it was the Russians turn. He could see the smoke and muzzle flash, followed by the grenade approaching them, as in slow motion. It was like watching a doomsday projectile approaching, against which they were helpless. He closed his eyes and braced for the impact. There was tremendous 'thud', the whole tank shook, but the grenade did not penetrate, just bounced harmlessly upwards. Thank god it was a 76mm Carl thought, the new 85mm equipped T-34 would certainly have split us open like a can of sardines.

"Reverse" he said to the driver. Their position had been carefully planned against the trees, with a narrow field of fire, which was just as well since the Jagdpanzer had limited traverse for its gun. It was a Panzer IV tank modified with a fixed superstructure. At this stage of the war, the Mk. IV was outmoded, at least against the latest Russian tanks. However somebody had the good sense to keep the production line open, and to modify it in a way that allowed it to keep fighting. The solution had been to remove the turret, slope the frontal armor, and put a small 'box' on top of the base vehicle. This allowed a more powerful gun, better armor protection and a low silhouette. It also made the tank easier, faster and cheaper to produce. Well needed at a time when the German Panzerwaffe (armored units) were heavily outnumbered on all fronts. The downside was that the gun would only traverse a few degrees to either side or the whole tank had to be turned. As such the "Duck" was useless in an offensive mobile battle. Its purpose was mainly defensive, but what the hell, all their battles were defensive anyway.

The driver shifted gear, gunned the 300 HP 12 cylinder Maybach engine, which responded reliably as always, and backed into their fallback position. To the right, almost a mile away, he could see one of the new Tiger II (Kingtiger) tanks positioned. A 68 ton monster with an extremely powerful 88 mm gun. A monster maybe, but a good one to lean on in a tight spot. He turned his sights towards the enemy again. The two sleek looking and deadly T-34's and the Sherman were racing towards them. He carefully aimed at the Sherman and fired. A hit, the tank stopped dead in its tracks, the crew jumped out and the tank started to burn furiously.

"Don't waste time on the crew" he said, as they were easy targets for the machine gun, but he really could see no point in it killing these guys, not now, not so close to the end.

"New target, take the next T........"

It was all he had time to say before the world exploded around them. It felt like somebody lifted him up, slapped him around, then threw him down on the floor. Slowly he regained his senses, realizing what had happened, the Russian got them first.

"Abandon tank, we are on fire", he heard someone scream, then realized it was Hans. He looked around in the smoke, the stench was terrible, Fritz was but a bloody mess, obviously dead. Peter was nowhere to be seen. He grabbed one of the escape hatches, but it did not move. He shook it with a strength born of desperation, swearing like a madman. Suddenly it came loose, and with a tremendous sigh of relief he opened it and crawled, or rather fell, out of the tank. Machine gun bullets from the approaching enemy tanks hit the side of Mutti like hail in a storm. Yet he was not hit and managed to crawl about 10 feet away from the burning tank before he collapsed on the ground. After a few seconds, that felt like hours, his head and sight cleared and now he became aware that the two remaining T-34's were boring down on him, their machine gun still blazing. To his dismay he noticed they had been joined by a third T-34, one that he had not seen before. This one was a T-34/85, probably the one that got them he determined. For tankers, as for pilots, it is the one you don't see that brings you down. Additionally, he could also see several squads of infantry. There was no reason to run, in his current state he would not get very far. This is it he thought, I've had it, but he was too shaken even to raise his hands to surrender. It was really too bad to die so close to the end, after having survived so many near hits and other dangers. His parents would miss him of course, but not many others. Suddenly one of the T-34's exploded, and it was as if it replayed the end of the IS a few minutes earlier, the turret flying upwards in a slow spiral against the blue sky. Actually it was rather beautiful to look at he determined in his dazed state, and then the other T-34 blew up a few seconds later.

"Fantastic shooting" he screamed, as much to himself as to anybody else, "Dank Gott for the Konigstiger". With the two lead enemy tanks gone, the remaining T-34 and the Russian infantry withdrew quickly. It became quiet, eerily quiet, only the dying flames of the burning Jagdpanzer hissed in the background. Even the Kingtiger had disappeared. He had noticed something similar many times on the Eastern Front. How the Russians came out of the steppes for an attack, and how, if they were repulsed, they seemed to disappear into the steppes, just leaving a heap of dead and wounded men in front of the German lines. He was used to it by now, but it never ceased to amaze him how even relatively large bodies of men could disappear so suddenly. Ivan was certainly brave enough, and they were fighting for home and country. Yet, the Red Army was also held together by a ferocious discipline, a discipline so hard they executed their own men at a rate that had not been seen since the days of the Roman army. They probably had to, Carl reasoned, considering that their tactics displayed a near total lack of concern for own troop losses. In fact he knew, like most German soldiers, that even at this late stage of the war their attacks caused higher losses for them than for the Wehrmacht. 'Zhukov has to be the only commander in history that is considered a military genius, even though he almost always loses more men than his opponent', Carl had said jokingly to his men at one stage.

"What a ride" Hans suddenly said and sat down next to him. Carl had not even noticed him before he spoke,

"Sure" was all he responded. Then they just sat there for what seemed an eternity.

"Fritz is dead." Carl said.

"I noticed him too, but I have no idea what happened to Peter" Hans said, "though he probably died inside Mutti. What now?"

"This is it for me," Carl said, "I am through with this war, they can continue without me."

"I thought the same. It won't last long anyway. What will you do? Go back to Norway or America? If that is the case we can travel north together."

Carl had told his crew in confidence that his parents lived in the US. He looked up at the alps, and it suddenly struck him.

"No, I don't think I will be welcome there, better to go south" he said, "to Italy. What about you?"

"Hamburg" Hans responded, "I have to see if my family is still around."

"Good, look out for the SS bands." Carl said. They shook hands quickly, then left in opposite directions. It was notable that they did not mention their dead comrades. Not out of disrespect, but simply self preservation. You always had to move on, push all thoughts of death around you out of your mind without hesitation. Nevertheless, it was a strange feeling, such a short farewell after so many years of friendship, so many experiences that could not be described. They were young men, but over the last few years they had been through experiences and hardships no men should have to go through.

He walked for hours, heading into the hills. When he checked himself he found that his uniform was pretty burnt and unrecognizable, as was he. Nothing serious, just a number of painful first degree burns. It was not easy to see that he was a soldier. The strangest thing was that he did not see any other soldiers, a few refugees and civilians, but no soldiers. Towards the night thirst and hunger started to bother him. He saw a small cabin in the hillside. It looked abandoned, so he decided to spend the night there. It had a small hill behind it, while a small stream ran close to it in the front. Staggering over to the stream, he lay down on his stomach and started drinking, thinking this was probably not the healthiest water you could drink. He did not care though, he was too exhausted and too thirsty. After drinking what felt like an ocean he felt better, and crawled into the empty cabin, rolled over and fell asleep. Exhausted after what was, even by his standards, a very eventful day.

He woke up with the sun high in the sky, feeling better, but very hungry. There was an old mirror on the wall, but looking into it was a shock. He had several smaller, if not serious, burns, was grimy and dirty, and in general looked much older than his 23 years. Looking around the cabin he noticed somebody had left their old work clothes there. He decided to put them on, and get rid of the uniform. They were ill fitting, but at least he looked more like a farm hand than a tank commander. Outside again, he went to the stream, drank some more and tried to clean up. When he continued he looked like a farmer, all his uniform effects gone, but he kept his 9mm Luger pistol. All German officers received a Luger as his sidearm, and by now it felt almost like an extension of his arm. He decided to continue south, and as he walked on a plan took shape in his head. He would go to Naples. They had been stationed there some time ago, in preparation for the expected allied landings. Actually it had been more like an R&R, but instead of facing the western allies they were sent back to the Eastern Front before the Allies landed. It had been the best part of his war experience, he thought as he let the memories flow freely.

Her name was Teresa, or so she had said. She was a dark haired bar girl he started hanging out with. He knew she only looked at him as a customer, but it was OK. She was the only one of the bar girls that spoke German, and after the nightmares on the Eastern Front he needed some female companionship. Sex was one thing, but he needed more so they walked around the harbor quarter of Napoli (Naples), chatting and looking at the old monuments and villas. His father had been (was, he corrected himself) a history professor, and historical places interested him as well. What better place to go than Italy. Despite efforts to the contrary, he became very taken with the girl, and it was during one of their walks it happened.

He was in civilian clothes, and they passed an old lady who greeted them and said;

"Ciao Rachel". He could actually feel, as well as see, her face turning white with fear, and knew the truth right away

"You are jewish" he stated, not even asking. She did not even try to deny it, just looked at him frightened

"What will you do" she whispered, barely able to speak.

"Nothing," he said," your secret is safe with me, I don't believe all that nonsense about untermenschen anyway. People are people, that's all. They should answer for their actions, not their origin."

It was true, he had grown up in a liberal family, and all these racial theories the Nazis had were stupid, though he was careful not to say so in the company of fellow SS soldiers. He had signed up for what he saw as the ultimate anti communist crusade, and besides, he had been impressed by the German military, the uniforms, the precision. All exciting stuff for an impressionable young mind. Teresa (he still thought about her as Teresa) was so relieved she cried when he said he would not tell, and looked up at him with tremendous relief. After that they had a different relationship, she saw him as a person for the first time, not a customer. They grew quite attached, but a couple of months later he was shipped to the Eastern Front with his platoon. They had continued to exchange letters after their paths parted, until the ever increasing chaos of the war made further contacts impossible.

Now that he was on his way south he thought about contacting her again. Should he contact her! Was she still alive? How would she react? He had nothing better to do so he decided Naples would be his goal, it was as good a goal as any and he wanted to leave all this madness behind him. The next problem was to find out where he was. The street signs gave it away. In Austria still, which meant he had a long, very long, way to travel. With his experience from hiking in the Norwegian mountains he would be able to stay out of sight, i.e. high up in the hillsides, and only get down to lower elevations when he had to. His other asset, he decided, was that he spoke

English as well as Norwegian and German, which would give him a much better chance to talk himself out of a difficult situation.

However there was one thing he had to do before anything else, get rid of his SS tattoo, i.e. the blood type all SS soldiers had tattooed into their arm. He knew that just to scrape it off would leave a very suspicious and obvious scar. He had to shoot himself in the arm. Even that scar would be suspicious looking, but at least a little less so. Carl was not a man to linger or revisit a course of action once he had decided what to do. He found a quiet little ravine to dampen the sound from the shot, then pulled his Luger and pointed it straight at his arm. Then he lowered the gun, thinking that he had to shoot in such a way that the bullet would hit flesh not bones. I better take off the jacket first, that will make the wound as clean as possible, he thought. He also cut off a part of his shirt to use as a makeshift bandage. Following that he once again pointed the gun and pulled the trigger. The pain was terrible, much worse than he had expected. Nevertheless he forced himself to cut off more flesh with the knife to completely remove the tattoo. Pain and sweat raced through his body and he started to feel lightheaded. Quickly he bandaged the wound, then everything swirled madly, and Carl passed out.

He woke up a little later. From the position of the sun it looked like he had been out a couple of hours. As soon as he moved the pain hit him again, and he had problems walking due to dizziness. He realized he had bled quite a bit, more than he had planned for, and felt weak and exhausted. He had to sit down, then he tried once more to get up, but it was impossible.

"Too goddamn weak" he swore to himself, realizing he was close to passing out again. Fighting the nausea he checked his bandage, then let his consciousness go. The next time he woke up it was dark, he drank some water and felt a little bit better, but not enough to move on. Hunger was once more starting to bother him and he ate some of the leaves from the surrounding trees, hoping they were not poisonous. Apparently they were not, and though not exactly tasteful he got rid of the worst feelings of hunger, then fell asleep again.

The next day he stayed put, his arm was thumping and aching and he decided to wait a little longer before he moved on. It was beautiful here he thought, spending the day looking at the grass, the birds, the flowers. The war seemed distant, very distant, yet he knew it had not gone away, the pain in his arm testified to that. The hours went by, the young man dozing under the sun thought back, wondering how it had come to this. It all started during a visit to Norway. His parents had emigrated to the US when he was a baby, and as such he had dual citizenship. To keep in touch with his Norwegian 'roots' he had gone to Norway to visit his family in January 1940.

On the morning of April 9th he left his uncle's house in Trondheim, only to witness a shocking sight. German naval ships, headed by the heavy cruiser Hipper, were at anchor in the harbor. After the initial shock of the invasion, and the following battles, he, like most people, settled down to life in an occupied country. He telegraphed his parents that things were quiet now, and he would stay in Norway for another six months to a year. At this stage many Norwegians were still trying to make sense of what had happened, and resistance to the Germans was not all that strong. Many felt that England would be unable to survive long on its own, so better get along with the German controlled authorities. An exciting thing to do in this period was to look at the impressive German military parades through the city, and the big map on the city hall outlining the impressive string of victories the Germans had won. He and his friends would walk alongside the parades, like boys often do.

He ended up staying in Trondheim, and a year later, just after Germany invaded the Soviet Union, Carl, like thousands of volunteers in occupied countries decided to sign up for what was being heralded as the big crusade against communism. He never told that his parents lived in the US, and apparently that fact escaped the German authorities as well. After a crash course in German followed by boot camp, he was sent to the front. After a few months there he decided to apply for the Panzer core, and take an officer course. A year later he was accepted and attended the Panzerschule Putlos. Initially a wireless operator, then trying out all the different positions in the vehicle, he was promoted to tank commander after 12 eventful months. With the ever increasing losses experienced by the German forces, promotions came fast, if you survived that was. By now he knew his decision to join the Waffen SS had not been too smart, and that he had been way too naïve, yet at this stage in his 'career' it was actually easier to stay in uniform and leave out any second guessing of his decisions. Nothing good would come out of it, as he was already branded a collaborator in his adopted hometown of Trondheim.

"Now you will die, traitor"

The shout shook him out of his daydreaming, and startled he looked around, thinking the message had been for him. Nothing could be seen, but he could still hear sounds so hecrawled up a nearby hill to see what the commotion was all about.

*

WEREWOLF

*

The young man was tied up like a hog, his Wehrmacht uniform dirty and shredded. His face was white with fear, as he watched the SS Lieutenant and his soldiers throw a rope over a thick branch.

"Warum, the war is lost," he said, his voice cracking out of fear and trembling.

"It is, and it is because of scum like you, deserters that have betrayed Der Fuehrer" the lieutenant said, the fanatical smile broad on his face.

His two soldiers were a little less enthusiastic, but 'befehl ist befehl' (orders are orders) was what they were thinking. Carl walked over to them and saluted to the lieutenant, then remembered he was in civilian clothes. The lieutenant looked at him suspiciously, then started to lift his gun. Carl pulled up his gun as fast as possible, his eyes black from shock following his sudden realization that he was in a 'deserter's uniform, i.e. civilian clothes. He fired first, and aimed straight at the face of the officer. It was as if the head in front of him came apart, spraying them all with red disgusting brain tissue. Then, as the lieutenant collapsed, he quickly turned and pointed the gun at the two soldiers, both of whom had been too shocked to move.

"Drop your rifles" he said.

After a little hesitation they did as he said.

"The war is over, you can all leave." he said as he untied the young soldier "but leave your rifles behind". The young man just collapsed to the ground from sheer emotion, gratitude etched into his face. The two soldiers, still confused walked off.

"My name is Jurgen, Who are you?"

Carl gave him a fictitious name, and helped him up.

"You should be careful when you go back to Germany," Carl said, "there are many SS bands like these guys roaming the countryside. They are more fanatical than ever, now that the war is lost."

With this they walked off, one heading north the other south. Though he got out of the situation without any injuries, it had been a warning as well. He had to come up with a cover story, and a believable one, fast. And, not least, he had to stop saluting. The solution came to him as continued his trail south. He would claim he was Swedish. Sweden had been neutral, and except in the unlikely event that he met somebody from Scandinavia, people would not be able to distinguish between Norwegian and Swedish. The two languages are quite similar, more like heavy accents, and only native or fluent speaking Norwegians and Swedes would hear the difference.

The next few weeks were remarkably uneventful. He walked and stayed to himself. In the euphoria of peace, nobody took much notice of a single man walking south. The allied soldiers were busy partying, or escorting captured German soldiers. The fact that he walked south also made him less suspicious, German soldiers would of course travel north. He had the perfect (to him) cover story. He indicated that he had been a captured Swedish citizen caught up in the chaos of the end of the war in Northern Italy, and was now on his way to the Swedish embassy in Rome. However, he did not have to use his cover story very much, just keep walking. At this stage most people just wanted to get back to their peacetime activities, so even if they were suspicious, and some obviously were, they did not bother to get involved.

After he passed Rome he changed his story to that of being on his way to the Swedish naval consulate in Napoli. (He was wondering if such a thing existed) People were friendly, by and large they were relieved the war was over, and often shared some food. At one place he helped a farmer with a fence in exchange for something to eat. Taken together it was enough that he survived, but that was all, he got very thin and easily tired. After several weeks of walking he was in the suburbs of Napoli. There were allied soldiers everywhere, and it looked as if most of them were constantly drunk or in the midst of a hangover. Winner takes all he thought as he saw a bunch of happy GI's with local girls hanging around them. Mingling with the crowds of people moving back and forth he slipped into Napoli. It was easy to find her apartment, and eventually he was in front of Rachel's door and knocked. His heart was beating, would she take him in, or would she call the soldiers and tell them what he was !! Slowly the door opened.

*

WE'LL MEET AGAIN
*

Rachel was shocked when she saw Carl again. The straight handsome young man with the charming smile was gone, instead she felt as if she was looking at a ghost. His face looked ten years older, and he was skinny and undernourished. She held the door open and helped him in. Her apartment was not much, just one room with a bed and a small kitchen with a sink. In his exhausted state he said a few words she did not understand, probably Norwegian, she decided. Their common language was German, but she would have recognized English.

20

"Hush," she said, "you need a rest. Drink some water and lie down."

He smiled, and did as she said. Then collapsed exhausted on the bed and slept for 16 hours straight.

Carl was slowly coming out of his sleep. He heard sounds, kitchen sounds. Was it his mother who was cooking? Then he opened his eyes, his confusion after the deep sleep disappeared, and he looked over at Rachel. She came out of the small kitchen when she understood he was awake. He hardly recognized her, she had changed almost beyond recognition. Much thinner, and with hair very short and ragged, scratches on her face and neck.

"What happened to you? He said, "you look worse than me." Not a very good way to address a young woman he realized, but he was just too surprised to hide it. She looked at him sadly, her previously beautiful face full of shadows and distress.

"I was branded a collaborator because I had partied with the German soldiers. With the other girls I was dragged into the square where they cut our hair off and slapped us around. It was ..."

She stopped, her eyes getting tearful. Then pulled herself together and continued,

"You should go on. You don't want to be seen with a girl like me."

He was stunned,

"That's not fair, you are Jewish, you had to do what you did"

"That's not how the good people here look at it! Leave now, before you are seen."

"What will you do after I leave ?"

"People will soon forget, and I am a bar girl, what do you think!"

He was quiet while he looked at her. Conflicting thoughts raced through his head.

"Do you really want me to leave?"

"Yes, Yes," but she did not sound convincing, and her eyes told a different tale.

Again it was quiet in the room. They were like two lost souls, both searching around, uncertain what to say or what to do. Eventually they sat down at the kitchen table, still without talking. The apartment only had the two small rooms, and the kitchen was definitely tiny, barely leaving enough space for the small table and two chairs. He reached out for her hand, but she did not offer it, just stood up and gathered some food. She put it on the table. He ate while he looked at her, still not uttering a word. But the longer he sat there not saying anything, the more he realized he could not leave her like this. The time with her were the happiest memories he had from the war years, the only happy memories in fact, the rest all involved killings and other horrors.

"You were all I dreamed about" he said quietly, "all that kept me going was the hope that I would see you again. And now you want me to leave."

Rachel started crying, she hid her face with her hands,

"It is for the best" she said.

But he knew he could not do it, not now. Then it hit him.

"We will leave together" he said, "like the people in all those old western movies. We will start over, you and me"

She looked at him with a glimmer of hope in her face. He walked around the little table and stretched out his hands, took her hands in his and gently pulled her up and towards him. She resisted a little, then stepped close to him and leaned her head on his shoulder.

"I always hoped you would come" she said, so quietly he could barely make out the words. "I did not believe it, but it was the only hope I had. But I have done things I should not have done, things I am not proud of, and I am sure your family would not approve of me."

"You are with me, not my family. Besides, why should they disapprove, I have been killing and fighting for years, and so should somehow be better than you ! Your sins are small compared to mine. Most of my family members are dead anyway" he lied "so we can go wherever we want to, well, except the US or Norway, they don't look too kindly at people who fought in the Waffen SS."

They were both thinking about solutions to the problem. Rachel started to feel hopeful again for the first time in months and years. She squeezed him and took in the smell of sweat and man. Normally it would have felt bad since he desperately needed a bath, but right now it strangely enough felt safe. In a way it was as if their planning washed away all the problems of the past.

"There is a lot of talk in the Jewish community about a new state in Palestine" she said "We could go there!"

His first reaction was one of surprise.

"I am not Jewish," he said, unnecessarily, since she obviously knew, "Besides I am sure they are not looking for old SS members to move there."

"I am Jewish, and I can teach you about the faith and what it means." She got more excited and enthusiastic the more she thought about it. A new start, it had a ring to it. She knew he would not take to the Jewish faith fully, but he was not very religious so would go along and make the best of it. Besides, Jews varied in their religious intensity, just like members of any other religious group. She continued.

"Our background will be our secret. Like you said, we will start over, but we probably have to get married to pull it off." It was formed as a sort of a question, and she did not look at him. He smiled and got down on one knee,

"Will you marry me?"

She suddenly got serious and asked;

"Yes, if you are serious, and want a girl like me"

He did not answer, just stood up and took her head in his hands, then kissed her on the mouth. Afterwards he lifted her up, carried her into the living room, and put her down on the bed.

"Why did you do that?"

"It is what you are supposed to do, kiss the bride and carry her into your house."

She laughed into his shoulder,

"But it is my house, and we are already in it!"

It was late afternoon before they got up. He looked down at her,

"I am a mess" she said, aware of his gaze, "I am surprised you even got in the mood looking at me the way I am"

"You are the one for me, and you are very beautiful, besides I am in worse shape than you, even if you are a bit skinny. We will fatten you up soon enough" he said jokingly, all the while letting his hand wander over her body "but first, let's take a bath."

*

THE STRAITS OF MESSINA

*

Months had passed by. They were approaching the straits of Messina, the narrow strip of water between Italy and Sicily. Their progress had been slow, as they were traveling on foot. It was made even slower since they took day jobs along the way, often with the occupying forces. His fluency in English had thus come to good use. It had been surprisingly easy to stay out of trouble, and she kept teaching him Hebrew as they moved south. She did not speak English, and he not Italian, so they were talking German between them, though she was also trying to learn English. For safety reasons it was definitely something they wanted to avoid in the future. During this time they also got in touch with, and were assisted by, the Jewish escape network. Immigration to Palestine was forbidden by the Brits, and this had created a sophisticated network of illegal transportation. Their cover story was that he was a German Jew, one of whose parents had been Christian. That explained why he was not circumcised and spoke Hebrew so poorly. With his Jewish wife he had decided to move to Palestine. In the chaos after the war there were many stories stranger than theirs, which explained why they got away with it.

All over Europe millions of people had been displaced by the war and were now trying to find their way home, sometimes to places that had been completely erased or destroyed beyond recognition. Other millions were on the move to a new homeland following the changed frontiers that the victorious powers had agreed on for political reasons, often with little regard to the unfortunate people caught behind new borders.

They were a real couple by now. Rachel was very happy, despite their poverty, the everyday hardships, the absence of almost anything that a normal existence would have yielded. In a way she healed with him at her side, and came to accept her past and put it where it belonged, in another life, one that would soon be buried and forgotten. If he was not ashamed of her previous "activities", why should she be, she decided. Her hair had grown back, and though still undernourished, her old facial features had started to re-emerge, the shining eyes, the sparkling smile, all the things that he remembered so well. Besides, she did not seem "worried" any more, if that was the word for it. She had a purpose in life and she was in love.

For Carl it was not that easy. He did miss parts of his old life, the part before the war, and he also wanted to contact his family. Yet he knew it was too soon, in fact he figured he had to wait five to ten years before he could do so. After a war with so much hatred and cruelty, he knew the bitterness towards him for choosing the wrong side would take a long time to burn out, even from his own family members. The war stayed with him in other ways as well. The horrors and the fears somehow seemed more real now that it was all over than when he had been in the thick of it. Mercifully they were so busy during the day he did not have too much time to contemplate the war years. In the evening they stayed under a small two man army tent they had obtained, and he held her body close to his, letting her warmth and lovemaking drown out all the bad memories from the last few years. Still, at times, he would wake up soaked in sweat thinking he was back in "Mutti", grenades exploding around him, but then Rachel would take his head and put it towards her chest, her soft fingers stroking his face till he fell asleep again.

The hardships and memories brought them close, closer than most people ever become, and so these evenings were something they would remember for the rest of their lives. The warm weather, made even more beautiful by the peace around them, the absence of fighter bombers and exploding grenades, no marauding bands of soldiers raping or looting, all this caused millions of people all over Western Europe to remember the summer of 1945 as the best one ever. In the East it was different, as Stalin took his revenge and tightened the screws of oppression, enslaving millions once again. But in the West people did not know that, and the Western governments chose to be as blind to that as they had initially been to Hitler's crimes.

Reggio di Calabria was a sleepy town just after the war. Had it not been for the occasional traces of the recent war, you could have been excused for believing you were back in the Middle Ages, planning to join a crusade. In a way that was what they were attempting, to re-conquer Jerusalem.

Together with about 30 other Jewish refugees they were picked up by a small freighter, hired by the Jewish resistance movement. The boat left as planned, and so they were on their way, hoping to avoid the patrolling Royal Navy. The refugees were hiding out in the bottom storage area, well aware that a serious boarding party would find them without too much trouble. The hold was cramped and uncomfortable, the air stale. It was fortunate that it was a short voyage. Rachel and Carl were sitting close together, not saying much, yet both thinking about what they should do in the new land. After much discussion and planning they decided to start a small truck workshop. Carl had acquired technical skills during his time in the armored forces, and now he could put those skills to peaceful use, he hoped. They finally arrived in Haifa, supposedly in secret, but not in reality, since the British did not have the resources to stop the flow of refugees into Palestine. As they entered the dock Carl looked back over the Mediterranean and towards Europe. He was wondering if he would ever see his home again. Rachel understood his dark mood, kissed his cheek, squeezed his hand and said;

"It will be for the best, we will be happy here, you'll see."

*

PALESTINE 1948

*

Two years had passed since they arrived in Palestine, turbulent years, yet also fulfilling years. Carl, under his assumed name Fredrich, (using a version of his middle name) and Rachel had settled down to a normal existence as the owner/manager of a small truck repair shop. They used her real last name, Blumenkrantz. The highlight of their existence had been the birth of their little daughter, followed by a son. They were happy together, and for both of them the past was now behind a hidden and very high wall. A set of memories they did not share with anybody, friends, children or associates. Their neighbors saw them as a very quiet, yet friendly, young couple. That they did not talk much about their past was not unusual. Many people all over the world had nightmarish memories of the war years, things they preferred to forget, or just keep to themselves, and that was respected and understood. But behind their own peaceful existence, war clouds were gathering over Palestine.

Haganah, the Jewish defense organization was struggling on two fronts, against both the Arabs and the British authorities who tried to limit immigration of Jews to Palestine. They had avoided direct participation in the preliminary fighting, though they had come to desire independence for Israel as the upcoming State was called. Now the explosion had come, and Carl found himself in Latrun. As a mechanic for trucks, he had some time ago been asked to help out with maintaining the few tanks that Israel possessed, mainly left over Sherman's. He had taken a low profile, yet when the commander of the 7th Brigade had seen him work, and test the tanks, he had quickly realized that Carl was an experienced tanker, 'drafted' him into the army, and asked;

"Where did you acquire your skills?"

"I was in the armored core during the war, it was not a good time, I prefer not to talk about it."

"For the Germans perhaps" the commander said jokingly, but with an edge.

Carl shook his head, and looked at him. He did not answer as he did not trust his own voice, and could see that the officer was suspicious. Actually it looked like he suspected that Carl had indeed been on the wrong side. Though little known, there were Jews who had fought for Hitler, not willingly perhaps, but hiding their true background to avoid the concentration camps. After some contemplation the commander told him to take command of the "A" tank. In reality Carl was one of only two men with any tank experience under his command, and the Israeli commander was painfully aware of that fact. The demands of the struggling state was far more important than his suspicions about this rather Nordic looking Jew, so he decided to give him a chance to prove himself.

And so, just a few years after the war, Carl found himself serving in the 7th Brigade of the new Israeli army, in what had once been an enemy tank. He had seen the Sherman many times, not least during his last battle of WW II. It was fairly easy for a man with his tank experience to learn the different handles and controls, and the operational doctrine was otherwise similar. Now, three months after the 'draft' as he called it, he was almost an old hand at operating this machine. The Sherman was quite a different looking tank from his previous mounts, high silhouetted, but thin skinned and with a less powerful gun.

The German forces had called the Sherman's 'Tommie cookers' because of their propensity to catch fire when hit. It had the same size 75mm diameter gun as most German Panzers, but with a much shorter barrel. Consequently it was not nearly as powerful, with a muzzle velocity of 2000 f/s (feet per second) for its 14 lb. projectile. The 75 mm German L-70 as used in his Jagdpanzer IV sent out a 16 lb. projectile at 3,600 f/s, and even the standard Panzer Mk. IV gun, the L-48, had better performance than the American gun. Carl would have given his left arm to be able to install an L-70 in the turret, rather than this 'tooth pick' as he derisively called the main gun.

The Brits had equipped some Sherman's with a high powered 75 mm gun and called them Firefly's, but this tank had the original US built M-3. All was not bad though. They were not facing heavily armored T-34 or IS-2's and the Sherman had excellent mobility. That combined with its reliability and roomy interior was a blessing in the heat. It was easier to maintain and more comfortable, since they could circulate and cool the air more efficiently than in any of the tanks he had previously commanded.

Their order was to cover one of the roads leading to Latrun, which was a few miles to the east, against any enemy force trying to outflank the main Israeli force. An old police fort was the center of the fighting, though they were too far away to see or hear much. Latrun was an important way point, and one the Israelis put a lot of effort into occupying. Interestingly enough, and a bit unnerving to Carl, was the fact that several of the Israeli soldiers were survivors from the concentration camps. Though he had not seen any of the camps during the war, they were well known by now, and like most sane people he realized just how criminal Hitler's regime had been. They had a rifle company of eight guys with them as protection against enemy infantry, all that could be spared from the main force.

Both his tank and the rifle squad were well camouflaged and hidden around an old stone church. He had placed the soldiers carefully so they would not interfere with the operation of the tank or be injured by the gun blast. One good thing in this war was that the air forces, of both sides, were so small they did not really count for much. In a small skirmish like this, combat aircraft were highly unlikely to show up. As he waited in the ruins, he could not help but smile at the twists and turns his life seemed to be taking. He took out the little picture he carried of Rachel and the kids, kissed it gently and put it back in his breast pocket. Now he had to concentrate on the less enjoyable task of killing people. The tank was well hidden, and the old stone walls gave some additional protection. Sorely needed in such an easily seen (due to its high silhouette) and thin skinned vehicle. Unless a really large force showed up, which was not expected, he felt certain they could repulse any enemy attack. All the soldiers were highly motivated and well trained.

"There!" he called out over the intercom as enemy tanks suddenly emerged over the little hill in front of the adjoining village. Not many, just a few that rumbled in front of his binoculars as he peered out of the hatch. He had decided to take the chance and keep his head out of the turret. At this stage he preferred the full uninhibited view rather than the limited view from the scope. The scope was not any better than the one in his German tank, worse in fact, but he did not expect any snipers to single him out and so could avoid it for the time being.

The enemy tanks were rather disorganized in the way they approached, with little regard to field of fire, the safety of the 50 or so infantry that trotted along on both side of the vehicles, or mine clearing. The last point was not so strange as very few mine fields were deployed. The troops and the vehicles were too close to each other, and instead of having the main guns covering the opposite sides of the road, all three tanks had their main guns trained straight ahead. It was clear these crews were of a very different caliber from the experienced Soviet tankers he had opposed in 1944-45. It was more reminiscent of the way the Russians had mishandled their equipment and its possibilities in the early stages of the war, the period immediately following operation Barbarossa, the invasion of the Soviet Union. Just as well in Carl's mind since they were one tank against three, and his own crew was also rather inexperienced at this stage.

What !!!, was it, yes, it was. He could hardly believe his eyes when he realized they were three old ex German Panzer Mk IV's. They had not seen his tank, concealed as it was in the ruins. Somebody had mentioned that the Syrian's had received or taken over some abandoned German tanks, but he had written it off as rumors. Yet, here was the proof. Apparently they now supported the Jordanian Arab Legion which was moving toward the Latrun monastery. He continued to look at the type of tank that he had commanded just a few years ago, almost forgetting to prepare to fire. With an effort he collected his thoughts and prepared his next move. First of all he closed the hatch, 'button up' as they called it, then adjusted the aim of the main gun to 400 yards. Good thing was he knew all the Mk IV's weak spots. He laughed out loud at the irony of the situation, a complete reversal from his last action in Austria, then became aware that the crew looked at him nervously, wondering if he was going mad.

"Ha, hrm" he cleared his throat with an effort and tried, unsuccessfully, to hide his smirk, then called out;

"Kano...., I mean Gun ready?" He had almost used the old German command. In the stress of the moment nobody noticed, thank god. Hopefully they would not remember afterwards.

"Yes commander" came the answer. His crew were still rookies as far as actual battle was concerned, and relatively new to each other, so they still used military titles rather than actual names.

The first Mk. IV rolled across his sight. He chose to aim just below the turret ring, where he knew a hit would make the most damage. By taking out the lead tank the other tanks would be blocked and forced to get off the road to continue, thus loosing what little formation they had.

"Fire"

The tank shook, and it was almost as if the muzzle flash reached out and embraced the first Mk. IV as it blew up in a brilliant explosion. Thank God they don't have Panters or Tigers he thought to himself, there is no way this tooth pick would have blown up one of those.

"Back up, reload" he barked to the crew. He had prepared an excellent fall back position which would make it impossible for the enemy to see him without dangerously exposing their hulls. The driver gunned the 400 HP Continental 9 cylinder petrol engine and the tank backed up quickly. As soon as he was out of sight of the enemy he swung around the building.

When he came around the corner on the north side both remaining enemy tanks were aiming at his old position. These guys were truly untrained, and were still partially blocking each others line of fire. On top of that the supporting infantry had not spread out but instead lumped together behind the hulls. He fired the next shot straight into the side of the most exposed, i.e. closest tank, expecting another explosion. To his disappointment and surprise the grenade did not penetrate, just exploded harmlessly against the side armor. The result was not in any way lethal to the enemy, though the tracks were damaged. The turret started to swivel menacingly towards them.

"Shit" Carl swore, fortunately in English this time. They had used the wrong kind of ammunition. HE instead of AP, not an unusual mistake for a new crew, but one that could easily be the last mistake they ever made. Carl swore to himself again, it was his own damned fault that he had not checked or reminded the crew what ammunition to use, after all he was the one with the experience. Now it was the Syrian's turn. He had to act fast.

"Back up, reload with AP" he shouted. They backed behind the wall just in time, and the Mk. IV fired harmlessly into the stones shielding them, releasing a cascade of flying splinters. Deadly for any exposed soldiers, but not enough to damage the armor of a tank. The sound of stone pellets hitting the side was rather scary though, it sounded like a drum salvo. He hoped none of the rifle team supporting them had been killed by the shrapnel. The loader, Joseph, worked frantically while he was constantly talking to himself, alternately swearing and praying. It showed that he was nervous and well aware that he had made a big mistake. They had practiced reloading endlessly though, and now the training paid off.

"Gun ready" Joseph screamed excitedly a few seconds later. They were ready long before the enemy.

"Forward" Carl called out, and again the driver revved the engine and they emerged from the cover. This time Carl released the round straight into the lower hull of the Syrian tank which was still reloading. The enemy started to burn as the AP round penetrated and exploded. Carl's crew roared in appreciation when the driver (the only person apart from him that could see outside the tank) called out;

"Bull's eye, the bastard is burning"

Carl was not as elated, he actually felt a bit guilty. This was more of a turkey shoot than a war, he thought as he looked for the third tank. He was very aware that with a more experienced and better trained enemy his tank would by now have been a burning hulk. Three against one are long odds, unless you have a superior mount, and that he did not have. The crew were talking excitedly over the intercom.

"Quiet. Keep the tank moving forward. Can you see the third tank?"

Carl was very aware from his experience back in 1945 that it is the one you don't see that gets you. He was not about to repeat that mistake. He also wanted to keep moving, even if only slowly. To hit a moving tank requires considerable skill, something these guys did not possess.

"It is running away" the driver shouted, his voice so high pitched from shouting and excitement he sounded more like a teenager at a prom than a soldier. Due to their poor battle order, the third tank had been obscured by the burning hulks of its two partners. Consequently it could not participate in the fight. After what had happened to them, the crew had no intention to continue what they now feared was a suicide mission. Thus when Carl finally spotted the last Mk IV through the smoke created by the gun blasts and burning vehicles he realized the battle was over.

The enemy was 'running' away from the battlefield at full speed, the crew not caring that they were running over and killing some of their own infantry in the process. While the main gun of Carl's tank had engaged the enemy tanks, the radio operator, who manned the machine gun in the front of the Sherman, had simultaneously released a hail of fire into the enemy line. It added to the confusion and carnage, and caused full panic among the infantry. Carl found he actually felt sorry for these scared men desperately running away as fast as their feet could carry them. However, a combat situation is not a time to act on pity, and despite his misgivings he aimed the main gun at the rear end of the fleeing vehicle. He adjusted for distance, and knew it would be an easy kill. The engine compartment of most tanks is in the rear, and by far the most vulnerable part.

"Fire" he called out.

The circle was full, but this time he was the one fighting for home and family, not conquest......

*

HISTORICAL NOTES
*

During World War II, particularly the early years, the final outcome of the conflict was not as obvious as it appears with the benefit of hindsight. As such it is hardly surprising that many people in the occupied countries hedged their bets by cooperating with the Germans. In addition to the millions of collaborators, thousands of men and women went one step further and volunteered for service with the Germans. Their reasons varied. From strong anti communism to securing a place for themselves in the new Europe they thought was emerging Many believed that siding with Germany was the only way their nation could survive in the new German dominated Europe. For others, less honorable causes like racial prejudice or outright financial gain was the motivation. In some cases it could be sheer self preservation, as it probably was for most of the Jews that served in the German army. In other words, their reasoning was as varied as it was for those who served on the other side.

To facilitate the volunteers the Waffen SS, or Armed SS, established separate units with what was termed racial cousins. They came from Scandinavia, BeNeLux, France, Russia and other occupied countries, and also included Americans and British citizens. The most famous of these volunteer formations was arguably the 5th. SS Division, named Viking. In the years following the war, these men were portrayed as thugs, dimwits and criminals, but in reality most of them came from "normal" families. Opportunists and thugs do not usually volunteer for the dangers and hardship of frontline war service, they prefer to stay home and do their bullying out of danger. From Norway, more than 4,500 men fought for the Germans, and a high percentage of them, some 20%, paid the ultimate price. They sacrificed their lives for a lost, and in the final analysis, unworthy cause.

The Eastern Front, where the vast majority of these volunteers served, was the single most important theater of the war. In many ways it was a tank war, and the ferocity, scale and scope of the fighting staggers the imagination. From the Arctic to the Black Sea millions of men fought and died. Some 80% of German military casualties were in the East, and the enormity of the Soviet losses are well known. Millions of soldiers and civilians on both sides died unnecessarily due to the crazy, or outright criminal, decisions made by the two ruthless warring dictators. Throughout the conflict, in battle after battle, the tank forces were the decisive weapon. The vehicles used were constantly evolving, growing bigger, faster, heavier and with ever sharper teeth. The most common size of tank borne guns during the second half of WWII was the 75 mm diameter barrel. Guns (and tanks) were often described by adding the diameter to their name. i.e. the T-34 was described either as the T-34/76 or in its later up gunned version as T-34/85. Some tanks, like the Tiger, had a much larger 88 mm barrel. However, the diameter of the gun is not the only determination of its power, length and type of ammunition is equally important. In general the Germans had the most powerful tank guns, and the Western allies the least, though the balance between the three major warring groups changed back and forth throughout the conflict.

When the guns finally fell silent after years of bloodshed and misery, the end of the war naturally became the momentous event in the West, and huge celebrations were held in all the victorious nations. Forgotten in all the euphoria was the fate of millions of people displaced by the war, or displaced by the Soviet Union following agreements made between them and the West. Agreements often signed or quietly accepted with little regard to any actual war guilt of the people involved, or the welfare of the millions of innocents chased from their homes. Another dark secret from those days is how many of the concentration camps left behind by the Germans were being refilled by the Soviet NKVD. This time with so called 'enemies of the people' instead of 'racial inferiors'. These enemies included just about anybody disagreeable to Stalin and his henchmen, including East Europeans who had fought with the Western Allies or ex Soviet POW's. In this cruel and chaotic situation millions of Europeans, from both sides of the war, tried to establish new lives among the ruins. Many died, but most eventually made it, and they can today be found in North and South America, in ethnic enclaves in major European cities, and in Palestine! As such the story of Rachel and Carl is more typical than it may appear.

Steel Armageddon

STEEL QUEEN
*
ARRAS, FRANCE 1940
*

The mouse was peering out of its hole, carefully, not making a sound. Predators were everywhere. The mouse knew that, and what to expect. Yet, it was different now. Recently new and frightening noises had entered its habitat. The mouse did not know how to handle this situation and stayed in its hole, fearful and scared. The new noises did not disappear, and so the mouse remained in hiding for a long time. But it had to eat. Hunger was driving it out of the safety of its lair.

Once outside the little mouse head started moving back and forth, scanning the surroundings for enemies. They were many, foxes, cats, and occasionally birds. For a long time it looked nervously from side to side, but it did not look up. Eventually it decided it was alone, and ventured out looking for food.

The two crew members catching a few rays on top of their Matilda tank were quietly watching the little life and death drama unfolding only 10 feet away.

"That mouse has just committed the biggest and last mistake of its life" the tank commander, Second Lieutenant Tommy Fletcher (Fletch to his crew) said.

"I don't understand how it could avoid seeing that old, scruffy looking cat." Hank Derby, the driver, responded.

"Maybe it has some kind of a death wish." They both smiled. The two of them were indeed an odd couple. Hank was a tall, thin haired, chain smoking Yorkshire man, quite unhealthy looking, while the non smoking Fletch, a couple of inches shorter, had a healthy look about him. He had always enjoyed the outdoors, and it showed.

The cat they were talking about had been watching the mouse antics from a small branch above the hole, and now it pounced. Its patience had paid off. The sharp claws went straight through the little mouse. It squealed helplessly, mortally wounded. The cat sat back and watched the little rodent, spinning around its own axis, slowly dying. From generations of hunting, the cat knew subconsciously that the rest of the mouse family would soon come out as well. It would be a good afternoon.

"It was an unequal contest." Fletch mumbled as he and Hank climbed into the tank and joined the rest of the crew, already seated in their respective compartments; "The stakes were too different. The mouse was gambling with its life, the cat only with a meal."

He actually felt a little bit sorry for the mouse, but it was not only due to compassion. The contest had been a good illustration of their current predicament as well, a little too close for comfort in a figurative sense. The tank was in essence like the mouse where the crews gambled with their lives, while the German planes just sent off a bomb. The tanks had no defense of their own against an air attack, they had to hide or just risk it.

The exuberance over the outbreak of war was all forgotten. There was no more talk of a short war, or another war to end wars. No brave talk about how they were going to kick the "Boche" back across the Rhine. The Germans had gotten the better of them. Again. After Poland they had overrun Scandinavia, and now it was the turn of the Low Countries and France. By going through the Ardennes forest with their panzers "en masse" they had outwitted the anemic French and British Generals. Once out of the forest, the Luftwaffe bombers had gone to work, knocking out anything that had not been destroyed by the Panzerwaffe, the Wehrmacht Armored Corps. Now Fletch found himself on the outskirts of the village of Arras. They were supposed to stop the advance of the 7th Panzer Division under Major General Erwin Rommel. At the moment there was little to fear from snipers so he kept his head out of the turret. The crew was calm and sober, discussing the recent events and the impact of their own commanders as far as they knew them.

"Those arrogant idiots were too busy drinking wine and chasing French women to be of any use. They think they are fighting Napoleon and have time for their mistresses to boot!" as Hank so colorfully expressed the general opinion of the allied Generals. At least the way the rank and file saw them, and they were the ones who had to do the fighting and dying.

As always the Germans seemed to be one war ahead, using new tactics, new weapons and in general thinking about future warfare, like equipping all their tanks with wireless sets. Their officer corps was younger and in line with the latest developments. Allied officers, with some exceptions, and even more the senior French Generals, seemed like a bunch of geriatrics released from a retirement home.

"Oh Well" Fletch said optimistically, "Now the Germans will meet British steel, and that will teach them a lesson."

He had complete confidence in his Matilda. It was the new A12 Matilda II type, much better than the earlier two man Matilda I. Unlike many of the other tank commanders, Fletch did not name his tanks. For some reason he felt it would bring bad luck. Though small and cramped, the Matilda looked like, and operated like, the steel monster it was supposed to be. The internal layout was traditional and the tank was divided into three compartments. The front with the driver, the fighting compartment consisting of the turret with the commander, loader and gunner, and the rear compartment with the engine. At 27 tons it was heavier than any of the German Mk. II, III or IV tanks, and consequently much better armored. It had a couple of handicaps. The main gun was small and fired solid shots, not High Explosives, and the Matilda had a very limited top speed of 15 mph. The prevailing joke was that the manufacturer forgot to add "Top Speed" to the speed lever.

'What the hell, who cares' he thought to himself, 'you can't outrun an airplane anyway.' The German bombers had obtained a fierce reputation, first and foremost the dreaded JU-87 dive bomber, normally called the Stuka. He instinctively looked up at the sky every time he thought about Stuka's, or when somebody mentioned the word. Not that he had seen any of the dive bombers, but its reputation was already legendary.

He heard the wireless crackle in the background and looked down at the operator, George, who was busy interpreting the latest message. The No.19 wireless set was quite noisy and not always the easiest to listen to. George, who doubled as loader and wireless operator, always claimed to have a minor headache after using it. Eventually he looked up at Fletch and called out

"Message from HQ, they are coming, and the old man (Major General Harold Franklyn) orders us to move forward at 5 mph" No wonder, Fletch thought, 5 mph was about as fast as the Matilda would move, at least if you wanted to avoid over-heating and refueling problems.

The counter attack was under way. He closed the hatch and ordered Hank to follow the lead tank with the rest of the 7th Royal Tank Regiment. He heard the twin AEC diesel engines roar as they started advancing, giving the impression they had much more power than their actual output of 175 hp. Not that it mattered all that much, they were reliable and that was more important than pure power. As he looked forward through the 'scope' he saw gun flashes and enemy tanks appearing in the distance. The tank suddenly rocked as a grenade hit them with a large thud, almost immediately followed by two more. He stopped breathing for a brief second, but the Matilda kept moving forward undisturbed. Silently he sent a thank you to the engineers that had equipped the tank with its thick (78 mm) frontal armor and two reliable AEC bus engines. Reliability was not a trademark of the other British tanks.

A few minutes later they emerged from the smoke and he aimed the gun at the first German tank he saw, a small Mk. II and fired. A hit, but nothing happened. The loader put in a new grenade, and they fired again, still no effect. He could even see the bullet holes in the superstructure but it had obviously not hit any crew member or vital parts inside the tank. He swore like a madman, and this time he told the gunner to aim at the tank's rear, i.e. engine compartment. Again their aim was excellent and the shot went into the other tank just as advertised. It stopped dead, the crew jumped out and ran away.

"Shit" he called out, "these solid shots are useless, they should blow up the damn German's with one hit." They were well aware that the larger German tanks could fire both HE (High Explosive) and AP (Armored Piercing) rounds.

The battle became a blur of maneuvering tanks, infantry, and shots. His radio operator fired the 7.62 mm Besa machine gun almost continuously, making the tank both smelly and smoky inside. Fletch tried to find new targets for the small but accurate 2 pounder (47mm) main gun, but it was difficult to get a clear view. He did not want to open the hatch. Snipers were always on the prowl for careless tank commanders.

There, another medium tank, a Mk. III, wandered into his view. It was considerably larger than the Mk. II and had a 37mm. main gun. Good enough for most tanks, but not against the thick bosom of a Matilda. He realized he was staring straight down its barrel and they fired more or less simultaneously. Fletch could literally see the grenade coming and closed his eyes, but again it just bounced off the Matilda. He started humming, 'Waltzing Matilda' and somebody in the crew joined in. Over the wireless a sharp "Shut up" came in, and despite the stress of the moment the crew laughed out loud. They had all forgotten that the wireless was on when they started humming. Meanwhile the Mk. III took the hit and started a 360 degree turn. His grenade had cut off one of the tracks. It quickly stopped, and again the enemy crew jumped out. Two of them were cut down by machine gun fire as soon as they came out of the escape hatches on the side. He looked around, and could see the Germans were retreating; in fact fleeing was a better word. Dead German soldiers and burning tanks littered the battlefield. Finally somebody had shown that the dreaded German Panzerwaffe could be beaten.

Their luck ran out just there and then. A tremendous explosion rocked the tank. It started to spin around, one track obviously damaged, then stopped dead. They were all dizzy from the explosion, but no shrapnel had entered the fighting compartment.

"Abandon tank" he yelled as the tank filled with smoke. They all scrambled out, falling head over heel out of the escape hatches.

Not exactly the elegant escape we practiced, Fletch thought in the middle of all the confusion and smoke, but gratefully he noticed all four crew members had made it. He wondered what had hit them, and decided it had to be a bomb or large artillery round. No German tank gun had, to his knowledge, such firepower. Once outside he ran and crawled back towards his own lines. As he did so, he could see Hank running in the same general direction.

"Are you OK Sergeant?" Hank was unable to answer, just nodded and waved him on. With the Germans in retreat, nobody took any potshots at them. The rest of the crew was nowhere to be seen. Fortunately they did not have to venture far before meeting up with British infantry units. They told him that the Germans had recovered and were pushing forward again. They had taken heavy losses though, and in fact Arras was just about the only Allied success during the battle of France. The Enemy had fled the onslaught of the heavy British tanks, their anti tank weapons ineffectual. In response General Rommel had improvised and remedied the situation by leveling 88mm anti aircraft guns, as well as heavy 150mm artillery units, and used them in an anti armor role. Brilliantly done, but if the Allies had committed larger tank forces they would have overrun the enemy positions. This one temporary allied success did not alter the course of events, but at least it showed the troops that the Germans were not invincible.

Soon afterwards Fletch found himself on his way to England with the remnants of the 7th Royal Tank Regiment. Some well earned R&R (Rest & Recreation) beckoned, after which they were shipped off to Africa.

*

OPERATION COMPASS, 1941

*

The CO (Commanding Officer) was enthusiastic about the planned operation, but despite this the presentation was boring to the extreme. Actually the dullness of his high pitched voice was in line with the heat and Fletch found it difficult to pay full attention, On top of that the tent was hotter than hell, and that made his eyelids heavy. Not that Fletch really knew how hot it was in hell, cared, or even believed in the existence of the place, but at least the phrase sounded good.

Word had gotten through to them. The Italians were moving further into Egypt, and their force was far larger than the British and Commonwealth forces of the 8th army. In the tent the Colonel continued his briefing for the upcoming action

".... but Marshal Graziani's 10th army is moving slowly, so General Wavell has decided that we will strike first. Their army is enormous, we estimate several hundred thousand men, but their tanks, though there are 2,500 of them, are lightly armed, lightly armored and unreliable"

"Just like ours" somebody commented, drawing laughter. The Matilda was actually quite reliable with its commercial bus engines, but the cruiser tanks, like the Crusader, were thin skinned and known to break down frequently. Unfortunately the cruiser tanks made up the bulk of the forces.

The Colonel continued undisturbed, pretending he had not heard the comment:

"Our task is for the 7th Armored Division to attack the Italian camp at Sidi Barrani and kick the hell out of them. The RAF is softening up the Italian camps and that should not be too hard since the Italian Air Force is mainly equipped with biplanes"

"Just like our Desert Air Force", it was the same voice again, but this time the Colonel got annoyed, looked straight at the culprit and said:

"Shut your bloody mouth George, or I will transfer you to latrine duty, and I am not joking. Let's stick to the task at hand. The RAF has already reported some success, so we should be relatively free from air attack. Your main problem will be the artillery. The main gun of the Italian tanks, like the M.13/40 and the even lighter Fiat models can not break your armor. Be careful so you don't allow them a flank shot. The attack will start in 30 minutes. Gods speed, Gentlemen. Dismissed"

Another battle loomed, but Fletch was pretty relaxed about the whole thing. All information received regarding the Italian tanks portrayed them more as self propelled coffins (for their own crews) than as serious opponents. He was an experienced tanker by now, and had been promoted to Lieutenant. He was still with the 7th tank regiment, and still in a Matilda Mk. II tank. Hank was with him, but the rest of the crew had changed over. His relationship to Hank was one of mutual trust, but not friendship beyond the professional association. It was not that they did not like each other, in fact the only argument they ever had was over Fletch ban on smoking inside the tank. He claimed security concerns, but the real reason was it gave him a headache. They were just too different to be "civilian" friends, though they probably knew more about each others than most brothers do. Many tank crews became close personal friends, but at this stage Fletch had seen too many dead friends and colleagues. Almost as a sort of self preservation he did not get close to anybody, but preferred to stay aloof. Many of his fellow soldiers thus mistakenly considered him arrogant or callous. Fletch knew that, and accepted it. In reality he did not really care what the men thought. Most of them will be dead soon anyway he thought cynically, as he climbed into the Matilda. It was always the newcomers, the greenhorns, who took the heaviest casualties.

"Fletch, orders from HQ, we are to move forward." The wireless operator crackled. Funny enough his voice sounded almost as if it came out of the radio. He ordered the other two tanks in his platoon to follow him at 30 foot intervals. At 1600 (4 PM) sharp, supported by an artillery barrage, they entered the built up settlement, and ran straight into the first Italian Blackshirt Division.

"Take the side street to your left" he ordered Frank Cambridge in one of the supporting tanks. As Frank's tank veered off, he saw it stop after a few yards, then start to back up. He was wondering why. A huge explosion on the building behind it explained the situation; it could only have come from a large artillery shell, not another tank gun.

"Circle around him, Frank, take them from behind.

"That's always been my favorite part" Frank responded. He was not one to loose his cool. It had been a rather unnecessary order, Frank was keenly aware of the danger, and knew how to deal with it. His tank disappeared down another street, out of sight. Fletch was relieved, it had been a close call for Frank.

He decided caution was now the better option, and stopped behind a building where he jumped out of the tank. While the infantry looked at him curiously, he peeked around the corner, but could not see any artillery placements. He waved for the sergeant in charge of the infantry to come over.

"Follow behind the tanks, but don't get too close. I don't want to run over any of you if I have to back up. Likewise the gun blast can be pretty deafening if you are in front of us so stay to the sides."

Getting back into the tank, Fletch ordered Hank to carefully steer it down a side street, silently praying for no hidden guns. He was followed by the third Matilda, under the command of Jack 'Tex' Nelson, and infantry from the Indian Division. Tex got his nick name because he had spent some time with his grandmother in Texas. Consequently he could put on a fantastic Texan accent, something which typically happened when he had one beer too many.

"Tank at the left," the driver shouted, he had seen it first. Two Italian M.13/40's came straight at them. Both were firing. Fletch instinctively ducked, as if that would have helped.

"Clang, clang," the noise from the impact of the shells was deafening, but again Matilda's thick armor prevented any damage. Fletch leveled the gun and fired straight at the first tank. The effect was satisfying, he could actually see the shell hitting the wall behind the enemy tank, it had passed straight through he hull. The other tank was dealt with in a similar fashion by Tex in the other Matilda. Now Fletch knew this would be a 'turkey shoot' as long as they did not run headlong into an artillery emplacement. The enemy tanks were useless, but he could see Italian infantry in the windows and down the street. They could be dangerous for him, a hand grenade or fire bomb dropped on top of his mount could ruin an otherwise good day. A tank is not really suited for close quarter fighting.

"Stop, wait for the infantry" he ordered and swiveled the turret towards a third Italian tank that appeared at his 11 o'clock direction. To his astonishment he could see the crew jumping out, panicked when they saw the Matilda aiming the main gun at them. He changed the sight, and aimed at the enemy road block down the street.

"Fire"

The shell hit the roadblock sending stone and wood splinters in every direction, but the solid shot did not do the amount of damage that was needed. Solid shots were strictly meant for fighting other tanks. Against this kind of target a HE grenade would have been useful. He could see their own infantry catching up to them and called out:

"Slowly forward, use the MG's to suppress the enemy, forget the main gun"

They moved cautiously forward, and Fletch started enjoying himself, feeling snug and safe inside his Desert Queen. He felt a bit sorry for the enemy infantry, most of whom surrendered, but some died fighting. As usual he did not allow himself to think about them as real people, that would have been too emotional. Like most soldiers throughout history he had found his own way of justifying what he did, and thus avoided going crazy. He did not hate the Italian's, or German's, for that matter. Nor did he feel any particular love for the Poles, the French and all the other allied powers. If it had been up to him, they could fight each other all over Europe, as long as they left England alone, and maybe his mother's home country of Norway as well. But, instead Hitler had attacked just about every country in Europe, and his country, England, had declared war. The Germans were now the enemy, and he had been sent to win this war. That was the way it was, whatever his personal feelings told him about this mess.

Suddenly a small tank emerged from a building on the left side, obviously lost. The enemy tank commander, who had his head out of the turret of the tank, was close enough Fletch could see his eyes open wide when he saw the Matilda boring down on him. He turned the turret and let loose a hail of MG fire. It sounded like pebbles hammering their walls, but Machine Guns rarely do any damage to a tank. He then tried to reverse out of the way, but it was too late.

"Run down that piece of Italian Fiat crap" Fletch said, and Hank increased the speed. The impact, though not very fast pushed the Fiat light tank over on its side, spilling the still active commander into the street. He was a brave man, pulled his side gun, a German Luger no less, and started firing straight at the Matilda while he ran for cover. Several of the Indian infantry was firing at him, but by some miracle he was not hit and got into a building. Fletch was actually happy to see him get away, you just had to admire such bravery.

"Reverse", he called out, but the tank did not move. It had been wedged on top of the Fiat, and the belts were just whipping up dust. He looked for the other Matilda to push them off, but it did not answer.

"Damn, where are those idiots" he said, then instantly regretted it when saw a tank burning furiously behind them. Somebody had thrown a bottle of gasoline from one of the windows, with scary effect, and now the crew was scrambling out. A terrible sight. They were either caught in the crossfire or burned to death in the inferno that just a few minutes earlier had been a fully functioning tank.

"Bloody hell!" Hank said, in a state of shock, he had seen the fate that befell their compatriots as well, and did not fancy ending up like them. He tried every trick in the book to get them loose. Nothing worked. The firefight around them had increased in intensity. The tank that until now had felt like a place of safety suddenly felt more like a prison. The loader started to open the hatch.

"Stop that." Fletch ordered, "You are safer inside the tank. Keep firing the MG." It was too late, the loader, panicked, had the hatch open and tried to crawl out. The rest of the crew could see his body shake as enemy bullets riddled him. He collapsed halfway out of the hatch.

"Get him in before somebody drops a hand grenade down the opening" Fletch said. It was prophetic. Before they could get to the hatch, a hand grenade sailed in through the opening and landed between Hank's legs.

"Oh God" the fear and hopelessness in his voice was clear to all. Fletch closed his eyes. This is it he thought, I wonder what death is like. Time ticked by slowly, each second feeling like an hour.

Nothing happened.

Slowly Fletch opened his eyes.

"A dud" Hank said. They looked at each other in endless relief. He quickly picked it up and threw it out. Together they pulled the loader, John something, into the tank and closed the hatch. In his present state Fletch could not for the best of him remember his last name. The 'post action' reaction had set in, and he found himself sweating profusely and shaking. A barrage of bullets started hitting the tank, making them cringe down. They had a loud impact, heavier than a submachine gun, and based upon the rapid firing bursts he guessed it was one of the Breda 38 machine guns. That forced another thought. The Breda 38 was also carried by the Italian tanks, and if it was indeed an enemy tank they could get around him. Not good, even the Italian light tanks could penetrate the engine department. He pulled himself together, forcing himself to think about the situation in a rational way.

The machine guns by themselves would not harm them, and the odds of an Italian tank getting behind them unnoticed was minimal. Thus, the real danger was from the Italian infantry, if they could get close enough to plant a grenade. To restore some kind of fighting order, and calm his own nerves, he barked out orders:

"I will fire the MG and keep their infantry from getting on top of us. You have to look after John."

The gunner, Brian, was in shock, just sitting in his chair talking silently to himself, leaving him and Hank to do the fighting. Fletch let Brian sit there, rather than waste time trying to bring him to his senses. He eased himself into the loader's position so he could operate the coaxial 7.63 mm Besa MG. As long as they could keep the enemy at a distance they were pretty safe. He looked around. The inside of the tank was blood stained and disgusting, full of smoke from the gunpowder, but still fully functional. The engine was running. In many ways it felt like they were in an old fort, immovable and unconquerable, hopefully. He kept firing short bursts towards anything that moved in front of him, particularly the road block.

The Besa was reliable and had a higher rate of fire than just about any other machine gun used in North Africa. It could pump out 800 rounds per minute, and you had to be careful not to expend your full ammunition supply prematurely. Quick bursts were the way to go, and after a few more minutes it looked like the Italians were abandoning the road block. He stopped firing, afraid of hitting their own troops. Looking away from the viewing hole, he fixed his eyes at John, who looked dead, but was not. He was still bleeding. There was not much they could do for him though, there were just too many bullet holes on his body and he died a few minutes later.

He noticed that it was quieting down outside, and best of all, he could hear English speaking voices. As the fighting died down he opened the hatch carefully and peered out. Italian prisoners were everywhere, rounded up by smiling British and

Indian troops. He got out of the tank, and somebody handed him a bottle of scotch, while others slapped his back.

"Great show old man, you kept them on the run with your MG"

"Thanks for ruining their tanks, use the gun next time though"

"We thought you were planning some steel babies the way you were wiggling like a rooster on top of that Fiat"

"Any cute Italian women around, watching you guys on top of that tank gave me some ideas?"

The constant, if well meant, barrage of comments from the soldiers were getting on his nerves as the post battle reaction set in. With shaking hands he took a deep drink from the bottle of scotch, trying not to think about the butcher's bill inside his tank. Hank was helping Brian out, while they left the sad remnants of John 'what's his name' inside the tank. The Matilda was a 'goner' anyway; substantial work had to be done before it would be fit to fight again. He could still not for the life of him remember John's family name. Some medics came over and he asked them to take care of Brian, then sat down on the hull.

Behind them, Tex Matilda was still burning briskly. Nobody tried to extinguish the fire, it was too intense. He forced himself not to look for the burnt out remnants of the crew. The situation felt surreal, and he could not help himself for thinking that the mess tent would be boring without Jack's booming voice hollering out Texan rants. The contrast between the carnage that had just come to an end, and the now cheering soldiers was incredible. The wrecks of the Fiat tankettes and the M 13/40 he had shot up added to the mental confusion in his mind. A couple of hundred yards away he could see that the abandoned but intact M13/40 was literally crawling with curious British 'visitors'. It would probably be put to good use, but Fletch knew one thing, he did not want to be the operator of that piece of thin skinned crap!

"Hi Sir, looks like Jack bought it, was he in the tank?" It was Frank, surprisingly cheerful as always. Did nothing bother that guy!

"Yeah, unfortunately. Did you get the gun?"

"Sure, it was but a lonely 155, they had abandoned it by the time we came around. There is captured equipment everywhere."

Fletch handed him what was left of the Scotch bottle. Frank took a long drink, sighed, and finished the bottle.

"Now that's good stuff," Frank said, "kind of makes the fighting worthwhile. Was this better or worse than France?"

"Much easier, the Italians are certainly not as experienced as the Germans."

"I was afraid of that. We will probably see them here pretty soon. At least we can use the Italian equipment against them" he smiled "but from what I could see it is pretty useless." See you later Lieutenant, said Frank, saluted and walked off.

*

DEUTSCHE AFRIKA KORPS, 1942
*

Queen of the Desert, he realized he hated the name by now. Desert Coffin would have been a more appropriate name at this stage. The new German guns opened the Matilda tanks as if they were sardine cans, and unfortunately they, the crew, ended up being the smashed sardines. With its slow lumbering speed the Matilda could not outrun the German tanks and their high powered grenades.

Fletch had plenty of time to ponder the new situation while he was waiting for the signal to attack the oncoming DAK (Deutsche Afrika Corps). The waiting period is always the worst, particularly when you don't really know what to expect, except that it will be bad. As he was peering through the 'scope' he could see nothing but sand, and more sand. He knew the emptiness was deceiving, a lull before the storm, a storm of German tanks hunting for prey.

The outdated Matilda tank was not the only reason for his anxiety. Fletch was also bloody tired of sand as such. When this damned war was over he was not even going to look at a sand box, let alone a beach. If he had children they would be required to play with pebbles, snow, peanuts, anything but sand. He smiled to himself, first he had to survive this war though, and that was at best a 50/50 proposition under present circumstances. At least he was better protected in his Matilda Mk. II tank than his colleagues in the equally under-gunned but very thinly armored Crusader and American built Stuart tanks.

The Queen of the Desert, as someone had dubbed the Matilda a long time ago, was still the best survival option for an Allied tanker. The name lingered because some of the "higher ups" wanted to give the home folks a warm secure feeling, a sense that their "boys" were well protected. In reality the new German Mk. III and Mk. IV specials (long barreled tanks) had relegated the Matilda to a second rate vehicle, and the new 88mm gun now used by the Afrika Korps had completely outclassed its armor and low speed.

The glory days of fighting the Italians were also over. The fantastic victory of Operation Compass, with its 115,000 prisoners plus thousands of captured tanks and artillery pieces was forgotten now. It was only a little over a year ago, but already seemed like an eternity.

The Germans had arrived, and with it their old nemesis from France, General Rommel. From the beginning they had shown their daring and professionalism, and a willingness to exploit every weak point they could find. In the air the balance was somewhat better, but whereas the Italian Air Force had been so weak it was rarely considered in the planning stages, the dreaded Luftwaffe was deadly in every sense of the word. Consequently every operation had to be planned with air support and air attacks in mind. Rommel and his forces were known by a new name now, the Desert Fox. The Fox had already shown his expertise, and the soldiers of DAK and their Italian allies were the ones doing the pushing, with the Brits retreating. Interestingly the Germans used the same tanks they had used in France 18 months earlier, but they had been up-gunned and thicker frontal armor had been added.

The British tanks had narrow turrets rings, and consequently small turrets. Thus they could not be fitted with larger guns. The German engineers had been more forward looking, and the German Mk. III and IV tanks had been equipped with high powered long barreled 50 and 75 mm guns, both of which could penetrate a Matilda, particularly at short range. In short this meant that his Matilda was gradually getting obsolete. At times the Matilda did shine, as at Halfaya Pass where a few Matilda's had handled 160 German tanks so roughly three senior German commanders lost their job.

He became aware of movement, and squinted to see more clearly. His binocular had scratches in them, which made them worse than the naked eye. The shapes started materializing and became a squadron of Mk.III and IV's approaching them.

"Ready for action!" he called out and ducked into the tank, but left the hatch open to avoid the heat getting too oppressive. There were no snipers here anyway. He took careful aim at the lead tank, a fast moving Mk III and fired. A hit, but he could see the bullet bounce off the frontal armor. Several enemy tanks swiveled their gun toward him and fired in response. However, it was maximum range and only one scored a hit. It bounced off harmlessly; the Matilda was still a tough old lady.

Fletch leveled the two pounder gun and fired a second shot at the Mk. III, hitting the turret. Some damage was obviously done, the tank stopped.

New German tanks appeared. The whole scene was eerie. In one way it reminded him of France. The enemy tanks were basically the same, and he was in the same type of vehicle as well. That was where any similarity ended; the surroundings were sand and stone, instead of green grass and trees. Another Mk III crossed in front of him, an older vehicle with a short 50mm. It fired, and Fletch braced for impact.
Nothing happened, a miss.

He opened his eyes, and ordered the main gun to fire. Another miss.

"Reload, fast."

The training paid off, they fired before the enemy. The gunner that had replaced Brian was experienced and professional. Fletch could see the impact, but the enemy vehicle continued to operate as if nothing had happened. He swore in frustration:

"Oh how I hate these useless solid shots. Keep the damned front towards that Mk III, he can't penetrate us."

Hank kept the front in the right direction, and they all felt a shiver going through the tank when they were hit.

"Reload"

Suddenly he became aware that they had turned too much, they were presenting their rear to the other German tanks. He looked out of the hatch and realized there was a tank behind him.

"Turn the turret, enemy 7 o'clock."

They swiveled the turret toward a German tank behind him, but he could see it was too late. A puff of smoke and flames came shooting out of the barrel pointing at their tank. The grenade penetrated the soft side armor of the Matilda.

"Crap, he must have hit my ammo", was his last thought as an internal explosion rocked the tank and threw him out of the turret.

*

POW

*

Sweet music filled his ears as he slowly drifted around the clouds. Heavenly sounds seemed to surround him. It was very pretty to listen to, and he decided to continue floating along with the music. That was when the pain hit him, and the sweet music changed into Italian voices. As he slowly tried to understand what was happening, he realized he was in an Italian field hospital, a POW. However, he had a great headache and started drifting off again, and once more he was surrounded by heavenly voices, but this time one of the voices spoke English:

"High Fever."

"Don't know if he will make it."

"Lost a lot of blood."

"Could be malaria, or some other tropical disease."

He wanted all these ugly voices to disappear, and eventually they did.

When he came around this time, the whole world seemed to be moving. He was all alone. Had everybody died in this world, but then why was the earth moving, and why did he hear the rumble and humming of a large engine. It dawned on him that he had to be on board a train or a ship. The headache returned, and he drifted off.

The light was unbearable, shining straight into his face. Not only that, it talked to him:

"Wake up, wake up"

Why did they wake him, it was so peaceful here. The voice kept shouting, and as his consciousness returned he became aware of even stranger movements than before. With an effort he opened his eyes, looking straight into the face of a young nurse. She held a flashlight against his face.

"Gracie, you are awake. We have to get you upstairs, the ship is sinking."

He struggled vainly to get up, but felt weak and nauseous. The girl grabbed him with strong hands and helped him up. The sight that met him outside the door was something akin to getting a fist in the face. Smoke was bellowing out of the hull. People were screaming all over. Worse, the ship was listing, and prisoners and crew were streaming into the lifeboats. They tried to get into one, but a crewmember shouted something in Italian and pushed them away. The girl shouted back at him, and though he could not understand the words, the tone of curses are universal enough.

"Come here," the girl dragged him to the other side of the ship. With experienced hands she opened a canister that turned out to contain a small raft. She pulled it towards the back of the ship, but he was too weak to help, and could do no more than pulling himself along the railing. The stern of the ship was dangerously low in the water by now, and she threw the raft in and pushed him down a short ladder hanging over the side. He more or less fell into the raft, pain shooting through his left hand. The girl jumped in, and pushed them away from the sinking ship. They drifted slowly away, faster as soon as the wind caught them.

Alone again, amazing. Fletch woke up, realizing he had dozed off once more. His arm was still throbbing, but not too badly, and with the headache and fever gone he actually felt much better than he had for days. He looked over at the girl, she was sleeping. But that was all he could see. No lifeboats, smoking ships, enemies, or other objects. Absolutely nothing, the horizon was empty all around. He looked over at the girl again. She was pretty, not beautiful, but very attractive, and he owed her his life. Trying not to wake her, he looked around the raft for some water or food. There was none. He looked back at the girl, her eyes were open now and she looked at him.

"How you feel" her Italian accent was strong, but her English easily understandable.

"Not too bad, what happened to me, and why am I here?"

"You had concussion when you came in, and many bruises. The problem was not your physical injuries, but you developed a high fever. We do not know what it was. Fortunately it gone now and you should be well fast. We put you on this prisoner transport bound for Sicilia, but as you can see your English planes attacked us."

"Successfully" he mumbled.

"What did you say?"

"Nothing, just that you can always rely on the Royal Air Force to show up when they are not wanted." he said and smiled at her.

She smiled back.

With that they both became quiet. He looked at her, the stillness became overpowering.

"What was the ruckus for when we left the ship?"

"He wanted to leave you, since English planes were the ones that sunk us. He refused to make room for us in lifeboat. I told him you were my patient."

The girl had saved his life by not leaving him. He told her he was grateful. Looking at her he noticed another thing, she was armed. A small Beretta in a holster. She followed his gaze.

"Don't get any ideas she said" but with a smile. He smiled back, they both knew he was not strong enough anyway.

The hours ticked by slowly, evening came. The ocean was still empty, no sign of life could be seen. He knew they were drifting west, that at least was a good thing. Thirst and hunger started to bother them. She had a little bottle of water, and they used it to wet their lips.

How long can we last? A thought shared, but not spoken. They sat close together to share body warmth during the cool night. Eventually they fell into uneasy sleep.

The morning was grey, and again the hours drifted by. They said little now. Suddenly he could see the girl raise her head and look towards the horizon.

Was it? It was. A small speck on the horizon that grew larger. A fishing boat, but from where. After half an hour they could make out three crew members.

"Give me your gun."

"It is mine."

"I promise to give it back to you if you want me to, but we do not know who these guys are and I am a good shot." He did not brag, just stated a fact. She understood that, gave him a long look, and eventually did as he said.

"What kind of a gun is it?"

"A Beretta Modello 1934, standard issue. Be careful, it has a tendency to fire if you touch the hammer, even if the safety lock is on"

"What caliber"

"9mm, 7 rounds"

That was good. A 9mm had considerable stopping power. He had been afraid it was one of the new smaller 7.62 handguns. He tucked the gun under his trousers. It was high time, the three rather dirty characters on the boat called over to them. He could hear it was a Latin language, but which one. As if she had read his thoughts she said:

'It is some kind of Spanish, but I think they are from Spanish Morocco, a rather long way from home."

They were helped on board, and he was pushed into a chair when they saw he was wounded.

The three of them barely bothered with him. In his obviously weakened state they knew he could not do much. The girl looked afraid, as the three men commented on her. That much he realized. The gestures were universal, and they could not be misunderstood. Suddenly one grabbed her from behind and pulled her arms back. One of the other men started tearing off her uniform. The girl was fighting and shouting, but the two men were stronger than her. The third guy gave Fletch a knock that threw him to the deck, he wanted to join in the fun. Fletch knew they would just rob him and throw him overboard after they had finished raping the girl.

But he had the gun.

He managed to get up, the three fishermen too busy with their 'prey' to take any notice of him. He moved slowly towards the fighting, screaming and laughing group, clinging to the railing. The girl was stripped now, and the men started loosening their belts. Her face was black with fear.

"Stop" It is a word that is understood by most humans, and though he was not shouting, but rather saying it decisively, it did the trick. The sight of the gun pointing at them changed their facial expressions from contempt to slight fear. Yet, when they looked over at him, they were very aware they were three, and he one. They started to spread out, and Fletch knew he could not let that happen. He fired the gun straight at the nearest man who was thrown back by the powerful impact. Half his face had been blown away and he tipped over the railing and into the sea. Now the other two rushed him. Fletched managed one more shot, a deadly one to be sure, before the last guy was upon him, knocking him down with ease. He felt his limbs going soft, and pain shooting through his body from the impact as he hit the deck. He knew the fight would be a short one, he was in no shape for any kind of physical struggle. As he was lying on the deck, he saw the fisherman lift an axe with a hateful grin.

I am done for Fletch thought, but the man waited for a few extra seconds, savoring his coming kill. That was his undoing. Suddenly he lost the axe and stumbled forward. The girl had grabbed a fish spear and rammed it straight through his guts. Fletch could actually see the point sticking out of his stomach. The man's face turned fearful, shocked and angry, all at the same time. He turned and tried to lunge at her, but she wisely held on to the spear. Without the axe he could not reach her. This went on for some seconds, but the blood loss and shock quickly got to him. With a fearful scream he collapsed on the deck where he twisted around in pain. For an eternity the girl and Fletch stood there, looking at each other. She looked magnificent, her bronze skin gleaming in the sun, not unlike a lioness who had felled a prey he determined. The sight would stay with him for the rest of his life.

Then, as if on command, they helped each other push the two men, one dead one dying, overboard. He was completely exhausted when they finished, and sat down against the wall outside the little cabin while the boat rolled gently on the waves. Some seagulls flew overhead, rather peacefully, and totally out of character to the gory drama that had just taken place. She sat down next to him and started crying as the reaction set in. He took her gently in his arms, held her close, stroking her hair. He was also trying not to dwell too much on the fact that he was holding a pretty naked girl in his arms. After a while she stopped crying and pulled herself together.

"You must think I am weak!"

"On the contrary, you saved my life again, and don't think about having killed those bastards." It was an idiotic thing to say, but he had never been very good at comforting others with deep meaningful phrases. He should have made her forget the action and killing, not reminded her about it.

"I have to get dressed."

"Not for me." That was the right thing to say, the girl laughed when she heard him, and she waved a finger at him. It was great to see her smile, and he realized that she was beautiful, much more so than he had observed when she was in her uniform. He could not help but stare. She let him, then picked up the remnants of her uniform and put it on. He became embarrassed by his own behavior.

"I am sorry" he said, "I have not seen a beautiful girl for a long time. Now, let's see if there is anything we can eat. Judging by that crowd it is probably poisonous. Ah, here is some water. By the way you can have your gun back."

"Keep it, oh, and I only have one more magazine."

Only 10 bullets in all, but it was probably all they needed for self defense. The water was not the cleanest, but they nevertheless finished the first jug very quickly, thirsty as they were. He looked around, the ocean was still calm, and they were drifting slowly west. Problem was he had no idea where they were. They searched the craft, but there was little to eat, though plenty of water in a container under the deck. The boat was not big, probably about 35 feet, lateen rigged, and had a small cabin at the front. Fletch decided he had to do something to get their thoughts away from their current problems.

"After all we have been through, I guess we should be formally introduced. I sincerely apologize for my lack of chivalry. My name is Tommy Fletcher, but everybody calls me Fletch. May I ask what your name is?"

"Constance Gallo, but everybody calls me Constance" she laughed mockingly.

"A beautiful name for a beautiful girl" What is this he thought to himself, why do I keep saying all these silly phrases in a situation like this. Yet the reason was obvious, he was fascinated by her. She smiled at him, then cleaned out the cabin for dirty clothes and what they naturally assumed were flea ridden blankets. As the night cool drifted in they sat close together in the small cabin. However, the image of her naked body kept dancing before his eyes. He could feel her eyes on him, and started to breathe harder. Then he felt her lips against his, and they kissed for a long wonderful time.

"You are my savior"

"No, it is the other way around, you have saved my life twice. You don't have to kiss me to say thank you"

She laughed softly.

"I did not. You are mine; I have known that from the moment they carried you into the ward. And now you cannot escape" They kissed again, but he would have liked to do so much more, yet knew he could not in his weakened state. Inside he cursed his own weakness. She felt his frustration, and could feel he was getting aroused, despite his exhaustion.

"Now lean back" she said, loosening his trousers as he did so, pulling them off. Her hands felt cool and wonderful, strong yet gentle. He let his hands wander over her body, creating a wonderful longing feeling. When she had finished, she kissed his cheek and whispered into his ear.

"Get strong soon, I don't want to wait for too long."

The next day the sun was burning down mercilessly, the ocean surface flat as a table. Just a tiny whiff of wind could be felt, but not enough to move the boat at anything like steering speed. Fletch just could not understand how the horizon could be so empty. There was a war going on, you would expect something, airplanes, ships, anything. A couple of times they saw what they thought were airplanes, but they were not certain and had no means to send out any signal.

Evening came, and now heat and hunger started to bother them. They had to start conserving water as well, not knowing when they would reach land.

"We must be drifting towards Spain," Constance said, reflecting his own thoughts. "Otherwise we would have seen ships or airplanes."

It was an uneasy night. Between the shortness of food, a diminishing water supply, and their general exhaustion, not much was said or done. By sun up the heat returned. A light wind still carried them west, but they were too weak to raise the sail, and were content just to let the boat drift along. It rolled quite a bit, but they were not seasick. 'We are probably too weak even for that' Fletch thought. 'What an irony it would be to have survived the battles in the desert just to die from heat and thirst, and in the middle of the ocean no less' He laughed quietly.

"What's so funny," Constance asked.

He told her, but she did not laugh, just shook her head. "I will never understand English humor."

The hours passed slowly by. Like the day before, the horizon seemed empty of life. Worse, the boat was also starting to fill up with sea water. If they had not been so exhausted they could have emptied it, but instead they only made some half hearted efforts, spending most of the time looking at the dirty water washing around the bottom. Then as they were both starting to lose hope a small speck appeared on the horizon, and their luck changed. It was a dark cloud, and while waiting they were alternately hoping and despairing, praying or swearing, but eventually it reached them and it started pouring, the way it can only rain in the south. They jumped around in the boat, held out their shirts so they could soak up the water, twisted out the water to drink, and repeated the process again and again. It was also getting cooler, a welcome relief from the heat. The life giving rainfall stopped after 20 minutes, but it had changed their outlook. They were full of hope again.

And there was more, they could see land to the south. Hours went by, and finally they were approaching the coast, but where?

*

THE ROAD

*

The road along the Mediterranean Coast of Africa is one of the oldest roads on earth, and one of the most unknown. It is not a defined paved road lined with monuments and past glory, like the Via Appia. Nor is it famous as a trade route like the Silk Road from Europe to India and China. It does not even have a name. Most of it is little more than a flattened trail, and it has always faced competition from the blue waters of the ocean.

But the road is older than its famous cousins, since Africa is the cradle of man, and the Mediterranean is the starting point of Western civilizations.

Around 250BC the road carried Carthagenian troops and their elephants on their way to subdue Spain and fight the Romans, as long as it lasted.

When Carthage was destroyed by imperial Rome, the road took on new importance. Grand cities were built, parts of the road were paved, and the Legions marched up and down the coast for the glory of the eternal city. But the empire was not eternal. Rome fell, like all empires fall, and when it did its monuments and cities disappeared, turned into ruins and covered with sand. The road itself drifted into obscurity. For hundreds of years it remained forgotten, ill maintained and less traveled.

Then, around 600AD, the road returned to life as Arab and Muslim armies used it on their way to conquer Spain and invade France. They did not return. Like previous invaders they were eventually overwhelmed and beaten on the killing fields of Europe. And so the road yet again lost its importance, only utilized by the local population. Less glamorous but more peaceful.

In the twentieth century the road once more drifted to the forefront of attention, particularly the section between Egypt and Tunisia. As in previous times not for trade but as a military highway. In their fights for empire, glory and wealth, the mechanized armies of Europe sent columns of troops and equipment up and down the road, from battle to battle.

The people living along the road watched all this activity with stoicism. Armies had come and gone over the centuries. They had seen it all before. How long would this incursion last, nobody knew. *Ins Allah*. It was in the hands of Allah.

For Constance and Fletch, their knowledge, sketchy as it was, about the existence of the road was their only hope. Their landing place, invasion point, as they jokingly called it, was literally in the middle of nowhere. The coast was rocky, and they did not see any life. However, they assumed the coastal road could not be too many miles away, so walked inland. When they found it, it was desolate and abandoned. No traffic could be seen, even if the marks left by man and animals over the centuries were everywhere. They decided to walk west, it was as good a direction as the east. They had packed what they needed when they left the boat, which was mainly a water can, so me loose copper coins, a bayonet somebody had left and the handgun. They also put some old dirty rags over their uniforms to be less noticeable. Just as Fletch headed toward the edge of the road, he heard Constance call out to him.

"Stop, we cannot walk on the road. We must walk a little distance away from it, even if it is difficult. We have to know who we meet before they see us. We will be recognized as Europeans as soon as we are close enough for them to make out our facial features"

"Why, who cares? We may be in Algeria, which is French, or in Italian territories, or even Spanish, which would by the way be the best, they are neutral."

"This is Bedouin country, and they hate us, regardless of whom or what we are."

"What are you talking about?"

"Just that, the locals hate us. Europeans have occupied and colonized the coast of Africa for hundreds of years, probably ever since the Romans. The locals have cultivated the hate forever, and when they find Europeans they kill them if they are alone, or worse. That goes whether we are in French, Italian or English territory."

"Or worse?"

"One of the nurses at our hospital was out with her boyfriend, and they probably got lost. We had dozens of soldiers looking for them, and they were found the next day. He was dead, and had probably suffocated since his testicles had been propped into his mouth. She had been tied up, beaten half to death and gang raped. Then left to die. She was barely alive when we found them, but it was too late so she died soon afterwards. They were both stripped for all valuables, including their clothes. It was a sight I shall never forget. Even in death, the endless fear and pain they had been through showed on their faces. I threw up when they were carried in, and I was not the only one."

"Oh my god. Did they find the culprits?" Fletch did not have to hide his feelings. He was shocked to the core, the images in his mind were uncomfortable to the extreme.

"Of course not. Our soldiers shot a dozen or so guys whom they said were guilty, but I know it was just revenge. They were probably innocent, just in the wrong spot at the wrong time. Revenge acts like that just add to the hate, it's a vicious circle. The French Foreign Legion act the same way, and I remember I read your countrymen bombed local villages in Iraq a few years ago. Don't believe all those Hollywood movies with Rudolf Valentino as the Sheikh. People have fought over and died on this road for hundreds of years. When the war is over all these people will probably rise up against their colonizers, it will not be pretty." She looked at him sincerely and continued,

"If we are captured, save the last bullet for me."

"Second to last," he said, "the last will be for me. I don't want to taste my own testicles."

When they started to walk west he still contemplated why the land was so empty. There was a war going on, hundreds of thousands of men were on the move in North Africa. Why did they not see any? Only one explanation made sense, they had to be much further west than he had originally thought. He tried to see the map in his head. They had to be west of Tripoli, where the Axis forces were disembarking and moving East. West of Tunisia came the French colony of Algeria, or rather Vichy French as it was right now. In theory they were allied with Germany, but of course many French people hated the Germans. However a large number of the French were also hateful toward the Brits for the sinking of the French fleet by the Royal Navy. So, he concluded, they had to be extremely careful, whether they were in Algeria or further west.

Towards the evening they started looking for shelter, and discovered a farm in the hillside. Hunger was bothering them, so they decided they had to risk it and approach the house. Fletch had the gun in his pocket, and unlocked it, just in case. They called out when they came closer, and the farmer came out with his family. Suspicion was on all their faces, but the fact that it was a man and a woman that approached them eased the tension. The age old custom of the Arabs living in the desert meant they were immediately invited in to eat and drink. It was a relatively modest farm, not wealthy not poor, by the standards of the area, but they shared what they had. Constance knew a few Arab and French words, and the farmer some Italian words, so they managed to make themselves understood. Afterwards they were given a room in the barn. As they put the dirty blankets over themselves, Fletch was thinking that it did not matter, since they were pretty dirty and stinking themselves. His next and final thought before sleep overtook him was that they would be easy to rob tired as they were.

What was tickling his nose! Fletch was coming out of a deep sleep when dawn was breaking over the mountains in the distance. He felt warm and surprisingly well, food, water and sleep had done wonders. Now he realized what the tickling was, it was Constance's hair, her head resting on his chest. It was wonderful lying there, looking out of the barn door at the approaching daylight. It was as if time did not exist. Judging by the animals and the farm buildings it could just as well be 1942 BC as 1942 AD. He also liked the feeling of Constance hair and body resting peacefully on him. The warmth from her body was going through him, leaving a good content feeling. He actually realized he was becoming a bit too warm as he started feeling her very feminine part pressing against his body. She smiled at him, when she could feel his reaction. Her arm moved down his body, and he let his free right arm move down hers from the shoulders to those wonderful breasts and beyond.

"I love you." He bent his head to kiss the top of her head, but she tilted her head so instead he kissed her mouth. It set off feelings in him that nearly overwhelmed him, even before the lovemaking carried him to heights he had never known existed.

When they finished, she looked at him and said.

"We are scaring the animals."

"Oh I don't know, they are probably used to worse"

They remained in each others arms and started talking about everyday things, like lovers often do.

"Where is your family from?"

"We, my parents, brother and me, live southwest of London, in a small place called Claygate, my father's hometown, It is a great little place with some shops, a train station, a great pub called "The Hare and The Hound', and that's about it. My mother is actually from Norway. Funny enough she has a sister who married an American. They live in New York. Like my mother, auntie has two sons. One of them, I think his name is Carl, is the black sheep of the family. He was visiting his grandparents in Norway when the Germans struck and apparently he signed up with the SS. That's about all we know though. What about you?

"Not very exciting. We are from a small village not far from Napoli called Castellabate. I was baptized in a church called Santa Maria de Castellabate. My parents live in a small house right next to Palazzo Belmonte, owned by the richest man in the area. It is a beautiful place, you will like it. I have a sister, younger than me, and a little brother. My parents can't stand Mussolini and his brownshirts, which is why it was easy for me to like you!"

"That's a beautiful name for a village, it rolls off the tongue. I would love to see it someday."

"You will, with me, when the war is over."

Almost reluctantly Fletch got up, stretched out, and went for a short walk. It was remarkable how good he felt, physically and mentally. This was a new situation, pleasant but also complicated. He wanted to be with Constance, but she was on the "other" side. Maybe they could get to a neutral country like Spain, and she could spend the rest of the war there. His deliberations had taken longer than he realized, judging by the sun. He turned and started walking back.

When he returned, the midday heat had set in. The moment he was within view of the farm houses he saw they had visitors. Three tired looking horses were standing in the yard. He decided caution was more important than valor, and slipped quietly up behind the main house. An incredibly dirty looking individual was standing by the door, talking to the frightened looking family which was lying face down on the floor. It was immediately obvious that a fight had taken place, the father had blood stains on his neck and clothes.

Fletch pulled back to gather his thoughts. He had not been seen. Where were the other two? The answer was obvious. He felt fear down his spine, and had to concentrate so as not to run in. He could not use the gun, the other bandits would hear him. What, what, what. There was only one possible course of action. He pulled out the bayonet and looked towards the stable again. Now he could hear loud voices, and fighting. He had to act fast. Quietly he went through the door, hoping the enemy would look the other way. He did, but one of the older women opened her eyes in surprise, and the guy noticed. He spun around, but Fletch was faster. He jumped forward and put his left hand over the mouth of the man. With his right hand he stabbed the bayonet into his guts, twisted, pulled it out and stabbed again. The man's eyes were round from shock, as he collapsed, dying, to the floor. Fletch did not wait, he turned and ran out of the door towards the barn. He dropped the bayonet and pulled out the Beretta on the way.

Just as he came through the door, the Beretta fired. Constance had warned him about the malfunctioning safety lock, and now the two bandits were warned. He captured the situation in one glance. Constance was up against the wall, she had marks on her face from the fight, her few remaining clothes in tatters, yet she was still fighting. One of the bandits had his left hand around her throat, the other between her legs. An old pistol was sticking out of his belt in the back. The other bandit was in the process of pulling down his pants, his erection showing through the trousers. A rifle was leaning against the wall next to him. They both heard the fluke shot and turned towards him, their smiling faces turning white when they saw Fletch more or less at the same time that he saw them. Both started pulling their weapons.

Fletch shot the man holding Constance, who looked like the more dangerous of the two, in the face. He was slammed against the wall, and a fine shower of blood drops spread out behind him like a mosaic. The other bandit was bogged down. He was trying to raise the old rifle at the same time as he was pulling up his trousers, hate and shame showing in his face. Fletch shot him in the crotch out of pure hatred and disgust. The man howled and screamed in pain and fear when he realized what was happening. He slid down on the floor, both hands pressed against his crotch where the blood was pumping out from the gruesome wound. Still full of hate and adrenalin Fletch walked over and lowered his gun towards the bandits face. The man's eyes rolled back and the vomit came out of his mouth like a fountain. Fletch took a step back, looked at him with a hateful grin and fired the 9mm bullet straight between the bulging eyes. The bandit's legs kicked a few times, then his body went limp.

Constance ran over to him, relief and gratitude etched into her face, kissing him and talking at the same time.

"I knew you would come back for me, but it took a long time. There is one more man, you have to get him before he comes back"

"Don't worry, I got him as well."

He held her tight as he led her out and away from the disgusting scene with the two dead bandits. After a while they both started to relax. Standing there he realized she was actually quite short, only reaching him to the top of his shoulder, and he felt good holding her. He felt his breathing getting normal, and to ease the tension said:

"This is the second time I have to save you from bad company. You have to be more careful about who you hang out with."

The joke fell flat on its face, she just looked at him. He could have kicked himself for saying something so idiotic. Finally she let go of him, collected the rest of her clothes and put them on. He watched her while he tucked away the Beretta which he still held in his right hand. The Beretta is great despite the malfunctioning safety lock, he thought. Even if it is not quite as powerful as some of the other 9mm handguns, its accuracy more than compensates.

"What about the family?"

"Oh crap, I forgot them, we have to loosen the ropes."

They went into the house and did so. The look on the faces of the family members when they came back was one of immense relief. They were extremely grateful, and rubbed their ankles and hands in pain when the blood circulation returned. Still, they wanted them to leave. They had brought trouble, and in this part of the world that was not what you needed. Before they buried the three bandits Fletch looked through their clothes and packs. Not much of value. Judging by these characters banditry was not a very lucrative business. Apart from the rifle, which he recognized as an old Lee Enfield, an equally old 0.32 in. Webley Bulldog revolver, a lot of rags and a little food, they only had a few copper coins.

"Tell the farmers they can have one of the horses," he said, "and also the old revolver. The Beretta is better and I have no ammunition for the Webley anyway. Actually they can have everything else except the rifle. By the way Constance, Do you know how to ride?"

"Yes, what about you"

"Not really, I have only been on a horse as a little boy, but you can probably help me. Did you get directions?"

"Yes, we are not far from a French Algerian town called Bouric, which means we have Spain right across the Mediterranean. I think we should steal a boat and cross over. Otherwise we will probably run into more Bedouins."

"Sounds like a good plan to me. Why do you keep calling them Bedouins? They are more like common bandits."

"They are, but we use the term Bedouins for everybody that are against us. I have no idea why, but the term stuck with me I guess."

They set off, their belongings and some carpets loaded onto the horses. Fletch looked at the rifle again, he was very familiar with it. It was a first world war Lee Enfield, the standard rifle of the British army, and one of the best bolt action rifles ever produced. This particular example was an old version and pretty beat up. To be certain it was functional he fired a bullet. It worked. British quality he thought proudly. They only found 11 bullets, not exactly what you needed in a war, but it had to do. To hide the rifle from view he rolled it into some of the dirty rags and put it on the back of the horse.

The trip was easy. After their earlier travails the ability to ride provided much needed respite for their tired legs. As they approached Bouric, traffic on the road increased. They were better disguised now, with additional rags over what was left of their uniforms. When they closed in on the town, they dismounted and led the horses on foot to create less attention.

The first obstacle came when they had to bypass a road block set up by some French troops. They did not seem too interested in the people passing them, so Constance and Fletch decided to just walk past with their horses in tow.

When they came close, so close he started to believe they would make it, one of the French soldiers looked at Constance and said something to her. She just shook her head. Despite the heat, Fletch could feel cold sweat running down his back. He kept on walking, looking down into the ground, but his heart was beating so hard he was almost surprised the soldiers did not hear it. Constance kept walking too, even as more comments came. He noticed that her face, which was mostly hidden behind a scarf, was quite pale. It is common for Arab women to look subdued and down into the ground, and that helped Constance, as she emulated their behavior. Maybe it was the heat, maybe just pure luck, but the soldiers were too lazy to get up to check them and they continued into town without any mishap. Fletch felt his heartbeat becoming normal. What now?

"We have to find the harbor."

She nodded, and they led their horses towards the water. With dozens of fishermen and other men milling around there was no way they could steal a boat in the daylight. For the next few hours they tried to stay unobtrusive, blending in with the crowd, and pick out a suitable boat at the same time. As darkness came they had their eyes firmly set on a small fishing boat anchored at the end of a pier. It was not too different from their earlier mount, and looked like it could handle the crossing to Spain. They had some food and water, and it was quite likely the Spanish coast guard would get to them before they landed on the coast. It was a good plan, and with a little luck it just might work.

Leaving the horses in a back alley, they entered the boat with their few belongings as soon as it got dark. They had expected more people around, but perhaps due to the war relatively few were seen, and nobody noticed the boat being manhandled out towards the open ocean. As soon as they passed the protected bay they were swallowed up by the dark and felt safe. It was a quiet night, with a light breeze, and it carried them out to sea. Fletch steered by the stars. He was not exactly a navigator, but all he had to do was steer straight north, and they were bound to hit Spanish territorial waters sooner or later. With the morning sun he looked around to find out where he was and became aware of a much larger boat following them. More than that, he could see muzzle flashes, though he could not see any effect or water splashes from the bullets. It had to be some kind of Vichy coast guard vessel. It was surprising that they had ventured so far out, and found them as well.

"Crap, we have been discovered. No more hiding I will return fire. Constance, stay low." He took off the old rags to let everybody see his uniforms, grabbed the Lee Enfield and started firing at the enemy. Sharp shooting from a small boat rolling on the waves is not an easy task, and after two shots, that created no visible effect, he knew he was wasting his small ammo stock. Even the accuracy and reliability of a Lee Enfield counted for nothing in this situation. They had to be closer before he resumed firing. He swore to himself. Why were they so unlucky? Why now, why being caught so close to freedom, it was just not fair. There was something like six to eight men on the Vichy vessel, more than he could hope to handle.

He decided to sell his life dearly. He was not in the mood to become a POW again. A kind of peace descended on him once the decision had been made. He knew Constance agreed, even if he had not asked her. She had on several occasions said that she did not want to be caught. In truth that had been in reference to the Bedouins, not the Vichy, something he would only remember much later. Just as he was preparing himself for the final fight, he heard engine noises that could only come from an airplane. He rolled onto his back and looked up. It was British, though he did not recognize the type, only the nationality markings. He waved to the plane, and pointed towards the Vichy boat.

Squadron Leader Charles 'Chuck' Spalding, 248 Squadron, was enjoying the morning in his two seat Bristol Beaufighter Mk. IV. The breaking dawn was always the best time of the day. He loved to watch the sun rise over the Mediterranean, it was spectacular, and the air was still cool and pleasant. Flying from his base in Gibraltar he had time to enjoy it. Enemy fighters would not be a factor until he ventured further east, they did not have the range to catch him this far out. Fortunately Spain had not allowed the Luftwaffe to place warplanes on her territory. In reality they were pretty safe from dangerous single engine fighters, but not long range twin engine planes like the Junkers JU-88 or the Messerschmitt ME-110. Flying from bases in France and Italy they could reach every corner of the Mediterranean if they wanted to. Unlike the single engine ME 109's and FW 190's, the heavy long range planes did not worry Chuck. With the speed and power of the Beaufighter, it was up to him if battle should be joined or avoided. Much better than the old Bristol Blenheim fighter bombers the squadron had used until last Christmas. That was not a plane you wanted to dogfight in at this stage of the war. According to P/O Peter Brown, the jokester of the squadron, the Blenheim could be shot down by a well flown barn door. An hour into the flight they could already feel the heat rising quickly, as was usual here, just off the coast of Africa. That meant the best part of the trip was over, and they were also closer to potential hostile action. Chuck smiled to himself, 'hostile action' was such a polite term, he preferred the sharper sounding 'deadly business.'

"Skipper, two small boats at 10 o'clock. Look a bit suspicious this far out."

It was well known the Italian navy used such craft to smuggle agents and mines. Chuck looked over the nose and to the left. He could just make out the two small craft below.

"Let's take a closer look."

He banked the Beaufighter (or Beau as the crews called it) left, dived down to 50 feet, and zoomed right between the two boats. One of the two people on the small boat was waving.

At their speed Chuck could not get all the details, but a few things stood out. The larger one had a Vichy flag on the side, which meant it was from Algeria and enemy controlled, and it was firing on the smaller boat. One of the two people on the smaller boat was apparently firing back. Despite this he was not certain if it was worth wasting ammunition on such a small patrol boat, which was probably just a converted civilian ship anyway. Maybe they were just chasing smugglers. When he pulled up after the pass he heard a couple of small "thuds' in the fuselage and realized the larger boat was firing at him as well. That did it.

"Damned, he is shooting at us. I will blow that bastard out of the water!"

Chris Shearn, The navigator/observer who was seated behind Chuck, did not answer, just nodded. He radioed their position back to base. Chuck turned the plane around in a leisurely fashion. There were no enemy fighters out here and the patrol boat did not have much in the way of Flak (anti aircraft artillery), only a solitary small caliber machine gun. Even if they had radioed for help, it would be at least 30 minutes before enemy fighters could reach them.

This gave him plenty of time to prepare the attack. He double checked that the safety hatch for the cannons were in the 'on' position, adjusted the two 14 cylinder Bristol Hercules engines to 85% power, went down to 250 ft. and lined up straight towards the craft. It had turned towards land and was going at top speed, knowing it was hopelessly outgunned. Yet compared to the almost 300 mph of the Beaufighter it was practically standing still. Flying like this was exciting stuff, Chuck thought. He could feel the adrenaline permeating every fiber in his body, and did not feel much compassion for the crew of the boat he was about to sink. His mission parameters had been "searching for targets of opportunity" and this was certainly an opportunity. The bastard had fired at him first.

At 800 yards out he pulled the trigger and the six 0.303 inch machine guns blasted away. His aim was slightly short, so he adjusted the nose of the plane 2 degrees up and could see the bullets crawling towards the boat. Just as they reached the craft, he engaged the four 20mm cannons under the nose. The crew was jumping overboard when they understood what was happening, which was just as well. The effect when the shower of machine gun bullets and exploding 20mm grenades hit home was dramatic. The coastal vessel literally disintegrated in a shower of splinters and flames as the powerful barrage tore it apart. Few airplanes in 1942 had the firepower of a Beaufighter.

'A little bit like shooting a bird with a cannon' Chuck mumbled to himself as he released the trigger and pulled up. He turned the plane around, throttled back and went down for a final look at the target. There was nothing but pieces left, yet he was happy to see some heads bobbing up and down in the water. He waved the wings to the guy in the small fishing boat, who was waving back, pulled up to 10,000 feet and headed for base.

"Radio the position of that guy to the navy" he said over the intercom, "I think he had a uniform on and that means he is one of ours. Do you still have some hot coffee left in that thermos?" He felt satisfied. Most patrols were boring and tedious, with little room for action. This one was certainly very different. All in all it had been a jolly good day.

"Wow, the RAF really delivered this time" Fletch said excitedly. He was still awed by the way the Vichy boat had been ripped to pieces. Constance did not answer. He looked over at her. She was lying quietly on the deck in a twisted position. With a shock he noticed the blood spreading over the front of her uniform.

"Oh my god, not now, not when we are as good as saved."

He rushed to her side. It was immediately obvious it was too late, there was nothing he could do. One of the many bullets from the coast guard vessel had hit her straight in the chest, and he had not even noticed.

The shadow of death was creeping into her beautiful face. She looked at him with tender eyes as she squeezed the amulet she used to keep around her neck into his hand.

"Give this to my parents!" she whispered. It was her last sentence, her eyes glazed over and life disappeared from her body, right there in front of him. He folded his fingers around the amulet while he looked into her dead eyes, tears streaming down his cheeks.

"I will"

He held her close while tears and sweat were dropping from his face to the deck next to her limp body. They evaporated immediately in the heat of the African sun, not even a wet spot could be seen. It was as if they had never existed.

*

HISTORICAL NOTES

*

The North African campaign was in many ways a strategic side show. At least for Hitler, whose plans were always firmly fixed upon Eastern Europe. After the Italians got in trouble following Mussolini's ill advised ventures into Greece and Egypt, it became clear too all, Allies and Axis, that the Italian commanders were not properly prepared for modern warfare, and their equipment was inferior to that of the enemy. Nor was Italian industrial capacity up to the task of keeping her armed forces adequately supplied with the huge amounts of materials a modern mechanized war required. To add insult to injury, a significant percentage of Axis supply ships never reached Africa. During a critical phase in 1942 only 20% of supplies sent from Germany and Italy to Rommel reached the front line. Most was sunk or destroyed during transit by the effective Allied blockade, carried out by their air and naval forces.

War and post war propaganda has always belittled the Italian army, but in reality the Italians were as individually brave as were the soldiers of any of the other warring nations. The Italians produced great air aces and the navy and army undertook many daring raids.

Only after the British had so comprehensively beaten the Italian forces in 1940/41, did Hitler dispatch what has become one of the most famous military forces in history, the Deutsche Afrika Korps. DAK for short. Together with the remaining Italian forces they battled the allies for two years until finally beaten. In many ways the German campaign was quite successful. The Germans initially committed very small forces, yet tied down much larger Allied armies. They also inflicted heavier casualties on the opposition than they lost themselves. For example, the 8ᵗʰ Army lost more tanks in the opening phases of the El Alamein battle than the combined German / Italian forces fielded in all of Africa. Unfortunately for the Germans, during the last stage of the North African campaign, long after the US entry into the war, Hitler ordered much larger forces to be sent to Tunisia as reinforcements. It was too late, and the forces that made it across the Mediterranean were beaten as soon as they arrived. When the end came, 250,000 Axis soldiers surrendered and were made prisoners. A better course of action for Germany would have been to pull the remaining forces out of Africa and then use these battle hardened troops in the following months, in the defense of Sicily and Italy itself. It was a major strategic mistake. Rommel was one of several senior German officers who argued against this late development. To the benefit of the Allies, Hitler did not listen to his Generals. It was neither the first nor the last time.

STEEL VENGEANCE
*
ITALY 1944
*

The girl was rough looking, marked by her profession. The gestures were universal. Some cigarettes, food and nylon stockings, and she would be his. For half an hour or so. He waved her off in equally universal gestures, and received what were obviously Italian obscenities in return, followed by insulting hand signals. The girl walked away looking for better customers. They would not be difficult to find, hundreds of soldiers had descended on the village.

"Remarkable how easy it is to manage without a common language" he said quietly, more or less to himself. The insults did not affect him. He had seen and heard worse.

It was getting hot and he took another drink from his 'secret' canteen as he called it. Not that it was very secret, nor was he the only one to carry some liquid energy, the pundits name for alcohol. While his normal canteen had water, the small bottle of Scotch was from time to time a life saver, and now he needed both of them badly. The southern sun burned down, and like many other crew members he had sought refuge in the shadow of the tank. HQ had ordered them to halt their advance while waiting for further orders, and the troops were taking full advantage of this unexpected, and short, respite. Some of the infantry soldiers were also relaxing, but most of them had spread out in the little town, benefiting from their short lived hero status. They were busy enjoying the victor's spoils, wine and women. He did not fancy joining them; the mental wounds from his North African adventures were still too deep. Not that he had any moral or other misgivings, it was just he could not do it. Instead he had taken to drinking, and got in trouble for it. He would have been a Major by now had it not been for his drinking issues.

The four crew members of his Churchill Mk VII tank, plus the crews of the other eight Churchill tanks, pretended not to notice Captain Tommy 'Fletch' Fletcher's unsocial behavior. He was not a loved commander, actually a bit disliked. He preferred to stay aloof, and to the rank and file he seemed 'arrogant.' It was easier that way he felt. Losses, unavoidable as they were, did not become so personal. Despite this there was no lack of men that wanted to be in his crew. He was a survivor. In fact he was the only officer left in his original platoon. Just yesterday Major Hawkens had been killed, leaving Fletch as the senior officer.

Sicily and Italy was not the 'easy' campaign the press portrayed it to be. Winston Churchill's speech about the 'soft' underbelly of Europe was showing itself to be somewhat premature. The further north they came the more Fletch and the troops realized they were in fact facing some tough old guts.

It was becoming too hot to sit still, even in the shade, so he got up and stretched out. That done he decided to have another look at the old road heading north. It was a road steeped in tradition and could be seen snaking its way through the valley. As picturesque as you expected it to be. Via Appia, the Appian way, is probably the most famous ancient road in the world. Over the centuries, everything from the glorious and victorious armies of Imperial Rome, to the common ox cart loaded with fruits, trinkets and screaming children had traveled its worn paving stones. For Fletch looking through his binoculars the sight of the road brought mixed feelings. While he would have liked to take a closer look at the magnificent countryside, he did not have the opportunity to do so. The problem was that a German patrol was blocking their approach a few miles ahead, and it had to be removed. Unfortunately most German blocking positions had one thing in common, they were usually damned effective. The excellent German anti tank guns could blast any allied tank in the field into oblivion, and their crews were quite good. Not as good as they used to be. The enormous losses the Wehrmacht had suffered on the Eastern Front meant Germany was now nearing the bottom of its manpower barrel. Yet the German army was still deadly, in every sense of the word.

"Cap," the wireless operator interrupted his deliberations, "HQ has ordered us forward toward the town of Cavello, and immediately."

"Acknowledge, and send out some men to get the guys. Fire one round from the tank. That should get their attention."

The crews came back, finishing their last wine bottles, pulling up their zippers, commenting rudely on their 'victories' which were mostly local prostitutes. They were laughing and talking, and Fletch let them have their brief moment of joy. They were young men in harms way, they deserved these stolen minutes away from death and destruction. Despite being only 23, and thus not really that much older than the rest, he was an old hand, and seen as such. It was not the years that had aged him; it was the length of service. The hours of fear, the number of people he had killed. It all ate into Fletch like a spreading tumor, like it ate into so many hundreds of thousands of other soldiers in his situation.

'Oh what the heck. I have to stop getting so damned sentimental' Fletch thought. He tucked his canteen away and gave orders to start up the tanks. The noise of all the 350 hp Bedford engines roaring to life was overwhelming, and after a couple of minutes the column moved forward. He took a quick glance back at the village from his vantage point in the tank turret. He had already forgotten the name of the place when its buildings and inhabitants disappeared in the dust behind the column. There had been so many towns, so many places. All of them easy to forget when you knew how to do it. By now he was an expert at forgetting.

Half an hour later, an infantry unit stopped them. Together with the Lieutenant in charge he went up to a small ridge overlooking the road ahead. From what he could see through his binoculars they had at least two or three 75mm anti tank guns, two tanks that looked like German Mk IV's and a monstrous tank destroyer. He did not recognize the unusual style of the tank destroyer, so would consult HQ. With this in mind he turned and walked back to his platoon of Churchill tanks.

"What does it look like Captain?"

"Trouble, but we can overwhelm them. It would be easier if we could get the RAF to soften up their position first. Radio HQ and ask if they have any air support available. Oh, and also ask if they know of any new German vehicles in the area, there is a huge tank destroyer down there."

"Does it have an 88?"

"Probably"

"Shit"

The last word was telling. The 88 was the scourge of allied armor. It would burn through anything at long distances, far out of reach of all allied tank guns. Yet in Fletch opinion, the German L-70 (75 mm) was probably a better anti tank gun. It had a lower profile and was therefore harder to detect and destroy. Due to its very high muzzle velocity, the penetration power was as good as that of the now famous, or infamous depending on your point of view, L-56 (88mm) used on the Tiger tank. It also had a higher rate of fire. All in all, the sad truth was that the new German tanks were far better than their own. Fortunately Allied airpower, when it could be brought to bear, turned the tables in most battles.

The hard fighting had also taught the Allied ground forces that the German strong points could be outflanked by the far larger Allied tank forces. Another advantage the Allies had was that the Luftwaffe was not too bothersome at this stage of the war. They made occasional appearances, but were mostly engaged in defense. Many of their best squadrons were engaged against the Allied bombers over Germany or trying to hold back Russian armor in the East. Consequently, land attacks could be planned and executed with minimal consideration of enemy air attacks. For the Germans as well as for the Allies, Italy was a secondary front.

"Captain, HQ says they have information the Germans have sent a few 88 mm self propelled guns here. Apparently they are called Elefant and Ferdinand or something like that. Sound more like a pub than a tank name. Should be easy to recognize, they have the gun in a huge box at the rear. HQ also says we cannot break their frontal armor, or even side armor."

"Gun in the rear, that's what I saw. We have us an Elefant down there. Well we cannot break the frontal armor of anything with our toothpicks, so this should not be that different. What about the RAF, anything?"

"They will send some Spits, should be here in 30 minutes."

"That's pretty good service."

While they waited he gave his orders. Two of the tanks would circle around the valley. That way they could hit the enemy from the flanks. The rest would move right down the mountain sides.

"You have to take the Germans from the side" Fletch told the tank commanders going along the side of the valley. "You heard HQ say we cannot break their frontal armor. Remember that even the front of the Mk. IV's can only be cracked at short range. Against the Ferdinand you don't have a chance, you have to immobilize the belts since it has no turret. Let's hope the RAF takes it out, but don't count on it. Let's light up the target area for them. Sergeant, radio the planes that I will fire some HE grenades to mark it."

"Yes Sir, right away Sir."

He went back to his own tank, climbed up and ordered the driver to move the Churchill forward, though also to stay out of the field of fire of the enemy guns. When they halted in their pre attack position he adjusted the sight and shot several smoke grenades towards the enemy. Just as advertised the Spits showed up. Four Spitfire Mk. IX's, each with two 500 pound bombs, zoomed in at 500 feet, blasting the enemy position with their 20mm guns before dropping their ordnance. For good measure they repeated the attack, strafing the enemy with exploding 20mm shells, then 'zoomed' over the British forces while they wiggled their wings. The infantry cheered. Very little flak (anti aircraft fire) came up from the German positions.

Everything considered it was a very encouraging sight to the British forces waiting to attack. From the distance it looked like everything down there was blown to pieces.

Fletch knew better. Air attacks almost always looked impressive, but in many cases they merely softened up the enemy rather than destroying him. Strafing with guns was useful against infantry, soft skinned vehicles and gun emplacements, but against tanks it did nothing. Only a direct hit from a bomb would damage a steel monster.

"Move out" Fletch ordered. The six Churchill's followed him, spreading out across the valley in a 'V' formation. The final two tanks were moving along the top of the hill as ordered. The infantry spread out behind and between the tanks. It was a classical broad front attack.

While they lumbered down, Fletch was once again brooding over the painfully slow speed of the Churchill. It was basically a sound tank, and great for infantry support, but in tank vs. tank combat it suffered from slow speed and an inferior gun. It repeated some of the worst faults of the Matilda tanks which he had commanded in North Africa. Ironic in a way since the Churchill had to a certain extent replaced the Matilda. The real design flaw was that the small turret ring did not allow it to be up-gunned. Why didn't those engineers ever learn?

That being said, the Churchill was a much more formidable war machine than the previous infantry tanks, the Matilda and the Valentine. The 75 mm main gun in his Mk. VII, though inferior to the German guns, was far superior to the measly two pounder in his old Matilda and also better than the 57 mm (6 pounder) main gun carried in many of the previous Churchill marks. It was the first British tank to have a cupola that allowed all round vision when closed down, a feature the German tank crews had benefited from for years. Another improvement was the Merritt Brown regenerative steering, which allowed sharper turns and more precise steering than had been possible in previous British vehicles. The lay out was fairly traditional, with driver and hull gunner in the front, a fighting compartment surmounted by the turret housing the loader, gunner and commander, and finally the engine department in the rear. Last, but not least, the Churchill was roomy, greatly appreciated by the crews.

While they were advancing Fletch decided to keep his head inside the turret, but took a quick 360 degree sweep of the advance to get a better view of what was happening. Just as he did so, one of the other tanks blew up in an unmistakable explosion. There was only one way that could happen, it had to be an **88**. The air attack had not been as effective as they had hoped.

"Look out" he said over the intercom," The Ferdinand is still operational. Tell the other tanks. By the way can you get some more speed out of this baby?"

"Cap, we are going flat out!"

"That's a laugh. Stop on my command, aim for the belts on the Ferdinand, then move forward as soon as we have fired."

It was kind of an unnecessary explanation. His crew had done this maneuver many times before. Some tank commanders preferred to fire while they were moving. It made them a difficult target, but also minimized their own chances for a good shot. Even with the new rudimentary gun leveling systems the odds of hitting another tank, or anything in fact, while you moved was at best a 1 in a 100 shot.

Suddenly another Churchill started burning. The Churchill had good frontal armor, but against an **88** nothing was good enough.

Now Fletch started to see the side of the Ferdinand, it was indeed a darn big monster. They aimed for the tracks,

"Fire!"

"Short, move forward 10 yards, gunner 3 degrees up"

The Churchill lumbered forward, not a second too soon, a grenade landed just behind them. A third Churchill was hit, veered sideways and started to burn. One, two, three, four, five he counted, relieved the whole crew escaped. That left only four Churchill's in the main assault, plus the two flanking tanks up on the hill.

"Stop, fire."

A great shot, he could see it hit the left track.

"Bulls eye" he screamed, "forward."

The shot did not destroy the Ferdinand, but a ruined track meant the vehicle could not move, thus limiting its field of fire to where the fixed superstructure pointed, and not much else. The eternal problem for turret less German tank destroyers was that they had to turn the whole tank if they wanted to traverse more than 10 degrees in either direction. Consequently Fletch's Churchill was now outside the Elefant's field of fire.

"Turn right, straight towards them."

The front of the Churchill had pretty thick armor, which provided some protection against the 75mm's of the Mk IV. Only one of them was operational, and he could also see the anti tank gun emplacements were quiet. The RAF had done a decent job after all.

They were only 200 yards away now. Several shots hit the Ferdinand and exploded as the two flanking Churchill's were firing down on it. He ordered the tank stopped, and then they started shooting at everything in sight. The other Churchill's pulled up next too his and joined in the firing while the infantry rushed forward. The shots did not penetrate the Ferdinand, but had to be frightening to the crew caught in the noise and shaking. After a few minutes the remaining Germans surrendered. Three crew members could be seen abandoning the Ferdinand, but one was gunned down immediately.

"Stop that' He knew it was useless, nobody could hear him. Even if they had, they would not have listened, but he did not like to see unnecessary slaughter. Before anything else happened, the radio operator called out:

"Cap, just received word from one of the planes, an enemy column is moving up the valley, probably German or Italian reinforcements."

"Let's give them a warm reception before they can organize an attack. Have the other Churchill's follow us."

They turned down the road and raced ahead, if you could call the top speed of a Churchill a race. Two of the Churchill's followed closed behind him. He certainly hoped the three of them would be enough. Within five minutes they met the German column head on. It was the strangest column of vehicles Fletch had seen. Some of them were box like and very square, while others were unfamiliar trucks and lorries. Then he realized what the box like vehicles were, SPU's, (self propelled artillery units) and they were intermixed with half tracks and lorries. Best of all, they were not battle ready. For once they had caught the enemy with 'their pants down' as the saying was. He stopped the tank square in the middle of the road.

"Block the front, take out the lead vehicle. High Explosives" he called out to the gunner. The 75 roared, the muzzle flash and smoke pointing straight at the lead enemy half track. It blew up in spectacular fashion, indicating it had been loaded with ammunition or fuel.

"Perfect" he yelled enthusiastically, then continued "What fools, why did they have an ammunition truck in the lead! Ben, take out the last vehicle to block their escape."

The 75 roared again, and a lorry disappeared in a maze of flames and splinters. Enemy infantry could be seen running away, and several trucks and SPU' s turned and fled as well. Ben had done his job nicely, and their escape was hampered by the burning truck at the end of the column. The three Churchill's now advanced abreast, guns and machine guns blazing. It was a mini-slaughter.

"Take out the half track 15 degrees right"

"Good shooting, next target"

"Another SPU moving over to the left, 10 degrees left, aim low"

"Perfect, the bastards burning."

"SPU at 10 o'clock, they are setting up, take him out before he takes us out"

"Fire at will"

"Two half tracks running, get their ass"

"You missed one"

"Forget the other half track, get the SPU straight ahead before it is out of sight".

"Crap, too late, pick another target"

It continued for what seemed an eternity, but was probably just a few minutes. Enemy vehicles were burning and crushed beyond recognition, panicked soldiers throwing up their hands to surrender. Eventually it was all over, the last fleeing vehicles disappearing back to where they had come from.

After the prisoners had been rounded up, Fletch surveyed the battle scene. It was complete carnage, the agonizing screams from the wounded and dying so completely at odds with the beautiful surroundings. Plenty of work for the medics, he reasoned rather cynically. When he looked at it more calmly though, the destruction they had caused was not as 'enormous' as it had looked like from inside the tank. However, no less than four SPU's and an additional 11 trucks and half tracks (trucks with front steering-wheel but tracked drive train) had been bagged, in addition to the Elefant tank destroyer and the Mk IV's and anti tank guns at the original road block. It was a significant victory in this area, yet he dreaded the future.

Like some of the previous road blocks, this one had not been too difficult to bypass. Still they had lost four Churchill's and several infantry soldiers despite overwhelming force and airpower. Rumors had it that the Germans were preparing several defensive lines north of Rome. Unlike individual positions like this, a string of gun emplacements giving each other mutual protection could not be outflanked easily. Nor were enemy columns likely to run straight into their arms in this way. The icing on the cake had of course been the destruction of the relief column, a mix of German and Italian troops and vehicles. It was defeated almost without losses to themselves. What a mistake their commander had committed by sending out a relief column without tank support. In all likelihood it would not be repeated, the Germans were fast learners.

He jumped down from the tank, walked over to the battle scene, forced himself to ignore the wounded and dead soldiers and started surveying the enemy equipment. It was a habit of Fletch to do that. It gave him an idea of what they could expect to run into over the next few months. There was something familiar with the SPU's. Looking at them closely he recognized the hull of three of them as being from old Panzer Mk II's, while the 4th was riding on an ex Mk. IV. They all had an enormous box like contraption for the gun. The manufacturer's plate on the gun emplacement said sIG 33 and it was a 150mm Howitzer as far as he could see. The whole contraption looked overloaded and bulky, particularly on the Mk. II chassis, but when set up probably worked fine. Most German equipment did. These vehicles were another sign of the often ingenious ways the Germans used and updated old designs, often creating some surprisingly effective hardware. The Afrika Korps had been recognized as masters of adaptation by the 8th Army. Despite this, the presence of the old Mk II frames was a good sign; it showed that German industry was running into difficulty supplying their armies with all the different equipment needed. They concentrated on the most important pieces, like tanks and aircraft, but improvised on just about everything else. That was why the lorries had been unfamiliar, they were requisitioned civilian trucks.

By contrast the enormous industrial capacity of the US, combined with the considerable production from England and the Commonwealth, meant that the quantity of material was not a problem for the Western Allies, only the quality. Before he became too philosophical, Fletch decided to continue towards the area of the original road block. The two German Mk.IV's were not very exciting to look at, he had seen them many times before. However, the Ferdinand was something else. It had been hit many times, but the only damage was to its tracks, not even the side armor had been more than superficially scratched.

Only the fact that the crew had abandoned it had kept it from causing more damage. He figured the weight had to be close to twice that of the Churchill, which meant it would be something like 70 to 80 tons.

His curiosity satisfied he walked back to his Churchill. It looked small in comparison. Yet the first time he saw it, it looked big compared to the old Matilda he had commanded in North Africa. It was a reasonably good tank at this stage of the war, had excellent cross country mobility and was very adaptable to different tasks. The 75mm when introduced in North Africa had been great, but now a year later it was already outdated and not powerful enough. Still, it was the main gun in all the most recent Allied tanks, like the Churchill, the Cromwell and the US built Sherman. The pace of development in tank warfare and equipment was just phenomenal, driven to a great extent by the relentless requirements of the Eastern Front. New tanks emerged all the time, faster, better armored, and with ever sharper teeth.

The problem was that the standard Allied 75mm gun could not crack the frontal armor of most of the German tanks they were up against. Consequently the majority of the Allied tankers were more than a bit frustrated. Overwhelming enemy positions through numbers and attrition might sound good in the government corridors of Washington and London, but for the guys in the field it had an ominous sound. They were the ones asked to be the 'attrition.' It was incomprehensible to Fletch that a nation that produced some of the best planes of the war, like the Spitfire, the Mosquito and the Lancaster, could not come up with a top notch tank.

Oh what the hell he thought, I have some R&R coming up and that will allow me to forget tanks and armor for a few days. The crew was going back to the rear area for some well deserved rest, but he had other plans. That brought his thoughts back to North Africa, a promise to keep, the warm body of Constance, and those eventful but ultimately tragic days. He took a small drink from his canteen as the memories came flooding back;

The RAF had saved him when they blew the Vichy patrol boat to smithereens and transmitted his position to the Royal Navy. A few hours later a Tribal class Destroyer, HMS Zulu, had picked him up. He was the only survivor; no trace could be seen of the Vichy sailors. The survivors of the air attack had probably drowned. He did not know and he did not care. The fishing boat carrying him, and the body of Constance, had slowly drifted away from them, and he was not bothered by their faint cries for help. They had killed Constance and tried to kill him. His compassion for them was non existent. The Destroyer Captain, Cdr. Richard Taylor White, had asked him about the dead girl, but he just said she was a local French girl who had wanted to escape to Spain, with him. He could see that the Destroyer Captain guessed there was more to the story than that, but he let it pass.

Since they were fairly close to Gibraltar she was not buried at sea. And so Constance was buried in a churchyard in Gibraltar, the first girl he had really loved. He gave her real name for the gravestone, but not her nationality. It would have been too much to explain. They had offered to send him back to England, but he said he preferred to stay in the Mediterranean. He had not revealed his true motive, fulfilling his promise to Constance of returning her amulet to her parents. Not that the 8th Army cared, they were short of trained tank commanders and happy to keep him.

In fact the CO commended his fighting spirit, which he thought was kind of a laugh. After he rejoined the army he had been assigned to an operational conversion unit as a tank instructor. After some months doing that boring and uneventful job, they considered him fit to fight and he found himself back in a front line unit. Just in time for the invasion of Sicily. Unfortunately, in this period he had also started drinking a bit too much. It was the only way he could avoid the ghosts in his mind.

He would keep his promise to Constance, he owed her that. Now he was as close to the town of Santa Maria de

Castellabate, Constance's home town, as he would probably ever be. The town was behind Allied lines now that the US Army had broken out from Palermo and moved north. He was just waiting for the right opportunity.

*

CASTELLABATE

*

It came two days later, when the unit was camped out in a small village called Potenza. From the map he figured it would take him four to six hours in a jeep to drive to his destination, though that was at best a guesstimate. In reality he had no idea regarding the condition of the roads. He told the Colonel in charge, Sanders, that he needed some time by himself and would be back in a couple of days. The Colonel was in an unusually good mood following the destruction of the relief unit, not a state of mind he often exhibited;

"A hell of a good show Fletch, the way you went on the attack right away, rather than wait for some bullshit permission. It is the spirit we need, and I will put you in for a goddamn medal of some kind. You deserve a little time off, but stay within a days range, who knows when we will be asked to move out. Look out for Fascist partisans, I am sure they would like to knock off a British officer, and my ass will be on the line if they do."

Regarding his choice of Castellabate, Fletch came up with a hastily improvised story of some relatives there. He indicated it was less than a day away, and promised he knew it was a peaceful village. He could see the doubt in the Colonels eyes, he smelled a rat somewhere, but could not quite put his finger on it. To Fletch surprise he nevertheless gave him the necessary permission to go see his 'relatives' without any further ado. Fletch knew he risked court martial by driving so far to see Constance's parents, but he had given his word. It had to be kept; it was a case of honor.

The trip turned out to be relatively easy, in fact much easier than he had expected. The American made Jeep had a hard ride, but easily handled the ill maintained roads leading there. As he came around a turn in the road and saw the village in front of him, he remembered Constance's word; 'It's a beautiful place, you will like it. We will go there together when the war is over.'

The war was not over, and they were not going there together. Instead Constance beautiful body was turning to dust in a small grave in a churchyard far, far away.

He parked the jeep and started asking the locals for directions to her home. They just looked at him when he asked about the Gallo family. Apparently it was a common name, sort of like Smith in England. Then he remembered another name, Palazzo Belmonte. Everybody knew that, and when he drove over and stopped close by he could see why. It was magnificent. Looking around he remembered something his mother had once said about Italy, which she had visited as a young girl;

"Even the dead flowers look romantic."

Now he could see that for himself.

Darkness was coming, so he decided to go from house to house asking for the Gallo family. An hour after he started a woman pointed towards a small house, just off the central plaza of the village, and a stone throw from the Palazzo.

When he saw the young girl who opened the door, he took a step back. It had to be the correct place, the girl looked very much like he remembered Constance. He remembered her telling him she had a younger sister.

"Do you speak English'?"

"No, Momento" She called out in Italian and an older man, obviously her father, came to the door. Unfortunately he knew less English than the girl. It became awkward. Then the father said something, and the girl ran out. Fletch was wondering what was happening, but then she came back with a young woman. Fletch stared at her, she was very pretty. Then he caught himself and tried again:

"Do you speak English?"

"Some, not very good, live next house. Me good friend Constance. Why are you here?"

He did not know what to say, just took out the amulet he had been carrying around. They all knew it, the father's eyes got teary, and both girls started crying. They asked him to come in and offered him a couch in the sparsely furnished living room. Constance sister left and fetched the mother. She started to cry as well. The emotion in the room was overwhelming and there was no way Fletch could avoid getting teary eyed. After a while the father brought out some wine, and everybody sat down around him. The girl from next door asked the questions and translated his words to them.

"You knew her? She is dead, yes?"

"Yes, I am sorry"

"Was you with her when she deaded"

"Died"

"Yes, yes, sorry."

He regretted he had corrected her, it had been automatic.

"Yes, we were on a boat and were attacked by another boat. She was hit by a stray bullet." Slowly he told the whole story, among many interruptions and breaks. He had their full attention. It was a painful story to tell, and hear. When he finished the mother, who had the same beautiful eyes he remembered Constance had, leaned over, said something, and kissed him on the cheek.'

"Constance mother say you are good man. She thinks Constance must have been happy in you"

This time he did not correct her. He stood up to leave.

"Stay for night."

It was tempting. It was past midnight, too late to go back to the base, and he did not have a place to sleep. He accepted. They gave him their son's room. He was in Rome, trying to find a job.

"Wake up, wake up." For a brief moment the accent brought him back to the hospital ship, but then he opened his eyes and recognized the girl from last night standing in the doorway. It all came rushing back to him.

"Come to town with me, yes. Share glass of wine?"

"OK, just give me a chance to get my things and clean up first."

The house was close to the water, so he decided to go for a swim in the ocean. It felt magnificent, cool, but extremely refreshing. In the distance he could see the island of Capri. He had to pinch himself to remember there was a war on. When he returned to the beach the girl was waiting for him. She smiled at him, and gave him a towel. She was beautiful and her smile reminded him of Constance's smile. He had to turn his head away to hide the emotion in his eyes. It was two years since she had died, but right now it felt like yesterday He had to come up with something to get his thoughts away from the past.

"What is your name?"

"Theresa"

"A beautiful name!"

She smiled again, and what a smile she had. He felt fresh and clean when they walked towards the town and his jeep, which was only a couple of hundred yards away.

"Crap!"

"What?"

He pointed to the jeep. Somebody had slashed the front tires.

"Fascistas!" Theresa said. "Still a few are around."

Two thoughts went through his mind. One. He liked the sound of her voice, and the grammatical errors made her more sexy in a way. The second thought was not as positive. He could end up in a court martial for this. I am already in trouble for drinking too much, and with this added they will probably send me back in chains. Forcing himself to think about the situation calmly, he decided he had to somehow get in contact with the Brigade HQ and explain the situation.

"Are there any army bases around here?"

"There is American base in Salerno"

"How can I contact them?"

"Telefono"

"What? Where?"

"Maybe call Salerno, we try."

The telephone central, it was the only one, was located just outside the village. The operators decided to help them. Particularly after he softened them up with some lies about being on a mission for the British army and that they could be in trouble if they did not assist him. After half an hour they got a response. He was amazed, he had not expected it to work. After some additional back and forth he heard an unmistakable American accent. Helpful as the Americans usually are they would contact his unit and explain. His final question was:

"Do you know where I can get a spare set of tires?"

"Sure, we'll get you a pair. What did you call this place, Castebate?"

Relief was all over his face. He might still get in trouble over the incident, but at least they would not charge him with desertion.

"They will get me a pair by tomorrow" he said to Theresa," any ideas where I can sleep tonight. I need a place to stay"

"You stay with me. I alone, my parents dead. Help you forget war."

Fletch looked at her. He wanted to believe what he had just heard, but was not certain if the language barrier had given the sentence a deeper meaning than she intended.

"I would very much like that."

When they walked towards the village she put her arm under his. It felt very comfortable. They walked for hours and she showed him the various parts of the town. Along the streets there were some restaurants, and when evening arrived they stopped and had a glass of wine in Ristorante Alexio on the Via Margherita. Some threw them hostile looks, or rather her, but most were friendly. However she talked with everybody and he heard the name Constance mentioned, so understood she told them who he was. Together they were watching the sun set in the west.

"Let's go home, I am tired."

He felt a bit disappointed, and guessed he had read too much into her invitation. It is probably for the best, I brought her friend nothing but misery and death he thought, but inside he felt a bit empty. She was not Constance, but she was so close, and so much like her. When they came back to her house, she showed him into what looked like a guest room. He put down his stuff, undressed, slipped into the comfortable bed, and pulled up the blankets.

He was about to fall asleep when a slight draft told him the door opened. It was her. Without a sound she slipped into the bed. He put his arm around her, she was naked. He let his hand slide down her back as her lips found his. His fingers started teasing her, and he could hear and feel her breathing fasten. Finally he rolled on top of her. Years of frustration and longing had built up in him and he thrust into her with an intensity almost born out of desperation. Her legs clamped shut over his lower back, spurring him on. They were two lonely people sharing a wonderful time in a crazy spinning world, oblivious to anything but this stolen moment of joy and happiness. The explosion made them see stars. They were both empty, the energy drained out of them.

"I can see why Constance liked you" she whispered to him, He loved the sound of her voice by now. She rolled on top of him and sat up. The outline of her shapely body against the moonshine from the window was like a sign from the gods. He felt like he had just made love to the Goddess Athena, though at the moment he could not remember if she was a Greek or an Italian God. The feelings she aroused in him made him short of breath.

"Wow, you are fantastic" he said "I love you and I am exhausted. Lovemaking makes me thirsty and hungry! Shall we grab something to eat?"

"No. Eat me first!"

Ever so slowly she lowered a firm round breast towards his feverish face. It was as if his whole life had been but a preparation for this night.

"What the hell happened, Fletch?" the Colonel was clearly annoyed. He continued before Fletch had a chance to answer.

"You were gone for three damned days, after giving me that BS about family obligations. While you were on your god damned sightseeing trip Captain Williams was killed by a landmine, and Major Jackson ended up with some fucking blood poisoning. Lucky for you we were not ordered forward. I would have put you in front of a firing squad. As it is you can forget any medals, though I know you don't care about that anyway. We have been ordered back to the front tomorrow. Despite all the fucking nonsense you are giving me you will be acting Major from now on; I am running out of officers. We are advancing north all over and against very little opposition, but intel has informed us the damned Germans have prepared new defensive lines up north. They are called the Gustav Line, Gothic line, Hitler Line and other bullshit names. We will move toward another monastery. Like Monte Cassino, it is probably another ratshit infested heap of old crap. This bloody country is full of old stones and ancient nonsense. We should just blow it all to pieces."

Colonel Sanders was clearly not a man of refined classical learning. He was also recognized as having the worst language in the 8th Army, which actually endeared him to the men. They felt they could relate.

"Yes Sir, Sorry Sir."

He saluted and was about to leave.

"Oh and Fletch!"

"Yes Sir?"

"You are my most damned valuable man right now. No more bullshit. Stay off the damned booze, don't get yourself killed, and I will make your promotion stick. Not that I really care if your ass is blown to shit, but I need experience, not some snotty greenhorn from Sandhurst."

Fletch saluted again, left the tent and walked back to his outfit. Well, one part was a definite lie, he was not sorry at all. It had been his best three days ever, and he would sacrifice anything to experience it all over again. The good-bye had been bitter sweet. They, at least he, had fallen in love in one day. Amid tears and kisses he promised to be back as soon as possible, and he meant it. Afterwards he said good-bye to the Gallo family. He was fairly certain Constance's parents guessed what had happened, but if they did, they were not saying anything. Not that it was any of their business.

He would try to stay off the booze. Things were different now. His outlook had changed. Until now his sole aim had been to survive this war. Now he had a reason, he wanted to go back to a magnificent girl in the town of Castellabate.

*

LINE UPON LINE
*

The Gustav line, the Gothic line and all the other defensive lines the Germans had created had indeed turned out to be hard nuts to crack. It seemed every hill and valley had to be paid for in blood. German Field Marshal Kesselring was a master tactician, and his forces made full use of every possible stone and rock for defense. They had not been assigned to the forces tasked with capturing Monte Cassino. Fortunately, as it turned out. Every story they heard was like a nightmare. The Allies had taken significant losses, not least the Polish units. In the end Monte Cassino had fallen, but by then it was nothing but a pile of rubble. The relief they felt when they heard about Monte Cassino's capture was short lived. New defensive lines appeared further north. It became an endless list of hills and valleys. Now, after many months of fighting, they had one more nameless hill to capture.

Fletch was observing the area ahead. It looked empty, but he could feel in every fiber in his body that was but an illusion. He was still Captain. The promotion was probably buried in some bureaucratic mess in London, but operationally he had a major's position.

"Cap, let's move on, nobody's there!"

"Hold on, I know something is out there. Give me a minute to think."

Not a very professional way of putting it, and certainly not something the army wanted to hear. They dealt with 'actual sightings' not 'feelings.' Fletch knew he had to order the tanks forward. The order could not be misunderstood. They had to take the hill ahead. He was afraid that if they spread out they would present too many targets, and they did not yet know what they were up against.

"Lieutenant, you take #three and #six tanks with you and move on the left flank. Single line."

It was brutal order to give, the lead tank was almost certain to "buy" it. With the time available they could not scout out the area, so frontal attack it had to be. To sacrifice the lead tank would give the other tanks time to react since they would be partly hidden by the lead.

"I will take the right flank."

"Did you say single line Sir, kind of dangerous isn't it?"

"Yes"

Fletch was not in a mood to explain every order. He mounted the tank, ordered the platoon to follow him, and moved forward. But toward what? He started sweating, and felt as if his heart was ready to jump out of his chest. The first 300 yards went by, and nothing happened.

"Sir, some shiny thing to the right, 400 yards or so."

He looked carefully through the binoculars, and suddenly he saw what it was. The turret of a Panter tank.

"Shit, it is a Panter, give it one HE and one AP in case they have infantry around there. Tell the other tanks to fire as well."

The shot rang out.

"Close, give it another one."

Fletch realized the Panter turret was turning against them. He could not see the tank. The hull had to be hidden down in a ditch. The other Churchill's were firing at the target as well now, and grenades were landing all around it. There he saw a puff of smoke as the Panter fired.

It was eerie, he could actually see the grenade approaching, as if in slow motion. He knew the Panter's main gun would break the front armor of the Churchill at this distance, and he could see it was going to hit them square in the middle. In fact it felt as if it was going to hit him straight between the eyes.

With a tremendous bang the AP round impacted the front and penetrated. Fletch could actually feel the 75mm grenade pass between his legs and the tank stopped short. In an instant his shirt was soaked with sweat.

"Abandon tank" he yelled.

He looked around the fighting compartment, it was a disaster scene. Shrapnel had crashed around, hitting other crew members. None of them were moving, and there was blood everywhere.

In shock he tried to shake the loader, all the time wondering why he had not been hit in a serious way. No response came, and now his sixth sense kicked in and told him to get out. The German gunner would probably follow up with another shot to secure the kill. He practically dived out of the turret, and fell to the ground.

Not a moment too soon, another 75 mm shell chewed its way through what had, just a few minutes earlier, been an operational war machine with 5 people on board. Now it was only a steel tomb for young dead soldiers. Half dead from all the explosions around him, he crawled away, while the tank started to burn fiercely behind him. Another few yards and he found a small ditch, rolled into it, and blacked out.

Water was splashing into his face as he regained consciousness.

"Hey Captain, wake up."

Almost reluctantly he opened his eyes. Two soldiers were standing over him and poring water from their canteens.

"Are you OK Sir?"

"I think so." Almost painfully he got up, and checked himself. He was not hurt in any serious way, but had several minor burns and scratches.

The battlefield was peaceful. I must have been out for some time, he thought. Two burnt out Churchill's were right in front of the Panter, which was about 300 yards away. He avoided looking at the remnants of his own tank and walked towards the Panter. Several soldiers were looking at it. Another Churchill, an operational one, was parked alongside. He recognized it as Sergeant Hill's machine. Some of the tankers were standing in a group around the Panter, arguing. They recognized him and called him over. To his relief he saw his own radio operator in the group as well, it was a good thing not to be the only survivor.

"Captain come and take a look at this contraption. It is only a turret, no tank. By the way you look like shit Sir, what happened?"

He felt like shit as well.

"We were hit by that Panter, or did you say turret?"

When he got close, he saw what they meant. The Panter turret was sitting on some sort of concrete pillar which had been lowered into the ground. A simple, yet deadly solution, as the burnt out Churchill's testified to. The turret had a ragged hole on the side, where one of the Churchill's had hit it with a well placed shot. He was curious about the inside of the bunker, if that was the word for it. However, the smell around the turret came from a lethal mix of burnt rubber, clothes, and human flesh. It was enough to keep him from any closer examination. He walked a few yards away and threw up. The desire for alcohol was overpowering.

*

GOTTERDAMMERUNG 1945

*

"Fletch, we have to get past these strong-points in a better way. Every one of those fucking Panter turrets cost me two goddamned Churchill tanks. The damned Germans are bleeding us white. By the time we get to Berlin the cook will be the only wanker left in this outfit. I think we have tried every trick in the book, rather unsuccessfully I might add. Any ideas?"

"I have discussed it with some of the guys. We have a suggestion, and it depends upon speed. A smaller gun like a six pounder can be quickly moved in and out of a position. If we bring it up without being noticed it should not be too difficult to knock out one of these turrets."

"How will you do that? We have already tried to use artillery, but with as much damned success as everything else. The turrets need a direct hit to be knocked out, and that means we have to bring up tanks. If you put 'your' gun within the line of fire of the turret, or indeed enemy sharp shooters and snipers, they will take out the gun crews as soon as they see them"

"We discussed that as well, and suggest that we drop a number of HE (high explosive) shells around the area. That will suppress the infantry and any snipers protecting the gun. It should not be too hard to keep it going for 30 minutes or so. We can use artillery, or if heavy guns are unavailable, use the tanks to drop the HE's from concealed positions. While this is going on we can bring up six pounders on either side. Even such a small gun caliber gun can do the job, and we can move it much easier than the 17 or 25 pounders. If we act fast we should get a couple of shots off before the turret crews detect us. Their side armor is thin, and unlike the front can be penetrated with a direct hit. By keeping the two guns separated the Panter turret can not present its front to both at the same time. We also avoid putting any of the tanks, or heavy guns, in harms way. I am sorry to say so, but we have light guns enough, and loosing one of them is a small price to pay for one of these turrets."

"Sounds good, let's give it a try."

The Gustav Line and all the other lines had given the Allies major headaches. Losses had been heavy in material resources as well as men, and the advance was slow. It seemed like every valley was defended. After the US 5th Army broke out from the Anzio beachhead and moved north, Rome had fallen and the new Italian government had sided with the Allies. Every time they received such good news the troops had hoped the end, or at least a German collapse, would occur. It never did. After the two Allied invasions of France, several units were pulled out and committed to the invasion force in Southern France. Consequently the Allied forces in Italy felt 'abandoned' with all the attention going to the Armies in France. In the press the Italian campaign was belittled and the opposition written of as 'light' or halfhearted. Yet men died in considerable numbers. Fletch was worn out and tired of the whole bloody mess.

His promotion to Major finally came through, but he had not been able to get back to Castellabate. Instead he had sent several letters. No answers had gotten through though, and he was wondering if he was just clinging to a lost dream. He was steeling himself to find out that she had found somebody else, or that something even worse could have happened. It was over a year since he had seen her, and this year, 1945 he had decided to go back to Castellabate, come what may. It was rumored that this would be the last year of the war, that the Germans were down to their last resources. That was what everybody said. They had said the same in 1944. In Italy all they had to do was to overcome these last dangerous German positions, and that would be it. Fletch had a hard time believing that.

They got their chance to try their new anti-turret technique the next day, when another turret was detected. The terrain was difficult, and the turret had a close to perfect position overlooking the only road leading through a narrow pass. Fletch left the tank, and took charge of a group of soldiers trying to manhandle a six pounder up on the east side of the turret. Another 6 pounder crew worked their way towards the west side.

It was brutal work, the area almost impassable for anybody but hikers. The good thing was they were not exposed to any snipers, but unfortunately it also meant they could not call down any protective fire. They were two hours into the job, when they heard firing. Fletch crawled up on a boulder. It was what he had feared; the turret had spotted the other gun, and was firing on it. They could not have seen the gun, which meant only one thing, they had an observer. He told the rest of the crew what the problem was, and what he planned to do.

"I will go and get their look out, before he sees us and direct them to fire at us as well. I am pretty experienced in mountainous terrain, so it is easier that I go alone."

The crew liked to hear that part, nobody wanted to risk their lives on a risky mountain climb so close to the end of the war. He brought along a Lee Enfield Mk IV rifle, and his personal sidearm, a Webley & Scott Mk. 6. Fletch had used a Beretta in North Africa, but after Constance died he had sent it to his parents for safekeeping.

When he took off on his hike he had a good idea where the lookout was and how to get there. Before the war he had spent many summers with his grandparents in Norway, often hiking up to peaks and high lying lakes. Now he put this experience to good use, staying out of sight of the anticipated look-out, while he climbed up and around. Finally he reached a plateau above the place he expected the lookout to be. Carefully he peeked over the rock in front of him. His planning had been perfect. Two Italian soldiers were on a boulder below him. Both had binoculars, and a radio set for communication with the Panter turret rested between them. Fortunately they were looking away from him and towards the British lines.

He put the Webley next to him, lifted the Lee Enfield, leveled it, and carefully aimed. He felt bad about killing these guys, enemies or not, so late in the war. It also felt a little bit cowardly to shoot them in the back. On a personal basis he had nothing against them, but they were the enemy. It was the age old soldier dilemma, them or us. While preparing his shot, his sixth sense told him something was strange. It was almost too easy. That was it, they probably had another observer on guard as well. The sense of danger was overwhelming, and he rolled quickly over to the side. Not a second too soon. An Italian soldier was only 30 feet away and aiming straight at him. He fired. Stone splinters were flying all over as the bullet slammed into the ground where Fletch had just been. A nearly perfect trap, and if he had not reacted so fast it would have worked. Fletch eyes were black from shock as he dropped the Rifle, grabbed the Webley and swung it towards the enemy. The Italian was preparing his second shot, but the quick reaction from Fletch, and the fact that the revolver was much easier and faster to operate, meant they fired almost simultaneously, with Fletch a tenth of a second faster. A short, but life saving, advantage. The Italian was thrown back by the impact of the bullet. One of the advantages of the Webley, compared to most other hand guns, was that its 0.455 caliber cartridge gave it considerable stopping power. Fletch felt a sting in the arm, but that was all. The Italian had been too hasty, and paid the price.

Breathing heavily, he looked at his arm. The bullet had bruised his lower left elbow. Though painful the wound was superficial. He tied his handkerchief around it to stop the bleeding. Throwing another look at the Italian soldier, he could see a huge blood stain spread over the front of his uniform. On top of that he was unconscious, so Fletch returned to the task at hand without worrying about him. Once again he crawled up the edge of the rock to look for the two soldiers below him. They had heard the shots, and were searching for the source. One of them was looking in his direction through his binoculars. He saw Fletch almost immediately and shouted something, then lifted his rifle and fired off a wild shot.

His buddy knew better, got up and started running down the hill. The first guy followed suit almost immediately, dropping his gun and running as if his life depended on it. Which, in fact it did. They knew they were at a disadvantage with Fletch hiding above them and 500 yards away. Fletch aimed carefully and started shooting. He did not hit any of them. Running men are difficult targets and he had no reason to go for a kill. That being said, his shooting certainly speeded up their departure as bullets ricocheted off stones all around them. After a few shots he stopped firing

What now! It was extremely unlikely they would come up again, so he decided to backtrack. The man he had shot was dead, so he ignored the body and took off, still shaky after the exchange of fire. The trip down was much easier than the trip up, and he reached the gun crew just as evening was falling. The men were curious having heard the shots, and he gave a quick summary of the events, omitting the ambush part that almost got him killed. Thus trying to give the impression it was nothing to talk about. However, some of the men noticed he was holding on to the handle of the Webley so tight his hand was white. They realized the incident had not been as easy as Fletch pretended, but were not so stupid as to press the issue.

"Major, the other 6 pounder is destroyed, we have to deal with this turret on our own. What do you want us to do?"

"It is too dark to start shooting now, let's wait till tomorrow. Not too early, we will be silhouetted against the breaking dawn, so we will wait till they have the sun straight in their eyes. Radio HQ that we will engage the target in the morning" The radio operator nodded.

It was an uncomfortable night, they were exhausted, and expected to sleep right away. Yet the area was filled with small sharp rocks, hard and uncomfortable to sleep on. Fletch arm was hurting, and combined with the lack of sleeping amenities he did not get any rest at all. Around 9.00 AM the sun was high enough in the sky, and they could see the target clearly. They positioned the gun carefully.

"Guys, we have to score on the first or second shot. If they turn towards us, we will pull the gun down. We cannot break the front of that turret, and have no back up from the other side, so let each shot count.

The plan worked perfectly. The first was close, the second very close, but since the turret did not move they put a third round straight through the side. A dull light explosion, that was it. Yet the barrel had been completely static, and suddenly it dawned on Fletch why. He started laughing, harder and harder. The troops looked at him strangely, until he told them.

"Crap" he laughed, "all that work for nothing. The turret is empty. We could just have waited."

After a while they went down. Just in case they were wrong they spread out when they were close to the enemy position, but nothing happened. It remained quiet. They all looked at each other. The turret was, as Fletch had said, empty. It had been left in a hurry, but organized. No sign of panic, just an orderly and quiet escape.

"I don't like this" somebody said "It is not like Fritz to give up so easily"

"They knew we would get them this morning"

"Even so, Fritz usually stays and fights."

Suddenly the radio operator, Sparks as they called him, came running up the road like a madman. When he reached them he was all smiles and they knew this had to be good news.

"It is over, it is peace, Germany has surrendered"

The troops started shouting and shooting into the air, cheering madly. It was incredible, unbelievable in fact. How could it have ended so suddenly, almost like a door closing?

"Are you sure it is not a ruse"

"Yes Fletch, I mean Captain, eh Major. The BBC reported that Hitler has committed suicide with his girlfriend. Admiral Donitz is the new head of Germany. He can keep it as far as I am concerned."

"What about the Japanese?"

"Nothing, they will probably do like the Germans, keep fighting till somebody reaches Hirohito's kitchen."

It took some time before Fletch and the rest of the troops could fully absorb the news. Over the last 12 months there had been so many rumors that the war was over, yet they had always been false. This time it was in fact true.

A few days later they were back at the main base. Unlike the initial reaction the mood was somber now. It became clear to all they had to prepare for a new existence, one of peace, almost a frightening concept in itself. The radio told of huge celebrations in Paris, in London, in New York, but after the first couple of euphoric days the soldiers had stopped celebrating. Too much had happened; too many friends had been lost. Instead they sat quietly with a drink or a beer, listening to the overjoyed reporters on the radio. The reaction was understandable, they did not blame the cheering crowds as such, yet they could not share the joy fully. After listening for hours, it became almost too quiet in the room. Nobody talked. It was too much of a contrast to the sounds in the radio. Somebody threw a glass of beer at the radio, and it became dead silent.

In the oppressive stillness Fletch decided to go for a walk. Once outside he looked towards his Churchill tank. It was sitting almost forlorn now, surrounded by rows of other tanks and military vehicles. The gun barrel was pointing down, almost like it was sleeping after a job well done. It was not needed any more, and it looked the part. He did not have any feelings for the tank as such, in reality it was just a steel monster. One of many he had commanded. Yet the sight of it brought memories, memories of sacrifice, defeats, victories, heroism and death, all of which had been so vividly displayed over the last five years. Now these memories would only exist in the minds of the survivors, and in the track marks on the ground. But soon the rain and the fragility of man's memory would wash even those away.

*

RETURN

*

Four months later he drove up to Castellabate in a surplus jeep he had purchased. He had asked for immediate demobilization, and it had been granted due to his long service. He would still be attached to the Territorials, the reserve, but they did not need him right now. They had more men than they could find work for, and demobilized surplus personnel as fast as they could. In most cases that meant as soon as they returned to England. Consequently he had asked for a six month leave the moment he returned home. His parents had been overjoyed to see him of course, and wanted him to stay. But he could not;

he knew he had to go back to Italy, to Castellabate. Now he was here. His heart was beating hard when he entered the town. Had she waited for him, or found a new man! With her looks he knew she would not have had any great difficulty finding another guy, if she had wanted to.

When he stopped the jeep he could see that the appearance of her house had changed, and the new owners did not speak English. Constance parents were not home either; maybe they had left as well. He looked at the people around him. They were going about their daily task, like they always had. If you looked around Castellabate you could be forgiven for thinking that the war had not happened. No battles had been fought in its vicinity, so there were no bullet holes, no damaged military equipment, no warlike reminders at all. Only an old stained Mussolini poster on a grey unpainted wall served as a reminder of the recent events. He tried to address a couple of people, but they shook their head when he said her name, then walked on. He felt a little bit depressed. He had told himself over and over that it was just an episode, but in all honesty he had hoped and dreamed it was something more.

Finally he walked down to the water and entered the little "Ristorante Alexio" where he had shared a bottle of wine with Theresa. He did not recognize the staff, not that it meant much. It was so long ago he could not remember many faces anyway, only one. Hers. Now he had to make new plans. Not that he had really had any plans beyond meeting up with her. Sipping his wine, he tried to assess the situation logically. It was not easy, several times he thought he saw her, but it was always somebody else. Eventually he concluded that only two options remained. Continue looking for her in the vicinity of Castellabate or go back to England. He would leave the decision to the next day, it was too late to do anything tonight.

It was a beautiful evening, the sort of evening you only experience in the Mediterranean. It was as if time did not exist. AD, BC did it really matter! The evening was warm and the wine was good, very good. Wine this good had not been available in England since before the war. Two hours later he was deep into his second bottle, and more depressed than when he started drinking. I have to leave before I am stone drunk he told himself, I cannot go back to the booze wagon. Just as he was getting ready to leave he could feel somebody looking at him. It was his sixth sense that warned him, the one he knew and trusted. It had kept him alive through a long war. Slowly he turned around.

It was her. Theresa. Thinner, dressed in worn out clothes, but definitely her. She was even more beautiful than he remembered. For a few seconds they were standing there, frozen. Then they were in each others arms, and life was wonderful.

"You came back!"

"You waited, I dreamed about it, but dared not hope."

The smell of her hair, the feeling of her body pressed against his, those deep brown eyes, all melted together in a torrent of emotions and feelings in his brain. Eventually she pulled out of his embrace.

"Come," she pulled him over, and pointed at what looked like a bundle of rags on a bench. Then he realized it, a baby, or rather a small toddler was sleeping there. She lifted the sleeping little boy up and handed him to Fletch. Carefully, almost afraid to hold this precious bundle in his arms, he cradled the toddler to his chest.

"I named him Tomasino, after you"

It was his child; he could feel it right away. He turned towards her as his eyes filled up and he started crying, crying like he had not done since he was a child. Years of stress, longing, fear and relief poured out of him. She held him tight as the sun sank below the horizon. Some of the guests looked the other way, surprised and embarrassed by this emotional foreigner crying on a girl's shoulder.

The night was even more magical than their first. He had such a feeling of happiness it was almost too much to handle. Yet for most of the night they were only sitting there, close together, holding on to each other, talking quietly. The apartment was sparsely furnished, but the couch was comfortable. The boy did not wake up despite all the commotion, and was sleeping in an old bed. She told him she had been shocked when she realized she was pregnant, and had sent him several letters. She had only received two of his many letters in return. Nevertheless it was enough to give her hope for the future, at least she knew he was alive. The Ristorante kept her on as a waitress until her pregnancy started to show, then she was fired. After that she took up sewing. The pay was barely enough to keep her and the baby alive, so she sold the house and got this little apartment. It had been a difficult time; an unwed mother was not welcome in many quarters. Fortunately Constance's parents had helped her when things got too tight, and it was Constance's sister that had spotted him and told her he had come back for her. There was so much to tell, so much to catch up on, but it could wait. They had a lifetime ahead of them.

Just before morning broke they made love in a way that made the long wait worth every minute. Finally she fell asleep in his arms and he enjoyed just lying there, looking at her. Even in sleep she had a smile on her lips, and he let his eyes wonder down her tanned desirable body. Almost as if she could read his thoughts she pulled him closer, while still sleeping. I will be able to make love to this beautiful goddess every day from now on, he thought, it was almost too fantastic to imagine. He felt he could spend the rest of his life on that couch, feeling her warm body and listening to the sound of Theresa and his son sleeping. His family. He liked the sound of that. There was no way he could sleep, he was too excited. He also wanted to be awake when the boy woke up. He still thought about him as 'the boy' rather than Tomasino, but that would change when they got to know each other.

It was strange to lie there and feel so lucky and fortunate. In many ways it was not fair. Millions of good men and women, much better than him, had not survived. Millions of others would still suffer for years to come. Yet somehow he was here, happy and content.

The stillness of the apartment, and the effect of the wine, made him more and more philosophical. Images from the long war that had recently ended flashed around him. The faces of people he had known and lost circled over his head. What had brought about this incredible amount of death and suffering, he wondered. Was it just some mad brutal dictators that wanted power? Could a couple of megalomaniacs cause the death of 50 million people! Why was he so lucky? What would today's children think about the war when they grew up? It was impossible to make sense of it all. He was reminded of the Greek statesman Pericles prophetic words 2,500 years ago.

"Future generations will wonder at us, like the present wonders now."

*

HISTORICAL NOTES
*

Italy was the weak partner in the Axis alliance. Italy's industrial capacity was not up to the task of keeping a modern mechanized army, plus navy and air force, adequately equipped. Neither did Mussolini have the cult like following that Hitler and Hirohito, and for that matter Stalin, enjoyed. After the Greek and North African debacles, most Italians were happy to see him go. Following the Allied invasion of Italy in 1943, the Italian people were divided in its loyalties, and from then to the end of the war Italian troops were fighting for the Allies as well as for the Axis. The Italian campaign reflected this, and the heaviest losses were among the Italian soldiers.

The British Prime Minister Winston Churchill famously saw Italy as the soft underbelly of Europe, and as a gateway to the Balkans. However, the campaign never lived up to its promise, and the Americans were not eager to commit significant forces in the Mediterranean. They feared a major effort would drain their forces of shipping and troops needed in the Pacific and in the upcoming invasion of France. Furthermore, the German commander, Field Marshal Kesselring, conducted a brilliant defensive battle in the hilly terrain of Northern Italy, an area well suited to defense. The

Allies contributed to the sluggishness of the campaign with some significant strategic blunders. The biggest were arguably the delayed break out from the Anzio beach head, which allowed the Germans to bring in large reinforcements, and General Clark's decision to conquer Rome first rather than cutting off the Axis retreat.

Italy was never considered the 2nd front, though the name is actually an artificial one. There were many 'fronts' in the war; The (main) Eastern Front, The Bomber Offensive, The Atlantic, North Africa, The Resistance Movements, all of them contributing towards the defeat of the Nazis. However, for those who wanted an offensive through France straight to the heart of Germany, it sounded better politically to demand a 2nd front than a 6th front

Likewise, the Russian and German General Staffs did not see the Italian campaign as the long expected 2nd front. That does not mean it was an insignificant or unimportant front. After all the campaign did knock Germany's only significant European partner out of the war and it was a constant drain on Germany's ever dwindling resources. In 1943 fully 1/3 of Luftwaffe aircraft losses occurred in the Mediterranean theatre of operations and no less than 28 German divisions were eventually fighting in Italy. Many argue that after Rome was conquered, and the primary allied objective thus fulfilled, they should have slowed down or stopped their advance north rather than committing additional forces to a grueling campaign in the alps. It is a point of view hotly debated among historians to this day. For the troops on both sides it was a bloody slogging match, and losses were considerable. Approximately 100,000 Italian soldiers died during the fighting. The US 5th Army had 188,000 casualties, the British 8th Army 123,000. German casualties came to 434,000, of which 214,000 were missing. In addition some 150,000 Italian civilians died. Propaganda during and after the war has belittled the contribution of the Italian forces, and the importance of the campaign. However, as can be seen from these statistics, the reality was very different.

STEEL TREK
*
NORTH KOREA 1951
*

With fighting vultures arrive. From time immemorial vultures know that when men are fighting, a meal beckons. As soon as the fighting is over they emerge, appearing mysteriously out of nowhere. Lurking in the outskirts of the battlefield, just beyond the reach of the living. It is almost like a dance. When humans move closer to scare away the birds, the birds move dutifully away. Then the humans move back from the stench of the dead and the birds move forward again. Vultures never have to rush. They know they will get their meal in the end.

Vultures do what nature has told them to do, a revolting but necessary activity. Yet humans all over the world find vultures disgusting, and have done so for thousands of years. Not only due to their activity, but because they remind us about our own end, our final destiny. In many ways they are the embodiment of the age old saying; from earth to earth.

Carl Fredrik, under his assumed last name of Rosenkrantz, looked away from the ugly birds and their grisly meal. The smell from the battlefield was overpowering his senses. It was a mix of dead bodies, burnt out rubber and rotting flesh, all of which combined to turn his stomach and make him nauseous. The vultures had won today. Their patience had paid off and nobody tried to interfere with their feast. There was nothing Carl could do about it, much as he wanted to. Instead he scanned the surrounding hillsides for Chinese and North Korean troops. It was all done from within the safety of several inches of steel, through the 'scope'. The tank provided the necessary safety, fortunately, since snipers were a constant worry. The cold rough steel surface, and somewhat stale air inside, strangely enough added to the crews feeling of safety. That was good. None of them fancied becoming victory marks on somebody's rifle. Judging by the number of dead soldiers, the snipers had victory marks enough.

The hills looked empty, but that was of little consolation; they were out there, he could feel it. Considering the carnage from the recent fighting, and the smell of death, his only wish was to get away from this place. He had no idea how far they had to go to reach safety, but had a sneaking suspicion it was getting longer by the minute. The enemy was advancing south, and so far nothing had been able to stop them. The problem was that his radio was out so he could not contact friendly forces. If it had worked, he would have asked for a helicopter pick up. Now they had to come up with another way of contacting the UN command, but it seemed to him that a helicopter pick up was still the only way out.

"Well," he said to the crew, "I believe we have the Chinese and North Koreans all around us, and they are moving south faster than we can. How about going west toward the coast and asking the Navy to pick us up?"

"Cap, we don't have any radio, how the heck do you plan to contact the Navy?"

"I assume we still control the seas, so if we can steal a boat and get away from land, we should have a chance. We have about 100 miles of gas left, and from what I can see on the map it is about 80 miles to the coast. The Chinese will be looking for guys moving south, not west. Any other ideas?"

He looked at the serious faces of his crew members. They were all acutely aware of the danger they were in. Fredrik Mortenson, the driver nodded, as did Pete Maclied.

"Let's try it, I cancelled my date for tonight anyway." Sam Grubley, assistant driver said, trying to crack a joke. Hank McWilliams, the loader, just responded with a short;

"Okay."

Their tank was a WW II vintage M-26 Pershing, which despite its age was still one of the best tanks in Korea. Only the British Centurion was comparable. That at least was lucky, the Soviets had not trusted the North Koreans with their latest tanks. The drive to the coast was not much of a hope, but the young crew was tired and frightened. Who wouldn't be, the thought of a Chinese POW camp was not one to be entertained with enthusiasm, regardless of how exhausted or dispirited you were. Thus, the drive to the coast seemed the best alternative

"Here we go, look out Tipperary!" Pete said, not very enthusiastically, and the 500 HP Ford GAF engine roared to life as the M-26 and its crew headed west.

"Shit, what a mess" Carl said silently to himself, "How the hell did I end up in such a god forsaken place as this valley, and behind enemy lines?" It was five years after the big one, WW 2, and at that time he had sworn never to be involved in a war, any war, again. Pressure, pressure and more pressure, that was it, and a secret that had gotten out. To top it off he was in a place he did not care about, or had even known much about before he was posted there. His thoughts went back to Israel, to that day several months ago when the two officer's came by his truck shop.

*

ULTIMATUM
*

The way they approached his workplace left him with a feeling of foreboding. This could not be good. It was not. One of the men in particular had an arrogant, and, was it, disgusted, look on his face.

"Lieutenant" they said, do you have time for a talk". Without waiting for an invitation they went into his office. He followed, closed the door and pulled up two chairs. The rather austere office felt like it was filled to the breaking point by the tension in the room,

"Go ahead"

"Your real name is not Carl Friedrich Rosenkrantz but Carl Fredrik Johnsen, and you served in the Waffen SS!" one of the men said in English. The way it was stated effectively ruled out any possibility of a denial. Carl nodded. Now he knew they were somehow involved with the intelligence service.

"As far as I am concerned" the other guy suddenly said, "we should line you up against a wall and shoot you"

Before he had a chance to answer, Rachel came into the office. The two officers stood up, but said nothing.

"This is my wife Rachel. Rosenkratz is her real family name. She knows the truth so you can say what you want in front of her. They know my past," he added for Rachel's benefit, "and now they want to shoot me."

"What!" Rachel looked at the two men with such fury they inadvertently took a step back. Then, with a ferocious voice, she addressed them in Hebrew which Carl had mastered with a heavy accent, but now she spoke at such speed he could not catch it all. However, he did pick up phrases like 'Latrun' and 'service to Israel' so the thrust of the tirade was pretty easy to guess.

The first officer responded, rather more politely now, and with an annoyed look at his companion.

"Sorry for my partner's outburst. He lost his parents in the camps. Nobody wants to shoot anybody. However, we are here on the command of brigade commander, Tal, (later General and known for his impact on the development of the Israeli tank corps) and he would like to see you. We are aware of your efforts during the liberation fight, and the commander wants to talk to you in person. It is regarding your continued services to the State."

"Korea," Carl said, as much to himself as to them. The outbreak of the Korean War was, for obvious reasons, all over the news, not only in Israel but worldwide. It had the potential of starting World War III

"I am not at a liberty to tell. Will you come with us?"

Carl nodded, kissed his wife and followed the two men out.

"You scared all of us" he whispered to her as he left. She smiled, through tears, knowing, like him, that their secret was out.

"Come back to me, or I will get really angry!"

The entrance to the base was modest, like it was for all Israeli military installations at the time. The money went into military equipment, not fancy facilities. Without any wait or hesitation, he was ushered into the office of the base commander with a;

"The Commander will be with you in a moment, Sir" by the staff sergeant.

Carl looked around the office. There were some pictures of various tanks, a pile of papers, and a window facing the training ground. He looked out as an old Hotchkiss H-39 rumbled noisily past the window. His curiosity was awakened, and he moved closer to get a better view. The H-39 was a prewar antique, the French had even brought a few to Norway in 1940. Behind it came a Cromwell. That was a real tank, even if he had not had any personal experience with it. In the distance he could even see some old Matilda's, another early WW II vehicle. But then the Israeli's made good use of every armored vehicle they could lay their hand upon. That meant tanks from just about every tank producing country in the world were present.

"Not quite a Panter or a Tiger, but good enough for our use, at least right now."

Carl had been so busy observing the action, he had not become aware he was not alone in the room any more. The General greeted him with a handshake, which took the sting out of the reference to his past service with the German Panzerwaffe. Commander Tal was known for not beating around the bush, and went straight to business.

"Your past is what it is. You did a hell of a job in Latrun, and in the preparation of our forces in '48. Your commander back then said you were the only one of his men who knew what he was doing. I am sorry to pull you out of retirement" General Tal had a faint, barely noticeable, smile on his face "but we need your help again. I understand you speak Norwegian, English and German fluently?"

A nod.

"Good. Well, where you are going you won't need German or Norwegian, but it may come in handy in the future. You know about Korea. It is not exactly tank country, but we still need information about the latest Soviet tactics and weapons. Eventually some of it will be cascaded down to our neighbors. We also need to measure how our own equipment stacks up against the opposition. Not the old H-39's," he laughed, "we all know that. With your knowledge and language skills you are the man for the job." There was no flattery in his voice, just a statement of facts. "I have arranged with the Americans that one of our men, you, will fight with their armored corps as a Captain. It will be sort of undercover in that you will also be an observer, and operate as a US tank commander. The odds of meeting anybody that can recognize you is miniscule, and we know that you are not wanted but presumed dead. Your adopted name of Blumenkrantz is fine, and the official story is that you emigrated to Israel with your parents before the war. I hope you can assess the American equipment in actual combat as well. We will take care of your shop for you while you are gone, though from what I heard your wife can manage it, and just about anything else, herself."

Carl smiled. Commander Tal's charm was undeniable. Yet, he was wondering what 'sort of undercover' meant. Moreover, this assignment was not a request, but an order. Carl wondered if the reference to him being shot had been staged, or just a slip of the tongue. He suspected that it had been planned, but only to be used if he had been uncooperative. The officer uttering the words had probably jumped the gun. It was all in line with President Teddy Roosevelt's famous phrase; *Speak softly but carry a large stick*. Well, the stick had been revealed.

And now, after several weeks of training and preparations in Fort Hood, TX, he was here, in Korea. It had been strange to be back on US soil, and the urge to contact his family had been strong, but it would have jeopardized the whole operation. Once the "cavalry" courses started, still called that even though the horses were long gone, he had been forced to think about other things than family. American operational tactics, as well as the cooperation routines with the newly reorganized air force, the USAF, had taken some time to learn, but, with his experience, it was still fairly easy. The operation of the new American tanks, the M-26 and M-46 did not cause any problems. They were fairly similar, the M-46 being an upgraded version, but they looked and handled more or less the same.

The most important part of his training was the intel regarding the latest Soviet tanks, some of which could be expected to show up in Korea. One heavy tank was mentioned, the IS-3, which had first appeared back in 1945. It had a powerful 122 mm main gun. A gun of that caliber would blow up any Allied tank in the field, a fact painfully clear to Allied commanders. A new medium tank, the T-54 with a 100 mm main gun, was more likely to appear than the heavy tanks. It had a low silhouette, a powerful gun and looked dangerous whichever way you looked at it. Finally there was a light tank called the PT-76 with a 75mm main gun. Except for the PT-76 all the Soviet tanks had more powerful main armament than the Allied tanks. The US built 90mm gun and the British 20 pounder were good, but in fact not any better than the German 88mm of WW II fame.

Fortunately the only Soviet MBT (Main Battle Tank) that had been identified in Korea was the old T-34/85. Carl pretended he only knew these tanks from what he had heard at Fort Hood, but in reality he was very familiar with the T-34/85 and its capabilities from WW II. The UN forces used a number of Sherman tanks, a few British Churchill tanks and some M-24 Chaffee light tanks. Against the T-34/85 the Sherman was adequate, but not superior. At the end of the course, it looked like they were going to miss out on the action. The UN offensives, the landing in Inchon and the break out from the Pusan perimeter, sent the North Korean's back in full chaos. Carl was pretty happy about that, but the rest of the cadets were disappointed, they were young and wanted fame and glory.

Carl did not comment, he recognized his own mood of 10 years earlier. Now he knew better.

A short time after their arrival in Korea they were 'shipped' north. Before they even reached the front, the Korean war took on a wholly new aspect. It was not the 'cake' walk they had expected with the North Korean army in full retreat. Instead the Chinese entry had changed the calculations completely, and now the UN forces were the ones falling back. Consequently Carl and the other replacements were committed as 'plugs' to slow down, or halt, the enemy advance. So far they had not had much success.

A 'clang' from the outside told him a sniper had taken a 'potshot' at them Nothing to worry about, but it forced him to stop reminiscing and concentrate on the present. They were now isolated as the only remaining tank from his platoon, inside what had become enemy territory. 'The IDF (Israeli Defense Forces) may not benefit much from my knowledge when I am dead,' he thought with irony as they started the drive westward towards the ocean.

It started out in a fairly uneventful way. They followed a road crossing down towards the sea of Japan, and relied on the map. Their two worries were gas, the M-26 had a rather short, 100 mile, range, and their own aircraft. Consequently they drove slow to conserve fuel, and had a large white 'US' painted on the top of the engine compartment. Probably not too noticeable to a pilot at 500 mph, but at least they felt they had done something. The Chinese had shown themselves to be expert snipers, so all their infantry had either fled, been killed or surrendered. Carl decided to keep the tank 'buttoned up' to improve their chance of getting away.

"Captain, there is some fighting ahead. Let's join in?

"No stop, I want to see what we're heading into."

Carefully he opened the hatch to assess the situation. Maybe they had not been discovered yet.

'Clang'

The bullet ricocheted off the turret ring so close he could feel the wind as it passed his face. With a:

"Damned, that was close" He slammed the hatch shut.

"Move on," he cried down to the driver, "Don't give them a sitting target. OK, let's do as you say and engage the enemy. What do you see, exactly."

"Three T-34's ahead, plenty of troops in the hillside"

"Well, we don't have any of those tanks, so smash them" Carl could hardly believe it, but here, five years after the war, he was back fighting T-34's. Korea was not really 'tank country', so up until now most tanks had operated more like mobile artillery than fast moving 'cavalry.' Actual tank vs. tank combat was relatively rare, but he had heard from other tankers that when it came to a fight the T-34 was not considered very dangerous to the M-26. It's 85mm main gun could not penetrate the front armor of the Pershing, and the crews were poorly trained.

The closest North Korean, or was it Chinese, tank swiveled the turret towards them. It did not stand a chance. Before they were anywhere close to firing, the 90mm gun on the M-26 roared, letting loose its deadly armor piercing grenade. The effect was spectacular, the enemy blew up, the turret blown off in a fireball.

"Bull's eye, turn 20 degrees left," Carl barked to Pete, he did not want to present his thinner side armor to the two T-34's he could see. The driver stopped the left track, while the right continued thus forcing the tank to turn.

One of the T-34's suddenly stopped and belched black smoke. The crew jumped out.

"They caught his ass" Fredrick yelled, "I never even fired."

Their, as yet unseen, comrade in arms had put a grenade into the engine compartment of the enemy, the most vulnerable part of any tank. The last T-34, fired, the grenade went wild, then started to pull back. It was too late. Carl's grenade went straight through the front armor, actually pushing parts of the engine out of the rear. A few seconds later he could see the enemy hit again, by the other allied tank. It was burning fiercely, reduced to a piece of scrap metal.

"Forward, stay on the road" Carl ordered. He was scanning the horizon through the scope, when the other tank came out from a side valley. It was unfamiliar, and for a second he felt a bit uncertain about what to do, but then he recognized it from pictures and diagrams. A British Centurion. He accelerated down the road, and to his relief the other tank crew understood, and followed him.

15 minutes later they were out of the valley, and into an open area where the road was emerging onto a plain. He stopped the tank, carefully opened the hatch and peered out. He could feel his shirt getting wet from sweat as he looked around, half expecting a bullet to slam into his brain. Nothing, no movement, no soldiers, nothing except the Centurion pulling up alongside him. He indicated that they should have the guns trained in opposite direction.

Then he jumped down onto the six foot clearing between the two tanks, the safest place around. It became quiet as the two tank engines stopped. The other tank commander (a Major, judging from the uniform) jumped down to him, smiling with an outstretched hand.

"Great show old man, you got us out of quite a jammy. Sooner or later they would have gotten in behind us. My name is Tommy Fletcher, everybody calls me Fletch, we are, or were, attached to the 8th Kings Royal Irish Hussars."

Carl smiled back. "My name is Carl Blumenkrantz. I had a cousin in England named Tommy Fletcher." He quickly shut up, realizing he was becoming careless with his background. It was too late, the damage had been done.

"And I had an American cousin named Carl, who disappeared in Norway." His face changed to astonishment before he continued.

"Are you him?"

It really was too late to try to deny it.

"Yes"

It became eerily quiet between the two men. Carl could see a million questions forming in Fletch's mind.

'Shit, shit, shit' Carl thought, why did I say that I had a cousin in England. I might as well have put an ad in the newspaper. That way the whole world can find me. Yet the odds of running into his English cousin had been so miniscule it was hard to comprehend. Fletch was looking at him with open mouth, then finally he said

"Then you must be the Carl that sided with, eh, the other side in the big one. I, we, I mean all of us, heard you were dead." Then, realizing it was not exactly a polite thing to say, and more than a bit awkward, he smiled and added, "but I am damn glad you are not."

They were interrupted by one of the crew calling down,

"Hey Cap, Are we leaving anytime soon, or do we have time for a cup of coffee as well? While we wait for the enemy to kill us I mean."

"Just a sec." Carl answered with a smile, then quietly to Fletch "I would appreciate it if you keep my past to yourself"

"Will do, you saved our bacon. We are trying to find out where we are. Where are you going, any plans?"

"The area between us and our rapidly retreating forces is swarming with Chinese, so we decided to try to reach the coast, and get a ride from there. Biggest problem is our radio is not working"

"Mine is. Sounds like a good plan. We'll follow you. How are you with fuel."

"Not good. This bastard drinks gas like an alcoholic let loose in a whiskey cellar. Should be good for another 60 miles or so. We have some jerry cans at the back so may stretch it another 20 miles. From what I can see, after looking at the map, just about enough to reach the coast."

"The Centurion is similar, only a 100 mile range. I have a relatively full petrol tank, but let's continue slowly to conserve as much fuel as we can. I will try to call our forces and see if we can get a pick up."

*
ODYSSEY
*

It wasn't much of a road, though it was an easy ride in the Centurion. All they had to do was follow Carl's lead, and that gave Fletch plenty of time to think about the strange meeting with his cousin, and also to reminisce about his own past experience in WW II. In some ways the manner in which they followed the road reminded him about a time long ago in North Africa. Together with an Italian girl, Constance, he had followed an ancient road along the Mediterranean coast to find a way to freedom. They had also headed for the ocean in hope of finding a way out from behind enemy lines. He did not like to be reminded about the trip, the whole affair was just too sad, even after all these years. Constance final minutes came back to him in an almost physical sense. He tried to force the thought away and think about his wife Theresa instead, but for some reason all he could see in his mind was Constance dying.

"Major, the other tank is signaling for us to stop. Were you sleeping?"

Fletch realized they had called him several times. He brushed the whole incident off with some BS about noise and hearing. Evening was coming, and Carl had spotted what looked like an abandoned farm house and headed straight for it. Fletch immediately realized Carl had picked close to the perfect resting place. Slightly higher ground than the immediate surroundings, and several damaged buildings that provided at least some cover. They backed the two tanks in between the buildings and covered them with some shrubs for partial cover. Not that they would be that hard to find, but at least they did not advertise their presence. Organizing guard duty came next. Between them they had nine crew members so they agreed on one from each crew being on watch for one hour at a time.

"Whoever falls asleep at guard duty will be dragged behind the tank to the coast" Fletch said, "and that is only a partial joke."

Tired smiles greeted his feeble effort at a gag. After a meal of ill tasting rations, Carl and Fletch sat down to talk. They found a place a short distance away from the others so as not to be overheard.

"I am sorry, I know it is not the time and place but I have to ask. How the heck did you end up in a US Army uniform, after you sided with the Nazis?"

"I made a few mistakes along the way. I saw the war with the Soviet Union as a crusade against communism. Norway was under the heel, and most of the volunteers thought they would improve Norway's position in the new German dominated Europe. I considered the US my home country, and we were not at war with Germany, so the whole thing was exciting to me. By the time I realized what a mistake I had made it was too late. I had realized what a bastard Stalin was, but was a bit late in making the same discovery regarding Hitler. Of course Stalin has been revered in the West, but I think this war will change many peoples opinion of him. He is just as bad as Hitler, but was on the 'right' side back then. I spent most of the war on the Eastern Front, and in '45 I was in Austria. When peace broke out I decided to go to this girl I had met in Italy while on R&R. I married her, and since she is Italian Jewish we moved to Palestine. Blumenkrantz is actually her last name."

Fletch looked like he was about to fall down.

"Crap, you have to tell me your story some time. Actually I am hitched to an Italian girl as well. As you have probably guessed, you were in some ways the black sheep of the family, but your mother always said you were tricked into it. Both she and your father were certain you did not participate in any of the atrocities. I never met auntie, your mother I mean, but my mother is writing back and forth to her all the time."

"Did you hear anything about my brother?"

"Yeah, he served in the pacific someplace, he was, is, a pilot. I believe he is married and has kids, and from what I understand lives in New Jersey. What about you though. How did you end up here?"

"Like I mentioned we moved to Palestine and I ended up fighting the Arabs for the Jewish state, kind of ironic in a way. Due to my service in the liberation fight in '48 the IDF figured I could be a valuable observer in this hellhole."

"Was the Eastern Front as bad as we have heard!"

"Yes, it was hell. No quarter asked for or given. The losses on both sides, and among the civilians, staggers the imagination" Fletch noted Carl got a distant lost look in his eyes. He has indeed seen hell, he thought.

"Despite what you may have heard, many of us knew it was hopeless fairly early on, 1943 or so. I guess Hitler was the only one who believed right to the end" He shook his head.

"Anyway, it is history now, Rachel and I have a good life, we have two kids. I am here on behalf of the Israeli army to catch up on the latest developments in armored warfare. Keep it to yourself, I am not exactly undercover, the US Army brass know who I am, well except for the SS part, but it is not something anybody wants to broadcast."

"Are you going to tell your parents you are alive?"

"I would like to, but how. I have kept my survival secret. If I had told my family I was still alive, I am sure it would have gotten out somehow. I do not fancy becoming a wanted man, in Norway or in the US, so early on I decided I would wait five to ten years to tell them. To be honest I don't feel I did something I have to be ashamed of, except bad judgment. Only a couple of Generals and you know the truth."

"Trust me, I will not tell anybody unless you ask me to. Many years have passed by now, so maybe we can come up with a way of telling your parents. While still keeping it in the family I mean."

"That would be nice, provided we survive this ordeal. What about you, you mentioned Italy as well."

"I had met this girl in Italy where I spent the last two years of the war, just like you, during R&R. We kept in touch, and strangely enough she waited for me till the war was over. We live outside London now, but have a summer house in a small place called Castellabate, which is where we met the first time. Most of our summers are spent there. Anything to get away from the London fog every now and then. We have a boy and two girls. I import and export scooters and motor bikes, but decided to stay with the Territorials, the reserve, which is why I am here. I am sure you can guess there is a bit more to the story, so I will fill you in when we are out of this mess and have more time. Like you say, if we get out."

They broke up and agreed on the final assignment of the guards. Carl had an early shift, Fletch from midnight to one. It was a long night, for most of the men. The tension was hanging in the night air, they knew they were in a way surrounded by thousands of enemy troops. A million sounds penetrated the night, most natural, but some human. However, the orders were clear, stay quiet and don't do anything noisy. Except for Carl and Fletch, the rest of the crew were young, relatively inexperienced, and jumpy. No mishaps occurred but in reality the commanders were the only ones who got any sleep. They had been in tight spots before. Their calm was comforting for the rest of the crew.

When dawn broke the plain was transformed. Just a few hundred yards away the valley seemed to be crawling with Chinese and North Korean troops.

Carl and Fletch stood inside one of the abandoned buildings, almost in a state of shock.

"How the hell could so many troops come here so quietly. I never heard a sound."

"Like Ivan out of the steppes" Carl mumbled.

"What did you say."

"I saw something similar in Russia in '43 and '44. The horizon was white and empty, then the Russkis came out of nowhere to attack. If they were beaten back they just disappeared into the steppes again, leaving their dead behind. It was scary, not least due to the total disregard they showed regarding their own losses. It was an iron discipline not equaled by any other army, or maybe by the 'japs'. Anyway, these guys have not seen us yet. If we don't start the engines, we may be able to slip out under the cover of darkness."

As if to mock him they could clearly hear an engine starting up behind them. To the two commanders it sounded like it could be heard all the way to China.

"Shit!" Carl ran back and soon afterwards the engine sounds died away. Looking at the enemy, Fletch was almost afraid they would be able to hear his heart beat, and held his breath as if that would have helped. Seconds ticked by but nothing happened. He let the air out of his lungs in a rush of relief. They had not been detected. Carl came back.

"That was a close call" Fletch said. "By the way, I agree, let's try to get out during the night. The headlights should allow us to see and follow the road, and since they are using it for infantry, I am sure it is not mined. It may not be much of a chance but we have no option. Let's make all the preparations in case we are discovered and have to leave in a hurry."

They told the crews, and after preparing the tanks they all sat down to wait. Quietly they discussed why nobody came over to see the farmhouse, but one of the crew members had a good answer.

"They are probably tired from all the marching, and this just looks like an old ruin to them." After meals, the enemy formations formed up and headed south. The tankers now realized they had camped at an intersection of two roads.

"I never expected to be happy to see Chinese marching south" Carl said. We may be able to avoid any fighting for now. He spoke too soon, their luck was running out.

"Cap, Look over there, I think our secret is out."

Even at this distance they could see the commotion. Officers were pointing and gesturing, Chinese and North Korean soldiers were milling around. As the tank crews started running towards the tanks, bullets started falling all around them. Worse, they could see a heavy gun being manhandled into a firing position. Carl and Fletch raced back as well, Fletch calling out orders while they ran,

"Start the engine. Carl clear the area down to the road, there is another gun down there. I will take out the gun behind us. Move down in the direction we planned." As the senior officer Fletch continued issuing orders while the powerful 650 HP Rolls Royce Meteor roared to life, spewing out black smoke. Practically diving through the hatch, he quickly closed it and was finally safe within the steel hull. It had never looked so comforting before.

"Crap," he called to the crew, "this was worse than an Indian gauntlet run. If I survive I will never watch another cowboy and Indian movie."

"Don't say that Major, your head would look good on a totem pole."

Meanwhile Carl's machine was also under power, and fighting hard.

"Target 30 degrees left, 400 yards, HE. (High Explosive)" he called out.

" Fire"

The shot was short

"Up one degree. Fire. Great, bulls eye." It was not a direct hit, but the blast and shrapnel from the explosion killed or seriously injured most of the crew. The barrel was pointing straight up.

"New target 24 degrees right"

"John, Engage the infantry with the MG"

Small arms fire was continuously hitting the sides of the tank, some with a deep rumble, probably 12.7's. It sounded like a thousand rattles being shaken around inside, a frightening sound even if it was harmless. John's 0.3 inch M1919 machine gun responded, and the deep 'cough as it released a hail of bullets was like music to the crew. Enemy infantry dropped in droves as they desperately tried to get out of the road in front of them.

'It really is a remarkable weapon 'Fletch thought. The M1919 had an effective range of over 2,000 meters, and a rate of fire of 50 rounds per minute. Not bad for a gun whose origins dated back to WW I. Unfortunately they could not use the heavy roof mounted MG without exposing themselves. It would have been suicidal. Thus only the main gun could be used to cover the rear. The two tanks swung out onto the main road, the Centurion first, the M-26 close behind. Carl swiveled the turret backwards, hoping the enemy did not have any heavy guns. The rear of a tank is the most vulnerable part, and even a smaller caliber shell can cause considerable damage to the engine compartment. He fired a couple of HE grenades more or less at random towards the pursuing enemy infantry, not expecting to cause much damage, but forcing them off the road.

"Cap, the Centurion does not seem to fire very much, I hope everything is OK over there!"

Just as they drew out of range, Carl heard some ominous sounds from the rear of the tank. There were no explosions. Probably some heavy machine gun bullets that entered the engine compartment he reasoned, and crossed his fingers hoping no vital parts had been damaged. For the time being at least the tank operated flawlessly. He had barely finished the thought when the driver called out,

"Cap, we are losing fuel."

Ahead of him the Centurion slowed down, and his driver, Pete, did the same. Another mile down the road, with no enemy in sight, the Centurion stopped completely. Carl wondered what was afoot as they drew up alongside it. He carefully opened the hatch, could not see any movement around them, got out and jumped down onto the road. It was safer to stand between the two tanks than on top of them. Fletch looked grim, when he jumped down next to him.

"Problems?"

"We have a dead crew member on board. Morgan, our loader, was badly injured when he entered the tank, though I did not realize it until later. We tried to help him, but it was too late. Any problems on your side?"

"We are leaking fuel"

They were both quiet, the situation was getting worse. Finally Carl said:

"I suggest we abandon one tank, mine, since we don't have time for repairs. We can transfer the fuel. Can you fit me and my four guys in the Centurion?"

"We have to. It is set up for four, but I am sure we can throw out some stuff. It should only be 50 miles or so left."

"Let's do it"

The burial was quick, one man dug a shallow grave while the others transferred fuel. The service was even shorter, but it was all they could do. They were acutely aware that the enemy was in hot pursuit. Unfortunately the ammo for the 90mm gun of the M-26 was useless for the 20 pounder gun of the Centurion. Finally they removed anything that could be removed from the inside of the Centurion, including any spare parts lying around. They figured there was little chance of getting into a tank vs. tank battle, so most of the unused AP grenades were removed as well. Space was tight, but at the end all the men were accommodated, if not in the most comfortable way. Carl ended up taking over the radio operators position, Finally they disposed of the M-26. Initially they had planned to rig a delayed charge, but there was no time for fancy solutions.

"Just put an AP through it," Carl said," I don't want those damned Commies to find a single useful part"

The AP did its job. It was almost sad to see the M-26 burst into flames, then blow up. The explosion was the most powerful tank explosion any of them had seen in a long time. It looked like it had been caused by a big airplane bomb rather than a grenade. Pieces of steel and track flew in all directions. They had placed the remaining ammo and fuel on the seats to be certain it went off, and it had done so in a spectacular fashion.

"Crap" Fletch said with feeling, "I hated to do that."

"As long as we were not in it I don't really care."

"Look, a truck is following us. I will try a shot."

With the tank moving forward, Fletch swiveled the turret.

"HE ready. Keep going, we will fire at the run."

The odds of hitting a moving target was at best 1 in 50, but even a close miss could damage a soft skinned vehicle like a truck.

"Fire"

It was a clear miss, but the truck pulled behind some stones.

"Crap. We missed. They will continue to shadow us, but carefully. Can you get anything on the radio?"

"Nothing but static"

"Crap."

It was becoming obvious to Carl and his crew, as it already was to the Centurion crew, that Fletch overused the word 'Crap' for just about any good or bad occasion.

They swiveled the gun forward again and continued. Since the truck by itself could not harm them, there was no reason to speed. Consequently they continued at a slow 10 mph, which gave a comfortable ride. The leisurely pace gave everybody plenty of opportunity to talk, and Carl also took some time to look around the inside. It was obvious the Centurion was a damned good tank. Not revolutionary, but a very well thought out package. The big wheels gave a smooth ride, and the turret shape and general interior was better than on the M-26. Fletch and Carl were chatting over the intercom during the ride.

"I like the Centurion"

"It is a great tank. For the first time in my career I am operating the best of the crop. In North Africa and Italy I was running around in a Matilda, and later on the Churchill. Both are so called Infantry tanks, and semi decent war machines, but nothing more. Unlike some of the Cruiser tanks, they were reliable, but we were always behind the Germans in so far as the main gun was concerned. Believe me, there is nothing quite as uncomfortable as being in a tank battle where you cannot destroy the enemy, even if you shoot first"

Pete broke in

"Hey Cap, Didn't you mention that you operated the Sherman, and tested some German tanks, back in WW II?"

Carl could feel Fletch looking at him."

"Yes, I did command a Sherman, but only faced the German Mk IV in combat. The Mk IV and the Sherman were fairly evenly matched though. The Mk IV had a slightly better gun than the Sherman, but it was nothing like what was fitted to the Tiger or Panter tanks. The Sherman was faster and more reliable, so as long as you could stay away from the Tigers and Panters you were OK. I tried, eh tested, a Panter, and that was one hell of a vehicle. Same engine as the Tiger, but 10 tons lighter, so it handled much better. The gun, a long 75mm called the L-70, had superb AP (Armored Piercing) properties, even compared to the 88mm fitted on the Tiger I. I know you Brits had an excellent 75mm gun fitted to some Shermans, the Firefly, right, but they were the exception. Even the Sherman Firefly was of course very vulnerable to just about every German anti tank gun. I saw the Koenigtiger, I mean King Tiger but never fought it, fortunately. I understand it had a better gun than the ones we use today. The King Tiger was underpowered and only really fit for defensive operations."

"Where did you operate the Sherman," Fletch asked, being careful not to say when. In fact he mostly asked to get an answer to a question he had. Had Carl fought tank battles for the Israelis as well as the Germans. If so, that would be quite a story.

"In the Middle East, I never used the Sherman in Europe."

I have to get the story from that guy some time. He did use the Sherman for the Israelis, Fletch realized. Too bad the story could never be told. He was pretty impressed about how convincingly Carl responded, avoiding the full story while not directly lying.

"Hey Cap, how old did you say you were"

You could always count on Pete for a good comment. They all laughed. After that they rumbled on for hours, and as the miles disappeared behind them the small talk did as well. It was actually becoming a bit boring and monotonous.

"Any slower and we will risk scurvy among the crew" Fletch joked.

Not that anybody longed for action. It was so peaceful they even opened the hatches, and Fletch had his upper body out of the turret. Carl decided to try the radio again.

Nothing! He was starting to worry a little, but not too much. They had to be close to the sea but were still shielded among hills and mountains. When they reached the ocean the radio would work better. More worrying was that they were getting low on gas. The truck was still following them, out of range. It was obvious they were waiting for the tank to break down.

Suddenly the static in Carl's radio became audible, he smiled broadly as he could make out a familiar US accent.

"Bravo Alpha 3, come in." He repeated the call signs.

"Come in Alpha Bravo 3, this is Charlie Vector 45

Carl realized it was an aircraft carrier, they carried the insignia CV.

"Any of you guys know about an aircraft carrier around here, CV 45? I assume it must be the USS Valley Forge which I know is in the area. I will ask for a pick up"

The crew cheered in the background. Now they did not care about the truck following them, all they needed was a chopper. He passed their information and request on to the radio operator in the carrier. Things finally seemed top go their way.

Yet the celebration was premature, life was getting complicated. Just when they could see the coast ahead of them, they ran into a line of refugees. They were a pitiful sight, young and old, men, women and children. Some were injured. As soon as the refugees realized they were not Chinese or North Korean, they ran toward the tank, begging for food, treating them like saviors. Pete climbed out of the tank, just to have an older woman embrace him while she was crying her eyes out.

He ended up swearing like mad. Not out of anger, but frustration. The group was just too poor and miserable to be ignored. The desperation in their faces, followed by the relief and hope that the tankers presence had created, was overwhelming him. The old woman led Pete over to a young girl. He immediately noted that something was wrong with her. The glazed eyes, the frozen face. No emotions were showing at all. She had a baby in her arms, but seemed to hold on to it automatically, not as a mother. He gave her some biscuits he had. She did not react. Then he took her hand, and put the food in it. She looked at him with dead eyes. Looking around he saw Carl had climbed down from the tank as well, and called out.

"Cap, what do you think about this one?"

Carl walked over, and looked her over carefully. He had seen the 'eternal' stare before, many times, and had a pretty good idea what it was all about. To be certain he looked down at her legs sticking out of the old rags. They were bloody and dirty, beyond what would have happened during their trek.

"She has been raped, probably repeatedly."

The rest of the tankers looked at her, pity in their faces. Carl's statement had transformed the group in front of them. No longer a bothersome grey bunch of refugees, they suddenly became individuals, humans in need of protection.

"We will bring them along" Fletch said "Let the old and the children ride on the tank. How many are they, let's see, 14."

They shared what little food they had. Pete felt extra sorry for the girl, almost like she was his responsibility. He talked nicely to her, though she was still apathetic, and helped her up on the tank.

"Carl, call the Navy again, say we need a bigger helicopter, or maybe two. Let's go straight down there and wait. We just have to see what happens."

Carl was looking closely at the hilly coast.

"There is a small hill by the water. It looks like it has an open area right behind it, which could be a landing place for a helicopter. It may just be a defensible place"

"OK, let's drive down there and corral our wagons. It may be Custer's last stand."

They both smiled at the last comment, but the smile did not reach their eyes. It sounded too much like a prophecy."

Fletch looked back. He could see the enemy truck stopped a couple of miles behind them, half hidden behind some rocks.

"That damned truck is still hanging out behind us. I wish we could get rid of it. Not that it would make much of a difference, but it annoys me and they may have heavy MG's there. That could complicate any chopper pick up"

"I have an idea. I experienced a similar situation in Russia once. A Russian light tank was shadowing us for miles, radioing our position to their HQ. How much gas do we have?"

Well, I guess it is about 5 miles to our final resting place. We probably have enough for 15 miles. What is your plan?"

"Behind the next bend, when we are out of sight for a short while, I will jump out with a couple of the guys, and ambush it. You will continue for a mile or so, then turn around and come back."

"Maybe we can hide the tank" Fletch said.

"No. They have learnt their lesson, and will keep their distance. They will not go on unless they see the tank ahead of them. If they see it turn back they will turn around as well. However, if we shoot out the tires and thus immobilize it we should be able to hold the soldiers off long enough for you to come back and put a couple of HE's on top of them."

It was not much to contemplate.

"Good, let's do it."

They called the guys over. Pete and Hank volunteered, and they were both good shots. Their weapons cache was meager though. Two M1 Garand rifles, six hand grenades and their side arms. Pete and Hank both had standard issue 9mm Browning HP 1935's.

"Take my gun, it is better than the Colt you have."

Carl looked at Fletch's hand gun.

"What the heck is it, a Smith & Wesson?"

"No, a British Webley & Scott Mk. 6 revolver. The Webley has long been standard issue of the British Army, but this version is a personal gun. Try it, you will like it. It is a bit heavy, but extremely reliable under all conditions. It also fires a powerful 0.455 'slug' which creates a real mess whatever it hits, and has considerable stopping power to boot."

They mounted the tank, and Carl let one of the other guys take his seat. At the agreed point, the tank stopped briefly. The girl tried to hold Pete back. He released her hand, smiled to her, patted the baby's head, and jumped off. As the tank started he could feel the girl's eyes on him.

The place they had chosen for the ambush was not ideal, but the only one possible. They expected to have about ten minutes before the truck showed up. Carl sent Pete up on the shallow hillside, while he and Hank stayed about 20 feet ahead of him. Since Carl only had the Webley & Scott and the hand grenades, he had to be the closest.

The waiting time felt like an eternity, but finally the Russian built Gaz-5 truck showed up. The agreement was that Pete would take out the driver at 50 yards, after which he would go for the gas tank and tires. With a little luck they figured they could ignite the gas tank and blow up the truck.

Carl could clearly see the driver with two other men in the front cabin and 15 or so soldiers in the back. One of the men in the front seat looked like he was giving orders to the driver so was probably the officer in charge.

The next second the front glass exploded, in a shower of glass, the driver slumping back. Carl raised his gun and started to fire. Individual soldiers would have been difficult targets at this range. Even the Webley, though an excellent handgun, was not accurate enough. However, against a large target like a truck with a crop of soldiers on the back he was bound to hit something. Over the barrel he could see soldiers getting hit and fall. He fired his six shots as fast as possible, and for good measure threw one of the hand grenades. It came up short, and exploded harmlessly in the middle of the road. He sat down to reload. Hank and Pete continued shooting, but not as fast as he had hoped since they had to move from spot to spot to avoid the return fire.

Soldiers were jumping off the back of the truck and taking cover. Sporadic return fire had started almost immediately, and after a few minutes it became a steady withering volley of shots. He crawled back to their agreed fall back position. Carefully looking towards the truck, he could see four enemy soldiers down, including the two in the front seat. In other words they were still heavily outnumbered.

Carl pulled back his head, just as a bullet ricocheted off the stone in front of him, showering his face with stone splinters. Luckily his eyes were unharmed.

"Damn"

"Ahhh"

Carl looked up, and saw Hank down, a bullet had hit his shoulder and thrown him around. He was still alive and was trying to stop the bleeding. Carl crawled over and helped him. The wound was serious but not life threatening, so he took Hank's rifle and moved back to his previous position.

It was obvious they were losing. This part of their plan was not working as well as they had hoped. With over 10 soldiers firing at two, they were pinned down, and it was now but a question of time. He looked down the road to see if their savior, the Centurion, was returning, but the road was as open and empty as any road he had ever seen. What had happened?

He peered around a stone, rifle at the ready. There, he could see a uniform under the truck. He aimed and fired in one fluid motion before he pulled back under cover again. He could hear from the impact he hit something, and the uniform disappeared, but he had no idea how seriously he had injured the enemy soldier. Several bullets whined off the stones around him.

"Shit" he swore aloud.

"I'm with you Cap" Pete answered "Where is that damned tank! Shall we move back?"

"We can't, Hank is down and if we try to pull him along I am sure they will get us."

Another bullet whirred off a stone to his left. It had come from the opposite side, which meant the enemy was now in the process of encircling them.

"Something must have happened to Fletch and the guys. Maybe they ran into trouble."

Just then a giant explosion rang out. They looked at each other smiling,

"I guess the cavalry came to the rescue after all"

They looked over towards the truck. It had been shot to pieces and the enemy infantry started running away, spurred on by MG fire. A couple of minutes later the tank stopped in front of them, the enemy soldiers long gone. They walked down to the road and Fletch opened the hatch, smiling to them.

"Last train leaving the station gents, any takers?"

"You are the most beautiful sight I have ever seen, but what the hell took you so long?"

"I appreciate your description of me. Unfortunately it was difficult to get the refugees off our back, they panicked when we turned around. Probably thought we were abandoning them or something like that. I had to leave John and Fredrik to calm them down. It was difficult to operate the tank with only the three of us, but when there is a need! By the way, where is Hank?"

"Injured, took a bullet in the shoulder, he will live."

"Good, let's get the hell out of here. Carl you should clean your face, it looks like you have been fighting bees."

"I have, it was stone bees!"

It was strange how the rumbling noise and cold steel of the tank felt soothing in a way. They took the chance and were riding on top of the tank, agreeing that the fleeing soldiers from the truck would not stop running till they reached the Chinese border. Then, when they reached the area where they had left the fugitives, they stopped in horror. Just a few were still alive, and dead bodies were spread all over.

"Oh crap, crap, crap" Fletch swore "What has happened? I should have brought them along, maybe the snipers would have left them alone."

"It is not your fault, whatever we had done this could have happened."

Fletch and Carl stood beside the dead body of John Hardy. His face had a surprised look on it. The bullet had apparently gone straight through his heart, not even giving him a chance to react. They found Fredrik Mortenson only ten yards away.

"Those damned snipers! I guess they took John and Fredrik first as the only soldiers." He raised his voice, "Be careful guys. Turn the turret gun left, from what I can see they have been shot from that direction"

Not that they expected the snipers to try again. They were not suicidal, and knew they could not do much against a tank. With the large gun trained in their direction any sane sniper would remain in hiding. As they walked among the bodies, they heard a baby crying. Pete went over. The baby was still in the arms of the girl, but she was dying. Using her last strength she held the baby up to towards him. Pete, with tears flowing out of his eyes lifted up the baby, sat down next to her and started stroking her hair. She died after a couple of minutes, and he walked back to the others.

"Shall we bury them"

"Yes, but only John and Fredrik."

"The girl too!"

"No, I am sorry but we don't have time for the rest."

John opened his mouth to protest, but thought about it again and ended up accepting the order. They worked feverishly, and Fletch as the senior officer said a few appropriate words. Three of the refugees were brought along. The other survivors were too badly injured to be moved onto the tank, and they had no stretchers. They bandaged them as well as they could, gave them some pills for the pain, but that was all they could do. Then they re-boarded the tank and continued towards what would surely end up being their last stand. It was telling that nobody looked back when they left. They felt guilty about abandoning the wounded, but had no choice.

*
THE LAST STAND
*

Half an hour later they reached their destination. It was a decent place to make a last stand. Easy to defend as long as the odds were not too bad. The small open field in the back was indeed large enough for a helicopter, and the sea meant they could not be surrounded. They put the three civilians close to the intended landing spot. The entrance to the landing place was between two mounds with the ocean behind them They backed the tank in between the two mounds and started planning the defense. Fletch gave the necessary orders.

"We will use the roof MG towards the left flank, with the tank covering the other side. Pete, you and Charley remove the MG from the roof and find a place for it on the mound. Is there any way you can make that baby stop crying. Give it something to suck on, anything will probably do. Be careful when you pick the spot for the MG, you have to allow an escape route to the sea, as well as avoiding being hit in the back from cross fire. Carl, have you been able to get any suggested PU time?"

"The Navy has confirmed that they are getting a plan together. Problem is we are out of range for the Air Force choppers, but they say the Carrier task group should be able to help us. Tomorrow at dawn they say."

"Crap, that means the enemy will almost certainly get to us first. Tell them that we may need some air support to suppress enemy forces."

They finished the gun emplacements, and, in one way, it was easier to plan the escape now. They were only six left, plus the baby, and so could fit in one chopper if necessary. Hank's injury was not life threatening, but he was in no shape to help or assist the others. When darkness fell they were all exhausted after the day, but still found it difficult to sleep. The hill had been turned into a mini-fort, yet they were so few. A fact they were all keenly aware of. The next day was on everybody's mind, all they could think about. They had little to eat, and most of what they had they gave to the baby.

Fortunately they were well supplied with water, so mixed the food into a kind of a soup, which seemed to do the job. The baby stopped crying and was smiling for the first time. Baby, as they all called her, was probably close to a year old but underweight, weak and hungry. Yet in a way she was a blessing. It was almost as if she became the pivotal person of the group, the one they all decided should survive. Pete in particular swore to help her even after the PU.

"I will adopt her" he said.

"How, you are not even married! The authorities will probably not even give you custody. Remember you don't have the right equipment for a baby. From natures side I mean."

"True, but I have given this a lot of thought. Formally, I will have my parents adopt her, but I will take care of her as soon as I get hitched. My girlfriend Karen will accept it, and if not I have to find somebody else. Karen is game though, she will understand."

In the end they all promised to help him. It was a strange night in many ways though. They knew they were going through what might well be their last few hours. If the Chinese and North Korean brought forward any kind of a cohesive force they would be overrun. Even a couple of hundred enemy soldiers would be impossible to handle in a prolonged fight. In the darkness they were all in their own way struggling with their fears and what the morning would bring. For most of them, it was the longest night of their lives.

Carl was relatively relaxed. He had faced death so many times before, and was quite cynical regarding wars, whatever they were fought for. Death was almost like an old friend. In Russia he had seen dozens of fellow soldiers and comrades killed, and literally thousands upon thousands of dead corpses, Germans and Russians. Young and old, men and women, none of whom wanted to die, but died anyway. It did not really matter what uniform they wore, or if they carried a uniform at all, they were all slaves of circumstances. Fighting for the places they were born, and died if they happened to be in the wrong place at the wrong time. The whims and ideas of two tyrannical dictators had been enough to cause endless casualties, and for what? Honor, Country, not really. They died because two men saw themselves as infallible, and had convinced those around them that they were. It almost felt like he had cheated death in those years, so if this was the moment to die so be it. He knew Rachel and the kids were safe and that was all that mattered. Despite it all, if this was the end, his life had ended in a good way, and Rachel would manage alone.

Pete was almost angry. He was only 20, far too young to die, at least by his own reckoning. Unfortunately destiny does not really care what anybody thinks. It picks its victims without any consideration of how you live your life, no weighing of your good deeds against you sins.

Many men comfort themselves through religion in difficult times, but it is not necessarily real belief, more like an insurance policy in hope of a second chance. Pete was one of those that turned to religion. He prayed, though felt a bit guilty since he had never really observed any particular religion before, and also because the main thing he prayed for was his own survival, and the baby's. Above all else he wanted that baby girl to live. She deserved it.

Charley was praying continuously. He had grown up in a very religious family and the prayers helped. If he died it was for a good cause, God's cause. It gave him tremendous confidence, and when morning came he was convinced, in fact he felt he knew, he was going to survive. God had told him so!

Sam was thinking about his girl friend. He really wanted to cry, but managed to hide his fears reasonably well. He had peed in his pants earlier but fortunately nobody had noticed. It was embarrassing, but fear does strange things. He still could not hold his urine, despite having gone for 'leaks' a dozen or so times. Bottom line was he did not want to die, not now, not ever. He did not deserve to die, he had lived a good life, never hurt anybody, so why should he be here in this terrible place.

Hank was in pain. His shoulder was damaged, and he felt guilty because he could not assist. He knew he should not feel this way. It was not his own fault that he had been injured, but it felt that way regardless. With his usable hand he held on to the Browning handgun. Whatever else happened he was not going to end up a POW.

Fletch was not really thinking that much about the next day. Whatever was coming would be there, whether he wanted it or not. He might as well think about something else. And suddenly faces from the past appeared. Hank, his first driver, who had burned to death in a Matilda tank in North Africa. His crew in Italy waved, yet most of them were killed by ricochets inside his Churchill tank. And then there was 'Tex' the ever cheerful guy who switched into a Texas accent after a couple of beers. He had picked up the accent from relatives in America. Like so many others he had not made it, but burned to death inside his tank. Constance was there too, she called out to him,

"You did not come with me to Castellabate when the war ended"

"How could I" he answered, you died.

"But you promised"

"I know, I know, I said I am sorry", and then her grave came into view, and he was standing next to it. Theresa was there too, which was strange, she had never been to Gibraltar.

With a jolt he woke up. He had dozed off after all. What a dream it had been, so real, yet so sad. He looked around. Daylight was coming and he could see a light graying of the sky in the east. He got up and stretched out. Better get some activity going, The Chinese liked to attack at dawn, so they had to be prepared. Making the rounds he realized most of the guys were awake. He ordered them into their agreed position, and asked Carl to call up the carrier again.

"Let Hank do that" Carl said "it gives him something to do"

It was a good suggestion, and Hank welcomed it. They helped him into the tank. Fletch climbed in as well. Together with Pete he would operate the gun and MG.

Carl took command of the heavy MG, and had Charley and Sam with him. While he was sitting there, watching the grey sky in the east announcing the upcoming day, he thought he heard some sounds. Without thinking more about it he fired a flare, and sat back astonished.

The area was literally crawling with enemy soldiers. Once again the enemy had managed to get large numbers of troops into position, undetected, under the cover of darkness. While the flare lasted he could see they were getting ready for an attack.

"Crap" he heard Fletch say "We better get those carrier planes here, and fast."

Carl fired another flare.

"Charley, fire as soon as you are certain you can hit something, don't waste the ammunition needlessly"

Almost immediately the heavy staccato sound from the 12.7 thundered through the stillness of the night. A second later the tank fired a HE grenade towards the enemy as well. The North Koreans were still forming up, and the sudden onslaught of fire threw them into confusion, at least for a few minutes. It was rapidly getting brighter now, and no more flares were needed, which was good, Carl only had two more which he nevertheless fired just for the hell of it.

Carl raised the M1 rifle and started firing. He purposefully tried to pick out officers, but it was not easy at this distance. So far no return fire had come their way, but that changed and the enemy started hiding and only exposed themselves for a few seconds when they fired. They did not attack, which surprised Carl. With their numbers they could easily overrun their position. What were they waiting for!

Suddenly two T-34/85's emerged and came racing over the field at max speed. The infantry followed after the tanks but were too close together. It reminded him of the misguided operational doctrine the Soviets had used in the beginning of WW 2.

"Fire" Carl shouted, and Sam immediately pulled the trigger. The heavy MG bullets ripped into the close knit formations with devastating effect, and almost immediately he could see several soldiers losing their nerve and turn back. He was going to tell Fletch about the tanks, but then he saw the turret of the Centurion turning towards them. The gun roared, and the first T-34 turned to the left, stopped and started to burn. The second returned fire, but missed, the grenade slamming harmlessly into the area behind them The Centurion fired again, and the second T-34 blew up, the turret being blown off.

"Great shooting!" Carl shouted to Fletch, though he knew Fletch could not hear him. It had been close to a suicidal attack by the two enemy tanks. They must know by now that the T-34 is not up to the task of handling the newer Western tanks, Carl reasoned. Or maybe they thought it had been one of the old M-24 light tanks hiding out.

The enemy infantry pulled back. Carl was puzzled, what was this. One reason could be that they did not know what they were up against, but they had to know it was a small force.

Unfortunately the North Koreans seemed to learn from their mistakes. He could see the officers screaming and ordering the men around. They were spreading out, which meant that the defenders primary weapons, the 12.7mm MG and 90mm HE shells would not be as effective in stopping the next attack. It will probably be the last, Carl reasoned.

Relief was on the way. A screaming sound filled the valley as two US Air Force F-80 fighter jets flew in, firing their rockets and machine guns, forcing another retreat upon the attackers. The two jets banked, turned, and came in again. Having expended all their bombs they commenced firing their six 0.5 inch machine. Then they disappeared, as suddenly as they had appeared. Like all early jet aircraft they were short on range and endurance, and their aiming devices were better suited for the speed of prop aircraft than modern jets.

The attack gave a respite, but that was all. Afraid of hitting friendly forces the planes had dropped their ordnance too far back to be really effective. Nevertheless Carl became optimistic, again. He started scanning the horizon for helicopters, and sure enough two US Navy Sikorsky HRS-1's came into view.

"Charley, run back and get them to land back there. Bring the baby and Hank with you. We will stay here and fire to the last moment. Have the helicopter pilots ready to leave on short notice."

Charley took off. Carl saw him talk to Fletch, then pick up the baby and helping Hank out of the turret. No fire came from the enemy, who could not be seen.

Suddenly a whistle broke the silence of the battlefield. The whole plain came alive as the enemy got up and started advancing all over. Hundreds and hundreds of enemy troops attacked the small ridge. Sam and Carl started firing the heavy MG, and spread the fire in small bursts. The Centurion's main gun and front machine gun added to the devastation.

'They finally have their act together, unfortunately' Carl thought. The infantry attacking them was well spread out and the effect of the heavy MG's and the HE grenades were much less than during their earlier chaotic and improvised attacks.

He looked back and saw the Sikorsky landing. It took on board Hank and the civilians and took off, leaving the landing site for the second Sikorsky. Out of the corner of his eyes he could see Fletch and Pete emerge from the tank, then run back. Carl waved them on.

"Run" he said to Sam.

Sam did not need any further encouragement, just jumped up and took off. Carl looked at the oncoming infantry. They were close. He fired his last bursts to slow down the enemy a few more minutes and thus give the others a better chance. Then he got up and started running. He knew it was too late, but would try anyway. Bullets whizzed around him, and some stings told him that he was being hit. 'This is it, I am not going to make it" he thought 'Looks like I am not coming back to you after all Rachel.'

From 2,000 feet above the battlefield looked chaotic, yet Captain Derrick 'Drew' McConnell knew what to look for. Over the radio he had basically been told that the tank was friendly, while everything in front of it was hostile. Flying a Vought F4U-4B Corsair, essentially a WW II fighter plane, his speed, or lack thereof, allowed him more time to evaluate the situation than had been available to the F-80 pilots. It also facilitated a more accurate weapons delivery than was possible from the contemporary jets. In a hostile environment, i.e. one filled with heavy anti aircraft (AA) fire, the slow speed was a liability, but in a situation like this, with little or no AA, the slow speed was a definite advantage.

Thus he took his time and could make out the people running towards the helicopter. He decided to lay down suppressive fire behind the runners. Drew banked the Corsair 40 degrees left and zoomed in at close to 400mph, blasting away with his six 0.5's. His mere presence seemed to be enough. The enemy threw themselves to the ground under this new menace from the sky. He could see the impact of his bullets snake through the grass around the troops, and several were killed or injured. Yet the best was that he allowed the 'runners' time to reach the chopper, though one of them went down.

Carl heard the plane, and looked up. Maybe he was not doomed to die after all, he thought, and tried to increase his speed even more, but he was out of breath. It was only another 200 yards to the Sikorsky when he stumbled.

"Shit" He looked back and saw that he had stumbled over Sam. His head smashed in by a bullet. It was not a pretty sight, but he pulled himself together, got up and continued running. As he reached the helicopter Charley and Fletch pulled him in. He collapsed to the floor of the cabin utterly exhausted. Looking up he could see Charley, Fletch and a crew member firing out of the open door with their pistols. Probably did not do much damage, except making them feel good. Which was probably why they bothered to do it in the first place.

The 600 hp Pratt & Whitney revved up and the helicopter took off. I have escaped, a miracle such as it is, Carl thought. Hopefully we are not shot down. He looked at Pete clutching the baby. He gave Carl a slight nod. Charley had finished shooting and was sitting with his head in his hands, looking straight into the floor. Carl looked over at Fletch who smiled to him.

"That was one hell of a run Captain. If you sign up for the Olympics my bets are on you. Anyway thanks for holding them off for a few more minutes. Looks like Custer got away this time. Too bad with Sam, he was a brave man. I did not realize he was shot until I reached the helicopter. Are you sure he was dead?"

"Unfortunately yes, he had taken one to the head."

"Too bad, we left some brave friends and soldiers back there. I wish we could have given them proper funerals"

Carl nodded. It was too bad, but then all wars are bad. He knew the horrors would be forgotten, since he had long experience in forgetting. Looking around the helicopter, he noticed it was surprisingly roomy, but not very comfortable. Quite shaky and noisy, but who cared, it did the job. It was his first ride in a helicopter, and what a way to be introduced to one of the most recent developments in military technology.

*

ISRAEL
*

"So, you feel the Centurion is the best option for our army. I read your report, very well put together, but frankly I was bit puzzled by your recommendation. Besides, there was not much about enemy armor there."

Carl was back in Israel, and in Commander Tal's office. It was almost two months since the Sikorsky had pulled them out of the war zone, and delivered them to the Essex class aircraft carrier USS Valley Forge. After debriefing and medical attention they were sent back to their units and eventually shipped home. Only Hank had any serious wounds, and when they left it sounded like he might lose part of his arm. They all wished him well, and said they would keep in touch.

Fletch and Carl had ample opportunity to talk, and in the end decided that Fletch and his wife would visit Israel, or Carl and Rachel would visit them in their summer house in Italy. He had a suspicion it would be Italy. Despite some bad memories, Rachel still loved the place and often talked about going there for a visit. When they met again they would come up with a plan for how Fletch could tell Carl's family that he was alive and well, without alerting the authorities. WW II had been over for many years, but after such incredible amounts of bloodshed the wounds, and memories, ran deep.

Their trek had become famous. A group of soldiers trekking for miles through enemy territory and saving a baby went straight to the public's heart. The press wanted interviews and photographs. It was fairly easy for Carl to avoid them since Charley and Pete were more than eager to be interviewed, Pete because he was trying to build 'popular' support for the adoption of the baby. He had already named her Heather, after his mother, and gotten the 'lady' journals to publish tearful articles about her.

He will be a good politician some day, Fletch had prophesized, he knows how to create attention.

He turned his attention back to Commander Tal's question.

"Well, the Centurion handles better, has a superior lay-out and excellent turret armor, which is where most tanks are destroyed. It is not as fast as it should be, and the range is poor. However, if we put a diesel instead of a gas engine in it, at least the range problem will be solved. The layout is conventional, but everything is very well organized. The M-46 is good, faster and very reliable, but is based upon a somewhat older design. The turret is not what it should be, externally or internally. It is cramped and full of shell traps. A great tank in 1945, but not now. I know the Yank's are working on some improved versions, the M-47 and M-48, and they may solve the turret problem. Anyway, they are not available and the silhouette is probably still too high. The M-46 would do the job for us if we cannot obtain the Centurion. The M-24 light tank is good, but again it is a WW II design, and in my opinion, a light tank is not what we need for desert fighting. As for enemy armor, there is not much to tell. The Russkis have not given any of their newer tanks to the Chinese or North Koreans. They are always secretive and suspicious so I guess they are afraid of the West, and probably also the Chinese, copying their technology. The T-34/85 we saw were the exact same type as the ones I saw in 45. If they have been modernized it must be under the surface, like communications, aiming devices and the like, In addition to the T-34's there were a few old Japanese and other tanks, but the T-34 was the only one with any combat value."

"I also liked your comments about helicopters. You said they are mostly used for medevac and transportation, but you feel they can be useful as scouts and warriors as well."

"Yes, but probably not right away. The current machines are not powerful or fast enough, but changes will come fast and furious. They always do. The Sikorsky that picked us up could actually carry 12 troops or passengers. I was surprised to see how roomy it was, and the many tasks the US Army used it for. It was big enough that you can take a team of commandos and land them behind enemy lines, without the need for paratroopers. I also feel some of the smaller helicopters, like the Bell 47, the one with the glass front that you see in all the newspaper pictures, could be equipped as gun platforms and thus be useful in certain situations."

"Good Carl, we will talk more about this in the future. I would like to keep you attached to the army as an advisor. I know you are worried about getting recognized, but frankly the odds of that happening are slim and getting better every year. By the way, the English Major gave you a great review. Sounds like you guys became good friends."

"He is my cousin"

It was quiet for a while. He had decided to tell the truth right away, they would eventually figure it out anyway.

"What a coincidence. You could not even make up a story like that. Too bad it has to remain a secret. Well, good luck, I am sure he will not spill the beans. You are eager to see your family I know. One of my men will drive you back.'

Tal stretched out his hand."

"Thanks again Captain, we are very grateful for your cooperation and great service."

They shook hands and Carl walked out into the sunshine. An old Sherman rumbled past as he walked towards the waiting Jeep. He had talked to Rachel on the phone, and she was waiting for him. The sun was hot, a bit too hot for his liking, but that was OK. He had survived. Again. Undeserved maybe but that was life. But for the luck of the draw he could have been one of the unfortunate left in the dust in Korea. It had nothing to do with being good or bad, but he was nevertheless reminded of the old Greek saying;

'Those who are loved by the Gods die young.'

Apparently he was not loved by the Gods, only by Rachel. That was enough.

*

HISTORICAL NOTES
*

The war in Korea is often called the forgotten war. Following so closely after WW II it was small in comparison. The forces committed were a fraction of what had been engaged in its WW II predecessor, and the geographical area fought over was tiny.

But it was important, much more so than it is usually given credit for.

It was a clear challenge to the West from the communist bloc. Between the Soviet Union, China and their satellites, the communists probably controlled between a quarter and a third of the world's population at that time. Had the challenge not been handled so competently by President Truman and the

Joint Chiefs of Staff, under the able leadership of its Chairman, General Omar N. Bradley of WW II fame, it could have escalated out of control and gone nuclear. Fortunately it did not, and the war became a wake up call for the West in its dealings with the Soviets.

Technologically the war was fought with a mix of WW II and modern weapons. The ground fighting was in some ways a repetition of the previous war technologically. All the tanks had appeared in 1945 or before. The air war was a different matter, a harbinger of things to come. The first jet vs. jet fights took place, and the conflict also saw the first widespread use of helicopters.

The soldiers who gave their lives in the conflict did not die in vain. They stopped the spread of what President Reagan 30 years later famously called 'The Evil Empire' and subsequent Soviet leaders were under no illusion that their use of force would go unopposed. It took another 40 years before the communist block imploded, but Korea was the first step.

STEEL MENACE
*
MOSCOW 1952
*

He was boxed in like a rat. Quite appropriate in a way. Most of his life he had been forced to live like a rat. It was the way it was in Stalin's paradise of the proletariat. Unless you were among the chosen ones, the communist bosses, the secret police, the party members, groups better known as the 'apparatchiks,' life was hard and unforgiving. The majority of the population only existed to let these privileged few live in their own utopia, the labor governed state, the earthly heaven. But it was not heaven, nor was it the people who governed. It was only another dictatorship, and one on an even par with the worst dictatorship in recent history, the Third Reich. His parents had been arrested and sent to the Gulag, after he witnessed against them. Not because he wanted to, but because he was forced to. His parents told him to go along with whatever the secret police, the NKVD, said, when they realized they were about to be arrested.

"Say whatever you have to Nikolai, we want you to save yourself. Don't worry about us, we will manage."

They wanted to save him, their only child, the last of their blood line, even if it meant their own end. He was in reality the only thing they had left. So the NKVD fed him lies about them, lies that he had to retell at their trial. And they disappeared forever, their worn out bodies buried in an unmarked grave somewhere in Siberia's frozen soil. Unknown and anonymous like millions of other faceless victims, people who for one reason or another did not conform to the rules of the worker state. He hoped his parents had found the peace they wanted in death, they certainly had not found it in life.

So well had he told his lies, so well had he hidden his true emotions, that he was hailed as a 'Hero of the Working Class' following his betrayal. His good looks, blond and tall, made him a fine choice for the propaganda ministry, and he was often featured on posters and films as an inspiration to the communist youth brigades. But the reality was different. He hated the apparatchiks with intensity for what they had done to his family, and he wanted revenge. Step by step he became a spy for the west. Willingly. Anything to hurt Stalin and his cronies. His hero status, combined with a sharp mind, allowed him a top engineering grade, and that made it easier for him to gain access to secret information. Now he could finally get back at the party and its puppets, the betrayers of humanity, and also the betrayers of his homeland, Hungary.

To do that he first and foremost had to get the drawings and other information he had stolen to a western embassy. But now it would not happen, not if he remained down in this basement. Ever since he left his contact in Tankograd he had felt it in his bones, and now he knew. He had been betrayed. The NKVD had been hot on his heels, and he was surrounded. His options were limited, he was trapped, but he still hoped they would not find him.

Suddenly dogs started barking outside the building, and he knew it was but a question of time before the dogs discovered his hiding place. It was a bitter end. He certainly did not want to die here, not so close to the salvation of a Western embassy. Yet he knew it was too late, he would die here, alone. The embassies were only a couple of miles away, but they might as well have been on the moon. Those damned animals had sensed him, and followed his trail, probably ever since he left the train station. He could not let himself be caught alive, they would force the truth, and everything else, out of him. Nobody resisted the torturers and sadists employed in the headquarter of the NKVD, the Ljubljanka. Not for long anyway. He could not let that happen, they would roll up the rest of the network, and many of his friends would die. He knew he would perish whatever happened, so this was as good a time and place as any. The papers he carried consisted of drawings for the new T-54 tank, smuggled out of tank plant 75 near Kharkov. Unfortunately this important technical information would now be retrieved by the NKVD. If he had been successful the weak spots of the T-54 would have been revealed to the West and allowed NATO to develop countermeasures.

Stalin had big plans, it seemed, both in the Far East, in Europe and in the Middle East. There were rumors that the Soviets were building up their forces just outside Korea, and were planning a big push to finally throw the UN forces into the ocean. Other rumors told of additional takeover attempts in Europe. All the actions would be spearheaded by the new T-54 tank which was rolling off the production lines in increasing numbers, and had been in service since 1949. It certainly looked like it was superior to anything the West possessed. They had to be warned. He looked at his hand gun again. It was a Tula Tokarev TT-33, 7.62mm, standard issue in the Soviet Army from 1944. Reliable, if not exactly sophisticated. He loaded his last few bullets.

Only six left, not exactly the 'artillery' that was needed in a fight like this. Ironically, his pursuers probably used the same type of gun. If he could take five of the NKVD bullies with him, then use the last shot for himself that would be a good way to go out. At the train station he had written a card to a friend in Israel, and in code mentioned the new tank. Then he had dropped it in a mailbox in Moscow, hopefully warning all enemies of the Soviet Union of the new steel menace. Yet he knew it was a long shot, but it was his last hope, the one piece that would make his sacrifice worthwhile. The card, if it reached its intended recipient, would be a warning, but unfortunately nothing more.

A shadow materialized in the doorway leading to the stairs. He aimed carefully and fired. Bulls eye, the guy stumbled down, mortally wounded. Two new men jumped in. He fired again. A miss. He did not have time to aim properly.

'Shit, I missed them' he thought. More noise followed, and a fourth man emerged at the top of the stairs. Nikolai fired, another hit. The man screamed as the bullet smashed his knee.

'Ha, that bastard will never walk properly again! It was his last clear thought, as one of the two previous agents fired a shot that went through his chest. Nikolai fell down on the cold cement floor, unable to move while the paralysis spread through his body.

'I am sorry mom and dad,' he thought, 'I had hoped to avenge you for what those Soviet bastards did to us, but now it will not happen.' A few tears rolled down his cheeks, then stopped as his eyes glazed over. Nikolai had his peace.

"The traitor is dead, and crying as well. Too bad he died so quickly," Victor said, "but what the hell shall we tell the Colonel? He specifically asked us to get this guy alive." The two surviving NKVD guys looked at each other in fear, both wondering how he could get his partner to shoulder the blame. The State Security Service was an organization built on fear and brutality. You kicked down, and were kicked from above, but above all you avoided taking the blame for any botched operation. In the NKVD the old proverb: 'Failure is not an option' was adhered to with a vengeance. They had done their kicking, now they would be on the receiving end. It was not an enviable situation for someone who wanted a future in the NKVD, or any future for that matter.

*

IDF HQ, FOUR YEARS LATER.

*

The air was stale and smoke filled, the conference room small and crowded. To top it off it was way too hot. The newly installed AC unit, recently imported from the US, was totally inadequate for the job. Ripe conditions for a headache, and Carl certainly had one. It left him irritable and generally in a bad mood. The situation was not helped by the fact that he felt heavily outranked, being the only Captain there. Commander Tal had told him he would soon be promoted to Major, but it was not in effect as yet. Even though the Israeli army was less obsessed with formalities and ranks than most of its contemporaries, he still felt very junior in this company. The six men in the room comprised a General, four Colonels, and him. The entrance to the room was heavily guarded to avoid anybody listening in, and the men were serious, marked by the occasion. War rumors were in the air, and the fledgling IDF (Israeli Defence Force) could once again potentially be tied up in a two front war, i.e. against Egypt on one side and Syria/Jordan on the other. The reason for the meeting was threefold: First, the emergence of the IS-3 heavy tank in Egyptian hands and, second, the probable introduction of the T-54 medium tank to the Arab armies. Finally, a message from a well placed spy had informed them that the head of the Egyptian ruling military council, Nasser, was planning to occupy the Suez Canal zone.

"So how do you suggest we handle the IS-3?"

"The short term solution is for the air force to take out the few heavy tanks the Egyptians have. The numbers are still small, and the IS-3 can be knocked out from the side and rear. I include the SU-100 in the heavy category, even if they, strictly speaking, are not tanks. The Egyptians have received a number of them. It will also help that the Egyptian crews are not well trained. The longer term solution is to introduce the Centurion or the M-48. Even if we up-gun the Sherman, and we should do so, it will be inadequate in a few years. The AMX-13, (a light tank the IDF was receiving from France) though excellent for scouting and anti infantry duties, cannot slug it out with modern heavy or medium tanks." Carl felt he had answered the same question in different guises over and over.

"Well, we cannot easily obtain those tanks," Colonel Nerev, head of the intelligence gathering department of the army, said, "and besides the crews who tested them say the Centurion is overly complicated compared to the M-4, too slow and the engine too thirsty. The General of the Army feels that the tank is secondary, he favors infantry operations, commandos etc. I don't think we should even consider the Centurion, it cannot do the job."

Carl could not stand Colonel Nerev. He was tall man with close set eyes and an arrogant grin. Besides he was known as a die hard Zionist, one who felt the Jews were entitled to all the land they could gather. That made him a fanatic in Carl's book. Finally, Colonel Nerev mistrusted all non Jews, wherever they came from.

"You are wrong. It is only a question of practice and training. The Centurion is state of the art, the Sherman is history. Even General John O'Daniel complimented the Centurion in Korea, and the Americans are not keen on complimenting anybody else's equipment." Carl retorted, a little more abrupt and disrespectful than he had intended, but he found it difficult to answer in a neutral tone. The Colonel rose, red faced, and blurted out,

"I don't intend to have a prior 'Obersturmbannfuhrer' tell me about tank warfare"

Carl jumped up as well, angry about the sarcastic reference to his previous career with the Wehrmacht tank corps. He knew he could not change the past, but resented having it thrown in his face at every opportunity. Before he could respond in the same manner, Commander Tal, stood up as well.

"Gentlemen, stop this nonsense. We are here to discuss a serious situation, not history. Captain Rosencrantz is the only one here who has extensive experience fighting Russian material, and he has also operationally used the Centurion. His comments about the tank are extremely valuable in my book." Everybody in the room was surprised; nobody had ever heard Tal raise his voice like that. He continued on a lighter note,

"Carl, we cannot obtain the M-48 or Centurion in time. What other options do you think we have?"

Carl and Colonel Nerev both sat down, but the comments had been a thinly disguised rebuke to the Colonel, and Carl could feel him looking at him in anger. Ignoring the hostile stare he continued:

"We have to use special tactics, and maybe earmark part of the air force for tank killing duties. And yes, I know we don't have many aircraft, but with the heavy frontal armor of the Soviet heavy tanks our losses will be intolerable in a normal tank engagement. Our current tank guns will not crack the front armor of the IS-3 at normal battle distances. Unfortunately. That being said, the IS-3 is not as deadly as we originally thought. Its aiming equipment is rudimentary, as it is on most Russian tanks, the rate of fire is slow, and the size of the 122mm ammunition allows only a small number of grenades to be carried. Finally, it is cramped and not suited for high temperatures. " As he was speaking, an inspired thought came to him.

"But there is a second option for defeating the heavy armor. An Alliance. When Colonel Nasser, or President, or whatever he calls himself now that he is in full control, eventually takes over the Suez Canal zone, France and the UK will be very unhappy. The Brits have the firepower to take out the Egyptian armored forces, and we could give them some 'heads up' information to allow them to prepare for the showdown."

He noticed Colonel Hebron and Tal looking at each other, and realized something else was afoot. Considering the various options, there really was only one that made sense. Talks with France and/or Great Britain were ongoing. As if to prove him right, Commander Tal, who hosted the meeting, quickly changed the subject:

"OK, we will look into those avenues. Now to a subject that in the longer term troubles me more than a few Egyptian IS-3 heavy tanks, namely the new Soviet T-54 medium tank. Some years ago we received a card from one of our agents in the Soviet Union, warning us about a new super tank. He had infiltrated the tank plant, and was supposed to take the information to a western embassy. Unfortunately the letter was the last we heard from him, the agent just disappeared.

Probably killed by the NKVD. Since then we have desperately tried to get additional information. Unfortunately it is sketchy and incomplete, and it is not good. Just like the T-34 was the nemesis of the German panzers, and the IS-3 supposedly the potential scourge of Allied armor in 1945, the West is now obsessed with this new vehicle. They fear that the Russkis have once again come up with a world beater and that NATO may soon face thousands upon thousands of them. I have to admit that to me it looks deadly from every angle, though the pictures we have are pretty grey and foggy. With Carl's knowledge I found it useful to ask him to look into what little information we have. Go on Captain:

"Unfortunately, as you mentioned, we do not know an awful lot. The T-54 is, as far as we can tell, the intended replacement of the T-34/85. We observed in Korea that the T-34 is now well past it's prime, and not really useful against the later Western tanks. The T-54 is apparently a totally different beast. To start with its teeth, the gun caliber is 100 mm, and may be a version of the gun in the SU-100, we just don't know. Based upon our previous experience with Soviet guns, it is in all likelihood more powerful than the British 20 pounder or American 90 mm guns. The tank is small, so the interior must be cramped, but its size also makes for a difficult target. We are fairly certain the engine is a diesel, and the large road wheels indicate good mobility. As to armor thickness, actual gun velocity, operational range, speed, aiming devices and other features we can only guess. The Russians are currently manufacturing the tank as fast as they can, and indications are their allies and satellites like China, Poland and Czechoslovakia will soon do so. Within a few years it is a fairly safe bet that we will see them in Egypt and Syria, probably in large numbers. By the way, I forgot to mention that a particularly interesting feature is the shape of the turret, it is hemispherical shaped."

"It is what?"

Carl smiled.

"Like the top of a ball. Somewhat similar to the IS-3 turret, and it should have good ballistic protection properties!"

"You mentioned that we do not have much detail knowledge. Any idea how we can obtain that?"

"Yes."

"Well, how?"

"We can steal one."

The room went quiet. Only the humming from the overstretched AC unit could be heard. It was quiet for what seemed like an eternity. Carl watched the reaction of the other men with interest. He had not been shut down immediately, which he had halfway expected. There was one exception of course, and finally Colonel Nerev snickered,

"I thought this was a serious meeting!"

"Oh shut up." it was Colonel Hebron who spoke this time. Colonel Nerev's face went red. "Captain, I assume you have given this, admittedly wild, but yet interesting idea, some more thought?"

"Absolutely. There is a lot of misgivings in Eastern Europe right now. In fact I think it is fair to say that a large proportion of the population in most of those countries hate the Russians, and their NKVD enforcers. What we saw in Berlin seven years ago, open riots, will break out again, in my view at least. If we have an inkling where the riots will spread to, we could put a couple of guys on the ground under some business pretext. They could even bring some girlfriends to look innocent. The girls could be outsiders, not aware of the real reason they are there. Somehow the agents can use the chaos to capture a tank and drive it across a Western border, pretending to be deserters. The tank would eventually be returned due to diplomatic agreements, but before it is, our allies could learn a lot, most of the important stuff. I know the odds may be stacked against us, but the risk is not excessive and the cost should be low. Provided Britain or the US can be expected to share the information it may be worth a try."

Once again it went quiet. Finally Tal broke the silence.

"Well, General Dayan asked us to be innovative and daring. This scheme has all the ingredients and a little bit of madness added in. If we decide to bless this crazy scheme, you probably know you will one of the agents to go, so where and how do you propose to proceed?"

"Several East Bloc nations have borders with western oriented countries, but only four are even worth considering. However, Bulgaria does not use the T-54 and the East German border is heavily guarded by Russian troops. Whatever else happens they will stop any tank fleeing. That leaves only two countries, Czechoslovakia and Hungary, with a useable western border, i.e. the one against Austria. Since Austria is not a NATO member, the border is not as heavily guarded. An added benefit is that Czechoslovakia and Hungary are also the countries that seem to have the strongest civilian opposition to the Soviets.

We could work with the Brits or Americans and have them meet us at an agreed border crossing. The Austrians will not be thrilled, but they would allow the US and or Britain to investigate the tank before returning it, or at lease share any information gained with them. Besides, our crew would also learn a lot while operating it."

"You realize that whoever tries this will be executed in secrecy by the Russians if they are caught!"

"Yes, but we can only do this if the civil unrest is so serious that it affects the armed forces. If that happens the chance of avoiding capture should be good."

"The fleeing tank, if the scheme works, may even be shot up by the Austrian border guards."

"Yes"

"What if the riots do not materialize?"

"Then all we have lost is a little time. The monetary cost is minimal, and would only come from a few trips behind the iron curtain, not much else."

The way the comments were worded, Carl could see that Tal liked the idea, and would go for it.

"There is a potential problem!" It was Colonel Mir, representative of the security service, Mossad. "General Amit has informed me we have a strong suspicion that the British MI-6 is still not secure. Though the two identified spies, Burgess and Maclean, defected and fled to Moscow, we are pretty sure they were part of a wider group. The British press is openly questioning some of their other Cambridge contemporaries. Until the rest of the group is flushed out we have to be careful. I know from my contacts that the Americans feel likewise."

"What about the Americans assisting us directly?"

"With the political turmoil following the Korean war, I don't think they will be dying to join us in something that could worsen their relationship with the Soviets. Particularly so since they want to give the new Russian premier, Khrushchev, some time to show his flag."

Carl could see a smug grin on Colonel Nerev's face. If the plan fell apart, it would suit him just fine, he would like nothing better than to see Carl fail.

Nobody could find a way around the partner problem, so it was decided to let everybody 'sleep' on it over the week end.

Despite being sworn to secrecy about the meeting, Carl discussed the general outline with Rachel. He had discussed the initial plan with her, so felt he did not reveal any dangerous information.

"Why not talk to Fletch?" she asked, "maybe you can deal with him directly and bypass the spies." It was typical Rachel to use the word spies rather than organizational names. She had mixed feelings about Carl's continued involvement in military matters, particularly clandestine operations, but knew she could not keep him from it. Even as he tried to come up with arguments against her plan, little by little he realized she was right. He wondered why she seemed so eager to involve Fletch, but her next sentence made her reason clear.

"We could meet them in Castellabate, pretending to be on vacation, and I can hang out with Theresa. The kids will love it too."

She smiled mischievously to him, and as always he found her smile irresistible. They had become good friends with Fletch and his family over the last three years, and Fletch had even organized it so they met Carl's parents and brother in Italy. It had been a wonderful experience, and Carl's parents and brother had naturally been thrilled to find out he was still alive. His parents had aged considerably since he had left them in 1940, and Carl felt a bit guilty knowing that his 'disappearance' had obviously added to their aging. Yet, all was forgiven, and the joy of the seeing them was immense. Not least the meeting of the children with their grandparents. It was immediately agreed that they would visit them in the US, though Carl could not travel with them. He could not risk being recognized since they still lived in the same area where he had grown up. The summer of 1952 was the best vacation they had ever had, and Rachel had talked about it ever since.

Not surprisingly she got along great with Theresa. They had both lost their parents early, had no siblings, and in general had a challenging childhood. Between them they had driven husbands, children and grandparents 'insane' by talking Italian together more or less continuously. At one point Fletch had jokingly asked if there was anything they could possibly talk about that had not been argued over at length. He claimed he was afraid they risked running out of conversation topics. Theresa had thrown him a kiss, then told him not too worry, they were not even close to exhausting things to talk about. At that point Fletch pretended he had lost his wits and ran out of the house. Carl still remembered the whole amusing episode well, looked at his wife and said:

"Ah, dear, now I know what your plan is, and it's pretty transparent."
Instead of answering she pressed her body against his and whispered,

"Believe me, you will not regret it!" It was the last clear sentence he could make out before he buried himself in her warm soft body."

*

ITALY
*

The town's full name was Santa Maria de Castellabate, but they usually just called it Castellabate. Carl loved the way the name rolled off the tongue, it felt and sounded like it was another world. Tank warfare, cold war intrigues and Korea, it was as if the problems of the world did not apply here. He mentioned it to Fletch, who nodded and said,

"Exactly what I felt in 1944, another world. We were just a few miles from the front, yet here it seemed like nothing had changed for a thousand years. Almost felt like I could run into Cicero around the next corner."

They were walking from the beach to the house, and were just about to talk 'business.' Surrounded as they were by the classical Italian landscape, Carl felt like the final meeting with the IDF commanders happened a thousand years ago. As they continued up the hill his thoughts went back to that day. It had been telling that when the meeting reconvened the following Monday, only four men greeted him in the room. Colonel Mir, Colonel Hebron, Commander Tal, and, to his surprise, the General of the Armed Forces who opened the meeting. Colonel Nerev was nowhere to be seen.

"Captain, this is one heck of a crazy plan, but I like it. Unfortunately I will only be able to stay here for a few minutes so let's cut straight to the bone. Tal has told me about your great services so far, and he will brief me about the final plan. I know he mentioned to you that we are negative to the idea of bringing in outsiders, if something goes wrong the negative implications could be grave. Another problem is that we do not really have any agents with the necessary tank experience. Have you come up with an alternate plan?"

"Yes. Well, at least it is an idea. I have a cousin and good friend in the British Army reserve, the Territorials. Maybe we could deal directly with him and bypass MI-6. I trust him, and believe him to be willing to participate in this, eh, crazy plan."

After 15 minutes they had the outlines ready, and as soon as the General left the room the real operational planning had started. Now several months later he found himself trying to convince Fletch it was worth a try. Fletch was intrigued, but understood the dangers involved. As they looked towards the island of Capri, which could be seen clearly from their vantage point, Fletch said:

"Of course Theresa would probably try to kill you if she knew what we were talking about. But she is too busy showing

Rachel around so I will break it carefully when we are home. Anyway your idea is that you and I should travel as businessmen to Hungary, which seems to be the most likely hotspot for a rebellion. When the rebellion starts we steal a tank and drive it across the border to Austria."

"Something like that, and I am convinced it can be done, provided the rebellion is wild enough. If the drive is impossible, we can learn as much as we can about the T-54 before we abandon it and then slip into a western embassy. I do not have all the details, but a lot of improvisation is certainly needed. Photos by itself will not be enough, they say nothing about armor thickness, gun and technical matters."

"So they chose you, and you chose me!"

"Well, you know, I don't look Jewish and speak three languages besides Hebrew, so even if I am captured the link to the IDF will not be there. I can pass for an American, a Norwegian, or possibly a German."

"They would force the truth out of you."

"Certainly, eventually, but even if they do so and publish it, it will not sound convincing to a lot of people. The political fallout will be minimal. With everything else going on, probably not even noticeable. You are in, if you go along, for almost the same reason, and also because we don't trust the British security services at the moment."

"I can understand that, nobody does. Okay, I will do it. I owe you that for saving my sorry ass back in Korea. Besides, my day job of selling scooters and motor bikes is boring compared to the stuff you usually cook up, and the Territorials don't train too much these days. What do we do next?"

"Apart from some planning, and you coming to Israel to meet Commander Tal, who is technically in charge, we have to visit Hungary to scout out the possibilities. Our security service has found a factory that deals in trucks and cars. We will meet with them, order some parts, but mainly scout out Budapest. They are a legit business so know nothing about this. We also have a contact that can supply us with anything we may need. What about the British staff."

"I will discuss it with my commanding officer, but it will most likely be a 'private' operation. The army is too tied up with the Egyptian situation, and other former colonies and territories, so I doubt they will have any time or interest for something like this. However, I would like to have a technical expert join us when we examine the tank. Maybe he can be a military assistant attached to the embassy while we are there."

"Reasonable, but let's be careful about who and how many we involve. Let's rejoin the ladies. I am in the mood for some good Chianti."

The Chianti had to wait. The moment they came into the house, Carl realized Theresa knew this was more than a courtesy visit. He looked at Rachel, and the fact that she avoided his eyes was enough.

Fletch knew that the skeleton was out of the closet as well. He took his wife's hand and they walked out. When they came back, Fletch looked a little distressed, while Theresa had a determined look on her face. A little embarrassed Fletch said:

"Theresa demands to come along, or she will reveal the whole scheme!"

Carl was surprised. He had expected Theresa to refuse Fletch to participate in the operation. Not in his wildest dreams had he expected her to join them. When he looked at Rachel however, he noticed she was not surprised at all. He realized he had been outmaneuvered by his wife, and that she was planning to come along as well. He finally caught her eyes and said,

"What about the children?"

Rachel did not say anything. Instead it was Theresa who answered,

"You have a better chance of survival with us around. If it becomes too messy we can enter some western embassy. As for the children, we will leave them here. My mother-in law will look after them. Maybe her sister, eh your mother, can come too. She would like nothing better than getting to know her grandchildren."

So much for keeping this thing within a small group, Carl thought, though his mother and aunt would certainly not be told about the real plan.

It became a late night, very late. Yet it was magical, the soft Mediterranean air, the distant sound of the waves rolling onto the beach. Carl kept trying to keep Rachel from going, unsuccessfully, and all his objections fell flat. Finally he was down to his last defense, and getting a bit angry as well. The atmosphere in the living room was getting tense.

"Well if you don't want to stay for the kids, then remember you are Jewish, and we do not want any link to Israel."

"You forget I am also Italian, I can get a passport here. There is no way the Italian authorities have any record of people coming and going during the chaos in 1945, and we never reported that we left."

"But you do not have an address to show for it"

"You forget I 'worked' here all these years, for Theresa, as her housekeeper. Just ask her." she added with a smile. "Remember housekeepers don't pay any taxes, which is why I do not have any other papers. You know we can help you, so why not go along and stop this bickering!"

At this stage Fletch started laughing.

"Carl, you are a brilliant planner and operations guy, but at this stage you may as well admit defeat and surrender. We are up against some hardened criminals here, and they have obviously planned this well. I think we both know we have been outmaneuvered, outflanked and outgunned."

They all laughed, the tension eased, and Carl went quiet, asking himself why he had even gotten involved in this crazy scheme in the first place. Nevertheless, after a short while he decided to throw in the towel and accept that Rachel would come along. It was a relief to all four of them, and it meant they could concentrate and think about how to pull the operation off. Rachel and Theresa were both excited about what they regarded as an adventure, which even allowed for some trips to Hungary. Even Fletch seemed to consider it more of a 'cake walk' than an actual operation. Unfortunately Carl suspected it could be far more dangerous than Fletch and their wives seemed to think.

*

BUDAPEST 1956, FIRST VISIT

*

Budapest is one of the great cities of Europe, and one of the most troubled. Located along the border between Eastern and Western Europe, an area sometimes described as 'Bloodlands,' this region stretches from the Baltic to the Mediterranean. The population living there has been invaded time and again by armies from both directions, leaving its people, its farms and its towns devastated and traumatized.

Established at the turn of the first millennium, Budapest reached its zenith in the 15th century. After a tumultuous history the city and the country achieved greatness during the Habsburg rule, as part of the Austrian-Hungarian empire. When the empire died in 1918, the nation of Hungary emerged, much smaller, but with a rich heritage. The city is actually two towns, Buda and Pest, with the river Danube running between them. It contains magnificent landmarks from the Habsburg time, and before. During WW 2 Hungary was again allied with Germany, but when it tried to break loose, the country became one of the last to be occupied by the Nazi's.

By the end of the conflict the country was devastated, and occupied by the Red Army. They had traded one dictatorship for another. Initially opting for a democratic solution, the presence of the Soviet army soon brought the Communist Party to power, though they never achieved more than 22% of the vote. Not that a lack of public support ever stopped the communists. The communist rule brought total stagnation to the economy, and considerable hardship to most people. However, the security service, the AVH, (modeled after the NKVD) saw to it that any criticism of the government was quickly suppressed. In fact hundreds of Hungarians were executed following show trials in the decade after WW II, their crime being the 'terrible' offense of not belonging to the

173

communist party, or some other trumped up charge. The death of Stalin in 1953 brought some relief, and under the able leadership of Imre Nagy, Hungary became one of the more liberal of the communist states. A development watched with considerable unease by the Kremlin, particularly when it became clear that Hungarian students and other groups did not want reforms, but complete freedom for their country. The leadership in Moscow wondered, in fact could not understand, why anybody would want something other than the rule of the proletariat and their own brilliant leadership?

The train station in Budapest was dreary. The western station, Nyugati, dated back to 1877, and was a grand building back then. Now it felt more like a museum filled with ugly posters, unreadable to Rachel and Carl, but obviously extolling the virtues of communism. In between the posters the building showed significant neglect and damage from a war that had ended 11 years ago.

"What a sad sight," Rachel said, "such greatness buried in mediocrity and neglect. The dust and humidity reminds you that the glorious past is gone. Maybe forever!"

"Don't say that, we are in a workers paradise, I am sure they will fix it up. Eventually!"

Carl had tried to be cheerful, to relieve the tension, but did not even manage to cheer himself up.

"Let's find the hotel. The travel agent in Vienna said it was just a few blocks away, and it is already dark. Do you have the map?"

"Yes, Hotel Danubius is only a couple of blocks away."

The receptionist looked like he was about to die from boredom, as did the concierge helping them with the luggage.

"They must be brothers" Rachel whispered conspiratorially, "in the most bored family in Hungary. "

The concierge did not even care about the tip when he realized they were not tipping him in any Western currency, just mumbled something about communist junk money, and left the room. Carl smiled, the comments told a million words about the general mood in the country.

"Communist service," he said. "Good for us."

The room was sparsely decorated, a double bed, a couple of chairs, a desk, a drawer and that was that. All in light brown colors. Exhausted after the trip they went to bed almost immediately.

"Do you think they have bugged the room?"

"Probably, but I doubt they film it, probably just microphones," he answered.

Rachel giggled,

"That's kind of exciting," and then she continued with a mischievous smile. "We are certainly going to give them something to listen to tonight."

He realized that the excitement of the situation had actually turned her on. It was a side of her he had not been aware of. In the darkness she moved her hand slowly down his stomach, which was enough to make him react. When her hand reached its intended target, she felt how hard he was, and rolled on top of him. Then she guided him in and started moving. She exaggerated the love making noises, and even in the poorly lit room he could see she was almost laughing. With her rotating hip movements egging him on, and her beautiful breasts dangling in front of his face, Carl was not able to do any play acting of his own, all his senses overheated by her movements. Within a couple of minutes, faster than he had intended, he exploded inside her. She climaxed just after him, then collapsed on top of him, still giggling.

"That was fun she said. Without the children around I don't have to be quiet, and our lovemaking actually gets better every time. We should travel like this more often!"

He was unable to speak, still overwhelmed by the feeling of her body on top of his, so he just nodded.

The next morning they met up with Fletch and Theresa over breakfast. Afterwards the ladies went to take a look around town, while Carl and Fletch went to see Jozef Potesi, a jovial looking man in his fifties, almost fluent in English and the head of Hofherr-Schrantz. What used to be an Austrian corporation was now a nationalised Hungarian company, which Mr. Potesi jokingly called Hungarian Peoples Tractor Plant No. 1. The political opinion of Mr. Potesi was quite obvious, but it could be a façade, so they were guarded in their comments to him. Their cover story was simple, and it rang true. They were in the country to see if they could buy cheap Hungarian tractors to sell in England, Italy and Israel. They were both technically adept, since their businesses were automotive. In addition they had read up on tractor and tractor building to be able to ask the correct questions in the upcoming discussions

The meeting was a success, and afterwards Mr. Potezi invited them for drinks and dinner. His wife was a plump and cheerful woman, originally from a small town called Kalorovo in what was now Czechoslovakia. It became a 'wet' evening as well. Palinka, a double distilled brandy and Hungary's national drink, was consumed in liberal quantities. Mr. Potezi ("call me Joe, it sounds more cosmopolitan and less Russian") became very expansive as the evening wore on. A testament to the liberalising effect of Imre Nagy's premiership, and in his view it was but a time before 'those filthy commies went back to the steppes from whence they came'. At this stage his wife, who went by the name of Elena, tried to calm him down, afraid that members of the dreaded AVH could be listening in on their conversations.

Fletch was also getting a bit deep into the bottle at this point, but fortunately he got into silly behaviour, like singing Irish drinking songs, rather than discussing politics or business. With a fairly good voice, the songs delighted the crowd in the bar, and pretty soon a general British Hungarian crowd was belching out God Save the Queen, Blue Suede Shoes by Carl Perkins and Elvis Presley's Heartbreak Hotel. The band even threw in a couple of jazz tunes. Early in the evening, Carl, who was always careful with alcohol, had spotted a couple of men not participating in the boisterous singing and celebrations. It was also noticeable that the other patrons seemed to avoid them. Since they abstained from alcohol, it did not take much imagination to understand they were out on state business.

Around midnight Carl managed to get Fletch, Rachel and Theresa out of the restaurant. They were all in a high spirits as they walked back to the hotel. Fletch and Theresa had checked in that same morning, and met them later. As they walked back Rachel said;

"Carl thinks the rooms are bugged!"

"I would agree," Fletch said "we have to be careful with what we say."

"We gave them something else to listen to last night." Rachel giggled "Should keep them busy guessing for days. Carl really knows how to twist his tongue. We will do even better tonight! Right honey?"

Theresa and Fletch laughed, but Carl could feel his face getting red. He was happy it was dark, and just mumbled something that sounded like a yes. When they returned to the hotel and received the keys for the rooms, Rachel could hardly wait to get him into bed. She pushed him down on the bed, and pulled off his clothes and her own in a remarkably short time. Then she sat down across his chest.

"Your turn to begin, but we allow no hands tonight!"

This trip has created a sex monster, Carl thought excitedly, before he devoted himself to the task ahead.

The next day's meeting with 'Joe' was a boring technical and financial discussion. Which was just as well, they were all a little 'under the weather' following yesterday's party. They ordered one tractor to be delivered to Italy for evaluation purposes, and discussed the payment details. The Hungarian state required all foreign payments to be channeled through a particular bank account in Austria, to Joe's frustration.

"We will only receive worthless commie crap money, while the party keeps the real money" he explained.

At this stage Fletch carefully indicated that they could pay him a 'commssion' if he needed it for 'undisclosed expenses' in a separate bank account of his choice! The whole thing was done in a roundabout way by talking about bank fees and sales rep costs since they were aware of the possibility they were being taped. However, to the surprise of Fletch and Carl, Joe was quite open about it.

"Every 'convinced' communist like me has at least one bank account in the west," he stated ironically and laughed, "and don't worry, I have removed or neutralised all microphones in this room. Thanks to premier Rakosi, who ran the country for the Soviets, and his idol Stalin, we are poorer today than we were before the war. There have been shortages of just about everything. Even the Germans are becoming wealthier than us, and they lost the war. Not long ago we would have had a party boss sitting in on this meeting, but with Imre Nagy expected to be reinstalled as the premier, the 'party' has embarked on a much more liberal course. They think it will last, but most people hate the Soviets now, and they will always be seen as occupiers. Hopefully they will leave us alone, but I have my suspicions."

"Why would they not?"

"I have been to the Soviet Union many times, and despite Kruschev's softening up of the party, I can guarantee you that neither he nor anybody else in Moscow care much about freedom. They probably never will, and definitely not in their colonies, which is what Hungary is, a damned colony. This despite all the nonsensical talk about eternal friendship. Besides, many in the old party cadre openly disagree with Kruschev and loathe him."

A general discussion about the political situation in Hungary followed, and while remaining vigilant in their comments, both Fletch and Carl came to trust Joe. When they left his office they walked around Budapest to get a better feel for the city, and even stopped at a bar. When people realized they were westerners, they immediately came up and talked to them. Then, to his surprise, Carl recognized the two guys from the day before. He had mentioned them to Fletch, and now he discretly pointed them out to him. Fletch, who had downed a couple of drinks too many, walked over and offered to buy them a drink, which they declined. Looking more than a little awkward, they left the restaurant to the obvious relief of the rest of the guests. Once again they realised how negative the mood was to the party and the 'occupiers' which is what everybody seemed to describe the Soviets as.

When they finally returned to the hotel their wives were already in bed, and they followed suit. He carefully crawled into bed trying not to wake up Rachel, but quickly found out she was still awake as her hand searched him out and closed around his manhood.

"Did you really think you could avoid your husbandly duties tonight?" she whispered into his ear. Between making love to Rachel every night, the drinking and the spying, I will need a long vacation after this is all over, Carl thought merrily.

Their third day was easy workwise, they just worked through the details of the payment, including $2,000 to "Commerz Bank" in Vienna for Joe to cover his expenses, undisclosed as they were. Meanwhile Rachel had searched out their Mossad contact, and established means of communication.

Their final day was in essence the most important. They walked around the city, and, not least, figured out where the surrounding military barracks were. The important ones were the ones that housed Russian troops. Only they could be expected to use the latest tanks. Carl had brought his new Voigtlander Vito II camera, one of the best and most modern cameras available. He took numerous pictures of landmarks and points of interest, usually placing Rachel, Theresa and Fletch in the scenes. The camera had a flash shoe, which allowed it to be used in most light conditions, even darkness. A pretty good cover story he felt. Even if they were stopped or arrested, and the film confiscated and developed, most of the pictures were pretty harmless. Those that had a more sinister purpose still looked innocent and 'tourist' like.

*

BETRAYED

*

On the train from Hungary via Austria to Italy, they discussed their next step. They had to be back fairly soon, they agreed, the situation was explosive. They were also wondering what to do with the tractor which would arrive in a few weeks time, and actually felt a bit bad about having deceived Joe. Yet the trip had been a success, and on top of that both their wives were thrilled about the visit to what was still a beautiful city, despite the visible war damage.

"I will plan the next steps with my commanders," Carl said, "but I suspect they want us back in a couple of months."

Tal was happy.

"Your crazy scheme may actually work, and the situation in Hungary is deteriorating as we speak. The Russians just allowed a reburial of some of the people who were shot in the show trials a few years ago. It seems to have aggravated the situation, rather than calmed it, as the Soviets undoubtedly had hoped. How about returning in a few weeks or so to discuss another few tractors. All we have to figure out is what the heck we shall use them for. While you are there, I am sure you can find ways of extending your stay."

That was about it as far as Tal was concerned. With some of the operations guys, Carl reviewed the pictures and the city maps, and decided where the best spots for ambushing a tank would be. A tank alone is not much of a fighting machine in a city, so they knew the Soviets would have supporting infantry around it.

"If we cannot capture a tank in the general chaos, maybe we can get hold of some Soviet uniforms. That way we may be able to catch them by surprise." Carl mentioned, though he and the others carefully avoided mentioning how they could obtain such uniforms. They all knew there was only one way to do it, and it was not pretty.

As far as the trip itself, Carl was uncertain how to handle the logistics. He knew this trip would be much more dangerous than the previous one, but the addition of Rachel made him less suspicious looking. In the end Rachel demanded to go, while Fletch would be by himself. Theresa and their mothers would stay with the children in Italy.

Budapest had not changed much during their absence. The buildings and streets were just as dreary looking as before. Except for one thing, and that made all the difference. People seemed less subdued, and talked to them readily.There was a notable excitement in the air, but also an undercurrent of uncertainty. The question on everybody's lips: What would the Russian's do? As in the previous visit they met Fletch at the hotel, and then called Joe to set up a meeting. They were told he was out of town, but his second in command would be available for the meeting.

This was a bit puzzling. When they said their good bys after the first visit, Joe had mentioned that he looked forward to their next encounter and would not lose it for anything. Eventually they agreed it was probably nothing serious, and, over an evening drink, planned the next day's move. When they walked into the hotel room, Carl looked at Rachel as she undressed for bed, her outline against the soft light from the window making him short of breath, fit and well toned as she was. Yet this time she took her time getting ready.

"You are not as eager as last time dear. Anything wrong? Or rather, what brought about such urgency during our last visit?"

"I am nervous. This thing with Joe sounds a bit strange."

She finally got into bed, and looked at his face. He put his arm around her and she snuggled up to him. He could feel her warm breath against his chin.

"Last time was so exciting, I felt like we were young again. No kids around, no reason to be quiet. Just you and me, almost like a movie setting. I love you so much, and we have so much to be grateful for. We were both pretty close to skid row ten years ago, and now I have fantastic children and a wonderful marriage. Making love like that was almost like having a secret exciting affair, but since you are my husband, there was no feeling of shame or guilt, just a wonderful experience. It is difficult to explain."

"I understand," he said, wondering if he really did.

"And now?"

"Something is wrong! I don't know what, but it is a feeling I have."

After breakfast Fletch and Carl walked over to the office. It was a new secretary who showed them into the Managing Director's office. Two men were present, none of them looking like industry managers. As soon as they sat down, the door closed behind them and a third man entered, standing behind them. Carl knew the game was up, yet he had to try to play along.

"My name is Carl Rosenkrantz, we are ..."

"Shut up, you are an ex-Nazi officer, who together with this English spy are here to stir up unrest and obtain military secrets by infiltrating our armed forces!" the man in charge spitted out.

Despite his surprise, Carl still managed to answer;

"We are not ..."

The blow to his head threw Carl to the floor, his head ringing from the impact. Fletch remained quiet, though his jaw muscles were moving. Fortunately he managed to control himself and keep his mouth shut. Any action would have resulted in him getting the same treatment Carl had just received. With an effort Carl crawled back into the chair.

"You will be shot as spies in a couple of hours, together with the Italian whore you brought as disguise!"

Carl and Fletch were shocked. They knew they had been betrayed, but by whom! However, though they knew a lot, it was nevertheless obvious from the comments about Rachel that the AVH's information was sketchy and incomplete. That gave them an opening to at least gain some time.

"She is my wife," Carl said. "I can prove it. We have pictures showing us and the children. While you are at it, do you think the Israelis would hire a Nazi officer? I demand to see a representative of the Israeli consulate."

"You can demand nothing."

At this stage the door opened and another policeman pushed Rachel through the door.

"Ah, here is your Italian girlfriend!"

Rachel was unceremoniously pushed into a chair by another guard.

"She is my wife," Carl tried again. Another blow from behind sent him across the room. He had the taste of blood in his mouth. Rachel ran over to him. Carl shook his head:

"You can beat me to shit, but it does not change the fact. She is my wife and she is Jewish."

He braced for another blow. It did not come, and he managed, with Rachel's help, to get up. His head and body still aching. Fletch had watched the incident, and also noticed the uncertain look the interrogators sent each other.

"I don't know what this is all about," he said, "I only know these people as honest traders. If they are involved in any other activity, that is unknown to me. I am an English citizen, and demand to see a representative of the British government. You can check me out with your sources in England, and get it confirmed that I am dealing in trucks, motor bikes etc. You seem to have infiltrated MI-6 so you could even ask them."

The last sentence was a bit far fetched, but he figured it did not hurt to show some 'admiration' for the opposition. A short heated discussion in Hungarian followed, then the senior officer nodded.

"We will check you out, and if you are not an enemy of the working people you will be allowed to leave."

Fletch nodded. In the stillness that followed Carl said, as much to keep the cover story alive, as out of curiosity:

"What happened to Joe?"

"He is out of the tractor business. He is none of your concern."

"I was just curious!"

They were led out of the office in handcuffs, and pushed into a waiting truck, flanked by uniformed guards on either side. The staff looked at them, but tellingly with pity. However, the looks they threw the guards were full of disgust. The AVH was despised and hated, like their big brother the NKVD. They were not blindfolded, and in a short time arrived at the AVH headquarters on Stalin Avenue, renamed from Andrassy Avenue in 1950. The building was dark and threatening, if not as infamous as the Ljubljanka in Moscow. What went on inside was just as cruel and evil. In a way renaming the street to Stalin Avenue was a fitting tribute to one of the worst dictators of all time, though not in a way the 'stooges' in the communist party understood.

They were whisked in through the back door, out of sight of the general public. Right away they could feel and smell the fear that permeated the building. Almost immediately separated, Fletch was given a cell on the second floor. To his surprise it was quite bright and 'friendly', if such a word was at all suitable. An obvious sign the AVH was still uncertain about his status. Now he had to figure out a way to get out.

Rachel and Carl were led into the basement, a musty smelly dungeon, sounds of people in pain coming out from behind the cell doors. As he was pushed through the door he saw Rachel's face, her mouth forming the words 'I love you', and he responded in kind as her worried face disappeared out of sight.

With a still aching head he stretched out on the hard wood bench that passed for a bed, trying to think where the betrayal had occurred. It was difficult. He was worried about Rachel, and how she would be treated. Yet, he forced his brain to review every person that had been involved, even Fletch. Between bouts of self doubt and worries about their further destiny, he now regretted he had ever let Rachel join him. The facts as they stood seemed to him to be:

The AVH guys had apparently not been aware of Fletch's role. Which could be a cover for Fletch, and a way for him to escape.

They assumed he was a spy, but did not know about the plot they had planned. They were treating the affair more as a regular spying mission.

Finally, they had assumed Rachel was also a spy, and not his wife.

He dismissed everybody from the top IDF brass fairly fast. They had little or nothing to gain, and a whole lot to lose. Besides, they were aware of Fletch's role, as well as Rachel's.

He also dismised Fletch after some additional consideration. If only for the simple reason that if he had been the source they would just have executed or incarcerated Rachel and him right away. They would have had little to gain by interrogating him.

That left Joe, the head of the tractor company, and Fletch's military contact in Britain. He had informed his superior in the Army, but not revealed the whole plan, which fitted with the information the AVH had revealed. However, the only missing piece was that the AVH commander seemed surprised when Fletch confronted him regarding his innocence. Carl could not see any reasonable explanation for that, but finally decided that the AVH could possibly be covering their source in Britain. The only alternative was that Joe had guessed their real purpose, spying, and had informed the AVH. Neither of the two alternatives were very satisfying solutions to the riddle, but they were the only ones he could come up with at this stage. He had to leave it at that. The next step was to find a way to prevent all of them being shot or shipped off to Siberia. That was an even harder task, and at the moment he had no idea how to do it, except to keep insisting on their innocence.

While Carl was trying to figure out how they had been betrayed, Rachel was sitting alone in her own cell trying to come up with a plan. At this stage she did not care who had betrayed them, but concentrated on finding a way out of the mess. Her life had not been easy before she met Carl, or even in their first few years together when they escaped from Italy to Palestine, so she was well prepared to handle difficulties. Like

Fletch and Carl she realised the AVH only possessed a half baked story regarding their mission. Consequently she immediately decided to act like a frightened woman, willing to do anything to get out. She figured that would make the guards less observant, which could come in handy if an opportunity to escape came up.

It was a long night for the three of them. Not knowing what to expect is often the worst, so sleep was next to impossible. The next day Fletch was picked up first. Just like the day before he was treated respectfully. Between some general questions, nobody hit him or indeed threatened him with execution this time around. Without knowing it, his reasoning regarding their current predicament more or less followed the same line that Carl's had taken, and he had come to the same conclusion, i.e. that the traitor had to be either Joe or someone in the British army. His gentle treatment also indicated that the AVH was investigating his status and had not received any answers, as yet. If they figured out his real task, he could only imagine how gentle they would be.

As he was led down to his room, they passed Carl and his guards coming up from the basement. They exchanged a quick glance, just enough that a barely noticeable head shake from Fletch told Carl all he needed to know. Fletch had not changed his story. Loud noises came from the outside, and so Carl was led back down into his cell again, a rather unexpede delay. It was most welcome. but he was wondering what was afoot.

The next two days nobody talked to any of them. Some disgusting looking porridge, or whatever it was, was slipped into their cells three times a day. That was all. It was boring, and scary. After all they did not know if they would eventually be shot or imprisoned. The third day was different. Early in the morning two guards came into the room and pulled him roughly up the stairs, into what was obviously an interrogation room. It was white painted, had no windows, and only a few chairs. More ominous was the cabinet, and his supicions were confirmed when one of the guards walked over and picked up some batons and manilla ropes. They then stripped Carl's shirt off and tied him securely to one of the chaira.

"Now Mister spy, we will talk" the leader said in poor, but readily understandable English.

"About what, the weather?" Carl answered, then regretted his attempt at being sarcastic as a baton hit him hard across the chest, leaving a red mark.

"Who your boss is, and what you are after."

"I am here to order some tractors, that is all," he answered, as the baton hit him again. After half an hour his whole body ached, and he tasted blood. The guards talked together, but in Hungarian so he could not understand them. Then one left, but returned after 10 minutes with Rachel.

"Good, since you are so reluctant to say anything, we will now find out what your girlfriend knows. You can watch!".

"She is not my girlfriend, she is my wife."

"We shall see."

They stripped the shirt off Rachel, then tied her down the same way Carl was fastened. He had never felt so helpless before, but did not say anything, just looked at her, and Rachel looked back. They stared deep into each other's eyes. I have to stop this Carl thought, a little frightened about what was going to happen, but how?.

"We can have more fun with her than we had with you" the leader said with a cruel, nasty smile, then ripped Rachels bra off. Her firm breasts were pointing straight into the room, as in defiance of the guards. The other guards became quiet, but kept watching the scene interested, and a little short of breath.

"Stop this nonsense, there is nothing we can tell you."

"Ha!" the leader laughed, then took one of Rachel's breasts in his hand and squeezed, hard. She groaned from the pain. The leader laughed again, then stumped his cigarette on her other breast, the resulting scream shattering the otherwise quiet room.

"Commie bastards."

Carl was pulling his ropes hard, achieving nothing except pain from the ropes biting into his skin. He knew this was more or less what the torturers hoped for, but he just could not sit passively. He tightened his muscles waiting for the unavoidable blow. This time they hit him so hard he was knocked over still tied to the chair. His whole body was aching by now, but from what he could tell nothing had been broken. He knew he could not take much more of this beating. If he sustained any serious injuries or broken limbs, it would jeopardize any possibility for an escape should an opportunity to do so present itself.

As they pulled him up and placed him before Rachel, they all became aware of the sounds from outside the building. It was much stronger than in previous days, and sounded like throngs of people chanting, screaming, and not least banging against the outer doors. Though Rachel and Carl could not understand the chants, it was clear the tone was hostile. The AVH guys looked at each other nervously, discussing in an obviously agitated state of mind what to do. Finally they unceremoniously started to cut their ropes, indicating they were going back to their cells.

One of the guards pulled a gun and pointed it at Carl. He closed his eyes, but fortunately nothing happened. They just wanted to keep him from acting. Rachel was freed first, but while they were working on Carl's ropes, the door was kicked open. The deafening sound of a shot rang out. One of the guards fell, his head thrown back, a disgusting mix of blood and hair flying in all directions from the impact of the bullett between his eyes. The three other men were initially shocked, as were Carl and Rachel, but Carl had been in similar situations before and reacted faster. He threw himself at the guard who had a gun in his hand. His hands were still tied together, so he could not fight, but the impact knocked the guard down, gaining valuable seconds. Out of the corner of his eye Carl saw Fletch standing there, gun in hand. He was not alone, a number of people were behind him. All of them carrying weapons like knives and batons, but only Fletch carried a firearm. The two remaining AVH guys were still dangerous, and Fletch leveled his handgun towards the next man. He would not have time to shoot both as they had overcome their initial shock and were pulling their own guns. However, they had all but forgotten Rachel, who had jumped on top of the dead man and wrestled his gun out of his shoulder holster. She turned it towards the AVH leader, and felt nothing but hate as she pulled the trigger and shot the man straight in the shoulder. It saved Fletch who took out the last guy. Fletch, Carl and Rachel stood there looking at each other.

""Come," Fletch said "some kind of revolution or riots have begun. We can get out now." Behind him Rachel and Carl could see cheering people freeing other prisoners, and taking away AVH guards. Rachel grabbed her shirt and put it on, then threw Fletch a kiss,

"Thank you for saving us, but I have something to do before we leave!"

While Fletch, Carl and some newly freed prisoners looked on in surprise, she walked over to the badly wounded AVH leader, and leveled the gun right at his chest. His eyes rolled back in their sockets from fear as she fired three bullets straight into his body. His legs kicked a couple of times, then he was still. Rachel turned to the two stunned men, and said in a flat monotonous voice:

"I am not staying in this awful place another minute, let's get out."

The three of them ran out among celebrating Hungarians. It was the 23rd of October 1956. The Hungarian uprising had gone from protest to active resistance. The population at large was trying to retake their country from the communist party.

As they exited the building, Fletch felt a hand on his shoulder. He turned around. It was Joe, though hard to recognize, for he was thin and grey, and had obviously been a prisoner for a longer time than they had been. Despite his harried look, he smiled defiantly.

"Come with me, we can go to my apartment and then find a way to escape from this."

They followed Joe through the streets towards his home. Rachel walked ahead with Joe, asking how his wife and family were. Fletch turned to Carl as they trailed Joe and Rachel,

"Remind me never to be unfaithful to my wife. I was not aware how ferocius these Italian women can be, but looking at the way the two of you were treated, I will not lose any sleep over those guys back there."

Carl grinned, though to Fletch it looked more like snarl.

"She caught me by surprise too. I was wondering why she seemed so lost and frightened when they beat us up. It was so unlike her, and from our escape in 1945, I remember how tough she could be. Now I know she took on the little frightened woman look to make those guys lower their guard. It worked."

Around them people were hurrying back and forth. It seemed everybody who could walk or crawl was out and about. Yet despite the obvious euphoria, it was in many ways an eerie situation. A big cloud was hanging in the air, for celebrating democratic rebels as well as for hardline Moscow faithful communists. Would the Red Army intervene?

*
ENEMIES OF THE PEOPLE
*

The apartment was one of the older, and consequently larger, apartments in the city. It was pretty austere by western standards, but furnished with grand old furniture. Remnants of a rich past. To say that their return was welcome was an understatement. Joe's family was overjoyed to see him, the stress of the last few weeks separation etched into his wife's features. They discussed the situation over some food.

"I will leave my country," Joe said. "As long as the Soviet Union is around we will never have our country back. I hate to say it, but the people in the street who hope for an independent Hungary are dreaming. The Soviet Union will never allow itself to lose Hungary, or any other country for that matter. They are driven by a desire for expansion, by the expanding empire. They have nothing else to offer, and to show weakness will be their end. Kruschev is not as bad as Stalin, but he is certainly no democrat. He is also just as suspicious about everything and everybody as most Russian are. Actually, I think he is from the Ukraine, another State crushed under the Kremlin's heel. Ironic in a way. By the way, tell me one thing, did you come here as spies, or did the AVH bastards just get suspicious about you?"

Fletch and Carl looked at each other.

"I actually own a tractor and truck shop," Carl said carefully. They were not 100% certain about Joe. "And Fletch is in the same business. However, Rachel also writes for some journals, which is what they may have found out."

"You are pretty handy with guns for a couple of tractor salesmen and a journalist." Joe said dryly.

"We have all served in the war! If you leave for the west, look us up. We may be able to help you, and the addresses we gave you previously are real."

"OK, let's leave it at that. I am leaving with my wife and children for Austria tomorrow morning. I have the route planned out, and if you need the apartment it will be empty until the commies find out we have left. You may need it for some writing!" Joe responded.

They all smiled. From the street, singing and chanting could be heard, though at times it sounded like doomsday bells. Rachel, Carl and Fletch were talking late into the night.

"Rachel," Carl said" I want you to go with Joe and his family. This is getting more dangerous than expected. If something happens to me, the kids need you. You should leave too Fletch, no reason for you to risk your life."

They both looked at him.

"And leave you all the glory, no way. Besides, I want to get back at these bastards," Fletch said with an angry grin" but you should leave Rachel. As Carl said, the children may need you. Can you bring a letter to Theresa?"

"I am not leaving!"

It took them the better part of the night to convince Rachel, but in the end she agreed to leave. The next morning they said goodbye. Carl hated tear-filled departures, and, except for the time he went to Korea six years earlier, had managed to avoid them. There was no way to avoid it now. They shook Joe's hand and wished him and his family all the best. As they departed Carl kissed Rachel tenderly.

"I am sorry you ended up being treated like that. Try to forget it, and I will try to make it up to you."

"I will not forget it, I don't' want to. The scar on my breast will be a good reminder that this is still a difficult time for many. Don't feel guilty, I forced you to take me along. Still, I know exactly how you can make it up to me! Just save your balls out there."

Carl laughed quietly, then watched her leave as he blinked away some tears that had mysteriously showed up in his eyes. Just as they were about to disappear out of sight, he shouted:

"We will all meet up in Vienna!"

The next few days were uneasy and tense. People were building barricades, talking freely among themselves, and waiting. Rumours were constantly circling around. One minute somebody had seen the Russians coming, the next they heard they were pulling out of Hungary. People were even fraternizing with the Russian troops stationed in the city, while their leader Imre Nagy negotiated with the Soviet leaders. The most optimistic were hopeful a solution could be reached, that Hungary could be free. Few believed it, and Fletch and Carl were among those convinced the rebellion would be crushed. The Soviet empire was built on fear. It had to show what awaited any country that wanted to leave, or else it would crumble from within.

As the hours and days ticked by, the rumour mill grew more and more intense. Fletch and Carl had left the apartment for what they considered to be one of the most likely Soviet invasion routes. It was now known that the Russian army and their 'allies' had Budapest surrounded. They realised that under current circumstances they were unlikely to be able to leave the country, or even the city, in a tank, but figured they could gather some very useful information if they could only get their hands on a T-54. They were simply not in the mood to give up at this stage. Carl had ventured back to his hotel room, and strangely enough his camera was still there, film still in it. He brought it with him when he left, and he and Fletch started looking for a good place to make a stand.

Eventually they decided on the National Theatre as a 'good' place to be. It had a big statue of Stalin, which for obvious reason of symbolism would be a hot spot and gathering place for both sides. When they arrived it was something akin to a carnival atmosphere, though with an undercurrent of fear. For the rest of the day they partied with the Hungarians, and when night came they stayed with their new found comrades in arms, joining the discussions about the likely developments the following day or days. Everybody asked if they thought the US or Britain would intervene. Carl used his American accent to great effect, so everybody naturally believed he had been sent by the US embassy.

In reality neither Carl nor Fletch expected the Western powers to do anything, nobody would risk a nuclear war over one small central European country. Yet they could not bring themselves to say so straight out. It would dash all the hopes of the Hungarians. Instead they gave general and non committal answers. Finally, when the point came that rumours and rhetoric over the radio made action seem imminent, they and a large group of Hungarian patriots entered one of the buildings along the main street and spread out between the floors and aparments. The room that Fletch, Carl and seven young Hungarians occupied was the living room. The atmosphere in the room, and the building in general, was intense. To avoid early detection only one man was looking out, his task to keep them informed about any Russian, or Hungarian, army advance. The rest of them tried to get some rest.

Carl felt like he had only just fallen asleep, when he heard a sound he recognized only too well. It could only mean one thing, Soviet armor was coming. He noticed that Fletch was awake and listening as well. The lookout turned towards all of them, and in a low hoarse voice called out,
"Red Army"
It was Zero hour. The Soviets had decided to strike.
Within a few minutes everyone was awake. Gone were the nervous and uncertain, yet hopeful, faces from the previous day. Instead somber and determined young men and women were ready to face the enemy. They all knew it would be a hopeless task to stop the might of the Red Army alone. It was a force built to face the armed forces of the powerful western nations. To brutally crush the hopes and freedom of a small country like Hungary was not a big challenge, militarily.
Fletch, Carl and the young insurgents in the building remained in hiding. The cardinal rule for any good ambush is timing and surprise. They had to wait until the Soviets were just outside their windows before they opened fire. Short on armor piercing weapons like bazookas, they pinned their hope on Molotov Cocktails. An improvised weapon the Finns had

used with great success while fighting the Soviets during WW 2. It was essentially a bottle filled with gasoline or other flamable substances. It had a wick, actually a piece of burning cloth, in the opening, and when thrown at the enemy would burst in an intense fire at impact. In addition they had a motley collection of rifles, hand guns and a few hand grenades.

The most numerous weapon was the Hungarian built Frommer pistol. Model 1910 had been widely distributed in Europe, and was known as a simple, reliable gun. Unfortunatley Fletch and Carl knew hand guns would be of limited use in the upcoming battles. Fletch had been more excited when he saw one of the famous Russian Tokarev SVT-40 gas operated assault rifles, and grabbed it immediatly. It had most likely come from a Hungarian army depot, or perhaps been captured from Russian troops. Carl found a StG 43, better known as 'Sturmgewehr,' among the small selection of assault weapons they had at their disposal. The StG 43 was issued to the German forces from 1944 to the end of the war, and arguably was the best automatic rifle to come out of that conflict. Carl was very familiar with it from his service in WW 2. It was almost like recognizing an old friend. He slung it onto his back and walked to his assigned window, next to Fletch's, but was careful not to look out and risk being spotted. Most of the insurgents had to settle for standard bolt action rifles of various types.

Standing there he took a moment to look at the young people around him. Their teeth were gritted, their faces concentrated almost as in pain. Some were praying, some crying and some swearing quietly. It was a sight Carl would remember for the rest of his life, a heroic, yet sad group of idealists waiting for Armageddon. Yet it also brought him back to his own youth over ten years ago, when he had thought he was fighting for the right cause. Only later did he understand that he, and millions of others, had been betrayed by their leaders, suffering and dying for nothing. At least these idealists did not have to worry about that. With time, Carl was convinced history would be in no doubt as to who were the oppressors, and who the oppressed.

The roar from the diesel engines came closer, growing louder and louder. After a while it filled the living room to the breaking point. The defenders grew quiet, nobody looked at each other. Some were trying to eat a little more of the stale bread they had, but few really felt hungry, so were just waiting quietly. Directly or indirectly all eyes were on the lookout.

After what felt like an eternity he turned towards them. His face was ashen white, and he spoke quietly in Hungarian. The meaning was clear, even if you could not hear or understand the words. They all prepared for battle, and one of the girls walked around nervously lighting the wicks on the cocktails. Carl and Fletch grabbed two bottles each.

"What is your name?" Carl asked the girl in an effort to calm her down.

"Galina."

"That sounds Russian."

"It is. Laughable in a way, if it wasn't so sad. My parents were socialists, and believed in the Russian revolution. They admired Lenin, Stalin and their victory over the various facists, and gave me a Russian name in their honor. They learned their lesson though," her eyes were tearful, and her tone full of irony "when the NKVD bastards had them shot as enemies of the people. But here is the sad part. They were excusing Stalin to the very end, blaming everybody around him, but not the monster at the center. They were but two of the many hundreds of nationalists killed a few years ago. Enemies of the people, what a laugh," her eyes turned hateful, "but I will get my revenge now. I don't hate these soldiers out there, but they serve a sick regime, and now they will pay the price for it. We will probably lose our lives, but we will show the world what the communist party and their cronies are all about!"

"It is unfortunately the way it usually is," Fletch said quietly. "The men at the front become the focus for all the hatred and revenge, though the men responsible remain safe far behind the front lines."

He turned to Carl,

"Good luck old chap. By the way, I am glad we managed to convince Rachel to leave. I don't know what will happen from now on, but I want you to know that even if we don't make it, I am glad I joined you. Besides, I like to help these poor youngsters, even if it is a hopeless task. As the girl said we may die here, but it is a worthy cause, and it will be an experience for the ages."

They shook hands with serious faces. Carl did not trust his own voice enough to answer, just cleared his throat and nodded in response.

It became quiet, there was nothing more to say. As if on command they looked outside the window.

The sight that met them was almost like a physical blow to their senses. A tank, from intelligence pictures they immediately identified it as a T-54, was leading a long line of tanks, trucks and APC's (Armoured Personnel Carriers) down the street. The T-54 was already more than 300 feet past the building, but a huge self propelled howitzer, an ISU 152, followed closely on its heels, while a PT-76 light tank was further down the line. Hundreds of Russian soldiers were marching on both sides of the street. Further back additional tanks of different types were coming. The morning mist gave the scene a surreal atmosphere, almost like they were looking at a movie.

"I should have had a Panter."

"Or a Centurion!" Fletch answered with a grin. Carl looked at him surprised. He was not aware he had spoken out loud. Finally he managed to smile back, despite the tension, then called out in German, which most of their comrades in arms knew better than English.

"Do not concentrate on the big assault gun, it has no turret. We can take it out later. Go for the soldiers in the trucks, and the real tanks!"

There was no reason to translate for Fletch. He was experienced enough to know what lay ahead, and what to do.

"lo"

The Hungarian word for 'shoot' came from the room next door. Dozens of guns started blasting away. Fletch knocked out the window, then quickly threw the Molotow Cocktail straight at the PT-76. It hit the tracks, and covered the side of the tank with burning liquid. A few seconds later another cocktail landed on the engine compartment, the whole tank now engulfed in flames. Within seconds the scene was one of total carnage.

The Russian soldiers, and the few Hungarian troops that had come with them, ran for cover. Between the rifle fire and the burning gasoline, dozens of them were cut down by bullets or ended up like human torches. Several vehicles, plus the PT-76 and the ISU-152, were soaked in burning gasoline, and the crews were scrambling to get out. Few made it, bullets hitting them the moment they opened the hatches.

Fletch and Carl were shooting at everything they could see, but now the enemy started firing back. To avoid detection they moved from window to window, firing short bursts whenever a target presented itself. Though in a difficult situation, the Russians still had the heavier firepower, and several of the APCs had roof mounted MGs. Though they did not blow down whole buildings, the way artillery could, the powerful 12.7mm slugs sliced straight through walls and windows with ferocious power. The splinters and shrapnel flying in every direction injured several resistance fighters, some of them seriously. Under cover of this heavy fire, the Russian troops started an organized retreat down the streets, leaving the badly wounded to their own destiny.

During the following lull in the fighting, Fletch called over to the leader of the resistance fighters.

"We have to get out of here and find a new ambush site. We cannot win a firefight, they will bring in reinforcements and blow us apart with heavy artillery!"

The leader nodded. His face was serious, and he started yelling orders in Hungarian. They, that is everybody who could still walk, started moving towards the back of the building and down the stairs. As they exited the back door, they crossed over to another street where they came across some Hungarian patriots dancing on top of a tank with Russian identification numbers. It had been abandoned, but looked fully operational. It was another PT-76. Unfortunately vehicles like the PT-76 and the ISU 152's were well known to the west. Nothing interesting could be obtained from it.

"Pretty good going. I think we may be able to get you a tank after all. With this house to house fighting the Russkis will probably lose many more tanks. Too bad this one is a PT-76. However, the way this revolution is moving along I think we can once and for all dismiss the idea of getting any tank to Austria. Once outside the city we will be sitting ducks. The intelligence gathering is undoubtedly our best option."

Carl agreed, but he did not like it. The backup option had always been 'Intel' gathering. It would be useful, but they could only do so much with a camera and a notebook. He was formulating an alternate plan, but decided not to share it before he had thought it through.

In the distance they could hear firing and the rumble of heavy diesel engines. The rest of the day they moved carefully from house to house. Snipers were active on both sides, nobody dared to stay out of cover for more than a few seconds. The night was a better time for the rebels. The Red Army had taken control of the Parliament and several bridges, but they met stiffer resistance than they had expected. And, for some unknown reason, the military had opened fire on demonstrators in front of the Parliament, killing 75 and injuring close to another 300. This created enormous resentment and local resistance groups harassed and ambushed the Russians all over the city. It also caused many Hungarian military units to join the rebellion. The Russians brought in additional army units, and the confrontations intensified over the next days.

For the insurgents and soldiers on the ground, the battle became a blur of interconnected skirmishes, and short lived interludes. But despite local successes, it was clear to the rebels they were losing, and more and more people were abandoning the fight, trying to get their families over to Austria. The radio station in rebel hands continued to broadcast, as much to the world asking for help, as to the rebels to keep their spirits up.

Fletch and Carl were in the thick of it, and though they believed in what they were doing, they were tired of fighting and killing. This was after all not their fight. During one of these skirmishes the girl they had met, Galina, was killed by a grenade. Quietly the survivors of the group gathered around the lifeless body. It was not that long since their first ambush, but it felt like an eternity ago. Fortunately Galina had died instantly when an artillery shell blew her and two young men to pieces. They were caught hiding in a small shed.

"I hope Galina died still believing in her cause. She avenged her parents many time over. Yet, this is getting ugly, and it will only get worse." Fletch said to Carl.

"Yes, and it is not over by any means. I think we have to try to refocus, and decide what we want to achieve here. We have to face it is now a lost cause!"

They buried Galina hurriedly in a back yard, hoping she would be reburied in a more appropriate place when the fighting was over. In a way the sadness of her death brought home to Fletch and Carl that they were not doing what they were supposed to do. It was not for lack of trying. They were tremendously frustrated that they had not come across any captured T-54s, indeed had not even been close to any of the elusive steel beasts. A lot of older tanks were in rebel hands, but none of them were worth taking any unnecessary risks for. That they were among the survivors was not so strange. WW II had thought them both essential survival skills, like changing positions frequently, quick movements, and other ways of hiding their wherabouts. Knowledge most of the other freedom fighters did not have time time to learn, and that lack of survival skills caused them heavy losses.

A couple of days later, just as they had decided to abandon their mission and were preparing to leave for Austria, Lady Fortune finally smiled at them. It was during one of the many minor skirmishes, while they retreated down a back street, that they found what they were looking for. A T-54 had been captured when the crew realised they were trapped and gave up. Fletch and Carl pushed themselves to the forefront of the jubilant crowd of freedom fighters, then jumped into the tank with a couple of Hungarians soldiers who said they had served in tanks before. They started figuring out the controls, and told the two Hungarian soldiers that they had experience operating tanks.

The T-54 turned out to be an awesome machine, just as they had expected it to be. It was crude in many ways, like Soviet tanks often were. The reason was that the Russian population to a large extent came from the countryside, had a minimum of technical knowledge, and could not master a sophisticated tank without extensive training.

For Fletch, Carl and the two Hungarians, the simple layout of the T-54 was a definite advantage. Between the four of them they soon understood the controls, and Carl had been thoroughly briefed on, and even operated, some of the older T-34s as he prepared for the mission. That information now came in handy. The first thing they noted was that the turret was very cramped, despite looking deceptively roomy from the outside. Traversing the gun turned out to be electrical, and the gun elevation was power operated. The gun was a 100mm, as expected. After a few minutes, Carl decided to see if they could indeed go anywhere. With nervous anticipation he pressed the starter. A couple of 'coughs' emerged from the engine compartment in the rear, but, after a few anxious seconds, the 12 cylinder diesel roared to life.

"What a sound." Fletch said, "that roar is just exhilarating, I hate to have to blow up this honey," Fletch said.

"We will not, we will drive it straight into the US or the British embassy".

Fletch and the two Hungarians looked at him surprised, so he continued;

"We all know the revolution is almost over, but at least we can give the western powers a look at what they may be up against."

The last was as much directed at the two Hungarians as to Fletch.

"They don't deserve it," one of the Hungarians said "they did nothing for us."

"You are right, yet the knowledge of this tank will aid all the enemies of the Soviet Union," Fletch responded. He had realised that Carl's plan was simple, but also quite ingenious. If we make it, I , eh we, will help you get established in Western Europe. I promise."

The two Hungarians looked at each other,

"Let's go, and by the way the English embassy is the closest!"

He leaned out and shouted something in Hungarian, and though they did not understand it, they heard the word English so the meaning was clear. A number of cheering civilians jumped onboard. Carl took the steering, turned to Fletch and said;

"There is no time to figure out the intercom, so let's use the old fashioned method. You tap me on the shoulder, right or left, when you want me to turn. Both at the same time if you want me to back up."

It was a ride everybody inside and ouside the tank would remember. They went down back streets, around corners, crossed main streets, all without any major incident. It was not as comfortable a ride as it should have been, simply because Carl was not used to the controls and over steered, stopped too fast, turned too hard and so on. However, he still found the steering better than on contemporary American tanks, and his handling improved quickly. Ten minutes after they set out, Fletch called down to him.

"I love this thing, you can even clean the periscope from the inside. All the components are robust and straightforward. Hell, it even has back up systems. This is a real man's tank. Most important of all, we can fire now. I figured out the firing and reloading mechanism. If you see a suitable target tell me."

The opportunity came as they were about to cross Baross Square in front of the Keleti (eastern) train station. The riders jumped off the tank to take cover, as it became obvious heavy fighting was taking place ahead. Carl stopped the tank in a side street, then he and Fletch got out and carefully peeked around the corner. Four Russian tanks were parked alongside each other in the center of the square. Two T-34s, one ISU-152 and one T-54. A PT-76 was about a 100 yards behind the four main tanks, but it did not seem to move. Some 100 or so Russian and loyalist Hungarian troops were shooting from the cover of the tanks. Return fire came from the surrounding buildings, but the Russian tanks easily kept the rebels at bay. They were in the middle of the square, and thus out of reach of the Molotov Cocktails, which was still the main anti tank weapon of the freedom fighters.

"Tough odds," Fletch said, "and we are not exactly experts on the T-54. But I think we should go for it. We have the element of surprise and the T-54 is probably the only one dangerous for us."

"Agreed, let's take that one first, but you better score with your first shot. My guess is the other tanks will take off once we knock out the T-54, after all they are surrounded. Do you know which are the Armor Piercing rounds?"

"Yes, one of the Hungarians translated for me. You have to stop when we shoot though. With my T-54 experience there is no way I can hit anything on the move."

"Let's do it before we start calculating our real chances and change our minds. I will not waste time using the MG, there are enough rebels around us to take care of any Russian troops trying to storm us."

They got back onboard, and Carl drove the tank into the edge of the square. He stopped between two buildings, only presenting his heavily armored front to the Russian tankers. Initially they did not react, obviously seeing a comrade in arms. It gained them valuable seconds, but the moment the Russians noticed the turret swivelling towards them they realized it was a ruse. Carl felt like it took hours before Fletch had the gun ready, and watched the enemy tanks with a feeling of doom as their turrets started turning towards him.

Not a second too soon he heard Fletch shout 'Fire' and the 100 mm roared. It was loud as hell and the tank shook from the powerful recoil, but the grenade hit the other T-54 low in the hull. Strangely enough he did not see any explosion, but the crew started exiting the tank and smoke was coming out of the hatches. 30 seconds later it turned into a blazing inferno as the ammunition started to go off. Through the 'scope' he saw both T-34s firing at them more or less at the same time. It was uncomfortable in the extreme to be sitting there without any task at hand, just watching the enemy firing at them. One grenade missed, disappearing into the building behind them. The other scored a bull's eye. The hit was right in the middle of the front glacis plate, but where it is at its thickest. The tank shook, and Carl felt he was getting deaf from the noise of the impact, but nothing else happened. Behind him, Fletch and one of the Hungarians were feverishly loading another shell. It weighed almost 50lb and in the cramped conditions reloading took roughly twice as much time as in a comparable Western tank.

"Go for the 152, it is slowly turning towards us, and a gun that size (152mm) can blow the devil himself apart."

One of the T-34s and the PT 76, which they now realised was operational, were racing towards a side street, seeking safety. While he was waiting for Fletch to get the gun ready, Carl took a quick look around the compartment. His driver position was in the front left, while to the right of him ammunition and diesel fuel was stored. Practical maybe, but a bit 'awkward' to say the least, if the front was breached by a grenade. Furthermore, the driver was not separated from the fighting compartment, the turret, with a bulkhead. In a way that meant what happened to one of them happened to all.

Finally he saw the turret move, and he cringed from the sound as the gun once again roared. At this short distance it was easy to hit, and the engine department of the ISU 152 burst into flames, just as the remaining T-34 fired again. This time it hit the turret, and with the same deafening noise. A few seconds later he could barely hear Fletch, though he knew him to be shouting at the top of his lungs;

"The bloody turret is jammed, get us out of here."

Carl backed up, knowing they were now extremely vulnerable. However, not knowing their true predicament, the last T-34 had had enough, it was fleeing down a side street. Russian soldiers were riding shotgun. Fletch had realised that they could still help the rebels, and he and one of the Hungarians had climbed on top of the turret. From there he blasted away with the roof mounted anti aircraft machine gun in an almost contiuous barrage. The few remaining Russian troops, now without tank support, had no option but to flee. Pursued by heavy 12.7mm shells ripping through buildings and hastily built barricades, they disappeard into back streets and alleyways. Dozens of lifeless grey bodies lying in the street were a testament to the deadly effect of a modern tank. With no more targets, Fletch and the Hungarians, stopped firing. That changed the whole scene.

Jubilant Hungarians poured out of the buildings, and when they got out of the tank, people patted them on their backs, offered to share beer and cigarettes and waved flags singing and shouting. Both Carl and Fletch had trouble hearing due to the deafening noise when the main gun had fired, but knew from experience it would rectify itself in a few minutes. They knew the Russian army would come back in force, but not when. With a jammed turret they were defenseless, and had to avoid fighting at any cost. They had to leave, and fast. Nevertheless it took them close to an hour to get away from the celebrations in the square, and now they had even more civilians riding on top of the tank.

Fletch and Carl felt a bit naked, if that was the right word for it, now that they could not use the main gun. Yet the trip felt like a parade. With all the civilians running around, waving flags and banners, Carl had to concentrate to avoid running over any of them, and despite the cool air he was sweating profusely. Finally, luckily avoiding any mishaps, they found themselves in front of the British embassy. Follow behind the tank and don't get too close they told their passengers. Then they closed the hatches, gunned the engine, and roared straight through the gate into the embassy compound.

To say that their entry was a surprise would have been a gross understatement. Embassy personnel and armed guards were running around, trying to figure out what was happening. Fletch jumped out, and asked to see the Ambassador. He was followed by an Embassy Royal Marine guard with his gun ready.

"Sir, My name is Tommy Fletcher, I am a Major with the Territorials, and this tank is the latest Soviet machine, a T-54. We should get all the information we can, before the Soviets demand that it be returned. Could be seen as a payback for what happened to the Rolls Royce Nene jet engine Sir!"

Though it was officially a non issue, the sale of 40 jet engines to the Russians in 1946, which were then copied and used in Russian jet fighters, even the MIG 15 of Korean war fame, was considered the most idiotic give away of technology in British history. To add insult to injury, the Russians built them wthout permission and never paid any royalties.

The Ambassador frowned when the Nene sale came up, but fortunately he caught on fast regarding the significance of the T-54 in his backyard.

"Who are the rest of your crew?" You certainly look like you have been in combat."

"Only in an observer role! Most of the rebels just want to get some food, after which they will return to fighting the Red Army. However, many of them plan to get out of Hungary as soon as possible. As for the rest of my story, it may be best that we discuss it privately, Sir. My presence, or at least my military background, should probably be kept confidential as well. It may cause some misuderstandings!"

"That is probably the best, depite your accidental role as an observer. Fortunately for you we happen to have an army charge d'affair who is a technical expert. He was assigned here only a couple of weeks ago, another happy coincidence I assume."

Fletch realised his superios had pulled some strings. The ambassador looked at the guard.

"Not a word of this to anybody. Understood. Go back to the others, and tell your Commander we need that hole in the wall to be guarded until the gate has been fixed."

"Yes, Sir."

"When the guard walked back, Fletch turned to the Ambassador;

"One of the 'crew' members is an American. I suggest we let him work with us, under the pretext of being a Hungarian from the German speaking minority?"

"You seem to have thought about everything. Start now, while I go and contact my superiors. Anybody special I should refer to?"

Fletch gave the name of his commanding officer, but emphasized that he was there on his own merit, as was Carl. The Ambassador looked more and more ill at ease. While he was gone, Carl, Fletch and the military attache, First Lieutenant Baldwin, worked furiously to photograph and measure the tank.

"I was told you would give me some drawings and photographs of the T-54" Baldwin said "what a pleasant surprise that you practically placed the real thing on my pillow."

After a while, the Ambassador came back. He pulled Fletch and Carl to the side.

"The Home Office suggest that you," he nodded to Carl, "get over to 'friendly territory' by yourself, which should not be too difficult. It is still relatively quiet around this area. Officially everybody on that tank were Hungarians. We will supply them with food, and send them off, just as you proposed. I guess most of them will indeed try to get to Austria. Mr. Fletcher, I believe you will have an interesting time explaining your actions to the army brass. You look like you can handle it though.

A small piece of friendly advice, for whatever it is worth. I suggest you both claim you undertook this whole operation on your own. Whatever the original plan was, the result is not what the army expected. As for you Mr. Blumenkrantz, the US Army seems not to know you. However, your name corresponds to someone they said worked for the IDF, and interestingly enough, operated together with Mr. Fletcher in Korea. Another pure coincidence I am sure, but if I were you I would get the hell out of Hungary as soon as possible. If you are caught by the NKVD, or AVH for that matter, you will disappear forever. Good Luck. Quite a story Gentlemen, and Thank God a happy ending. The governments of all countries involved will probably choose to keep it out of the public eye, so, as long as you keep your mouths shut, I suspect no action will be taken against anybody. I shudder when I think about the implications if our Russian 'friends' had caught either of you."

Carl shook the Ambassador's hand, then Fletch walked him out towards the street. Just as they were saying good-bye, Fletch gave him his camera.

"Don't forget this. It would be an awful disappointment if, after all this, you return empty handed. I have also written down some last minute information on a piece of paper, it is stuffed down in the camera bag. Do you still have your handgun?"

"Yes I do. I will keep it until I get to Austria." Carl said.

"You know," Fletch said with a grin, "my victory tally now includes German, Russian, Italian and American tanks. Not bad for a London boy."

Carl laughed.

"You should not include my M-26 too often, people may get the wrong idea. Besides it was a pretty soft target, stationary and loaded with gas and ammo! Anyway, thanks for everything. I will see you in Italy. Tell Rachel I am OK when you call home, I am sure Theresa knows where she is and can relay the message."

It was two days before Fletch remembered something that had been in the back of his mind for some time. Who had betrayed them? He figured he would never find out, but somehow he had a suspicion Carl already knew.

*

END GAME
*

Israel was at war. It had started just a couple of days after the last round of fighting in Hungary. From the Israeli embassy in Italy, Carl had relayed all he knew about the T-54. As it was, the T-54 was not a factor in the Suez fighting, but his technical information was still invaluable to Israel in the struggle over Sinai and the Suez canal.

Their escapes had gone surprisingly well. Rachel had had an easy 'walk' over to Austria with Joe and his family, and the Austrians had handled the crisis on their border remarkably well. Refugees, many thousands of whom were Jews, were processed and passed on almost as soon as they arrived. There were some anti-semitic episodes, but everything considered, the Austrian border guards managed to act correctly, and avoid 'episodes' of any serious nature with regard to their neighbour. Not always easy in a tense situation with a couple of hundred thousand people fleeing across your border, and a suspicious superpower massing soldiers a few miles away. Carl had walked with a large group of refugees, and as soon as he crosssed the border, pretending to be an American businessman caught up in the chaos, he reported to a Mossad contact in Vienna. Within a few days he found himself in Italy.

It turned out Rachel was already in Castellabate with Theresa. After a joyous reunion, Carl and his family had to wait until the fighting died down before they could return to Israel. They did not see Fletch. He had to stay in Budapest as an advisor to the Royal Armoured Corps while they checked out the T-54. Diplomatic protocol demanded that it had to be returned to the Russians, so there was no time to loose.

However, Rachel, Carl, Theresa and the children had a relaxing time while they waited for a safe passage, though the dramatic newscasts from Hungary kept them 'glued' to the radio. They were a constant reminder that they were among the lucky ones who had escaped. The rebellion was being crushed, and Carl could not keep from thinking about the many brave people he had met and fought with, wondering who had survived and who had died. He decided that in the future he would try to help the Hungarian refugees in any way he could, and since many Hungarian Jews would end up in Israel the opportunity to do so would be there. Together with Fletch he would actively try to find Joe and help him getting set. Rachel had lost touch with Joe and his family after they crossed into Austria, but Fletch and Carl both felt they owed it to Joe to help him.

At dawn on November 4, the Russians captured the Hungarian radio station. Its last words to a sympathetic but inactive world:

"Help, Help, Help!"

Just a few days later a Russian controlled government was installed in Budapest, signalling the end of the uprising and a return to normal, whatever normal meant.

The Suez war ended on November 12, when a peace treaty between Egypt, Israel, France and Great Britain was signed.

Europe and the world was once again peaceful, but at a high price.

When Carl, Rachel and the children returned to Israel on November 15, the sunshine felt warm and invigorating after the dark fall days in Hungary. He had hardly set foot on Israeli soil before he was summoned to give a briefing to the IDF. Commander Tal was thrilled.

"That is a hell of a story Major. And yes, your promotion to Major is approved. Your information will allow us to develop countermeasures. From what you say, it is a great tank, though maybe not as formidable as the T-34 was 15 years ago?"

"That's correct. It is a real war machine, and the 100mm gun is the best gun found on any tank today. The standard guns on the US and British tanks are good, but inferior. The tank's low silhouette and thick armour makes it difficult to kill with our current tank guns. It also has adequate range, a diesel engine with an exellent power ratio, and most modern 'comforts' like electrical traverse, good speed and proper ventilation. Yet, the T-54 has some shortcomings that can be exploited. The Russians still have problems with rangefinders, and their optical equipment is crude. Consequently they have difficulties hitting anything beyond normal battle distances. The cramped interior makes for some inefficient practices, such as a low rate of fire and small ammunition stowage. Only 34 rounds are carried. Still, if you consider the three key tank ingredients; mobility, protection and fire-power, it is a leap forward in tank design. As things stand now, it is in my view the best tank around. If, or rather when, the Centurion and the American tanks are upgunned, I believe they will be superior to the T-54 though!"

"Carl, seeing how you pulled this operation off, I am glad you are on our side. By the way, did you find out how the AVH got hold of you?"

"No, I suspect it was only their usual suspicion regarding foreigners."

Colonel Nerev was walking home from the office late at night. He had to go through some poorly lit streets, but there were few assasinations these days so he felt safe. Only a year earlier he would have avoided these quarters completely, unless he had his gun at the ready. Just as he turned a corner, he became aware of a person hiding in the shadows across the street. He was about to say something, when the faint reflection of metal told him the person pointed a gun at him. The barrell looked a bit odd, but he soon recognized that it had a silencer. Gathering his wits he said with what he felt was a stern voice:

"If you fire that gun, you will be in a shitload of trouble!"

"I don't think so. Even if I am, it is worth it. You betrayed us, and this is the price of betrayal. For your own petty grievances you compromised the whole operation and thus your country. Nobody else could have told the AVH what you told them. We initially thought some of the Brits had leaked the information, but that was not the case. You see, you made a mistake. You told them too much. Not all of it was correct. They even repeated the errors, and one of them could only come from you. They thought Carl brought a fictious girlfriend. Since you were at the first meeting, but not the second, you were the only one not aware he brought his wife"

Nerev's first thought had been Carl, but it was not his voice. With growing panic he realised he was about to die, and there was absolutely nothing he could do about it. He felt like a giant fist of fear squeezed his chest, and he was unable to move or to utter a single word. Then a muzzle flash lit up the street, and the assassins face. To Nerev's surprise he recognized the person that fired, but it only lasted a split second before the flash reached all the way over to him. He felt the impact of the bullet throw him back. It was like a hand from hell calling him home, and his legs buckled under him. Faintly he heard steps moving away from the scene, and a short greeting:

"Ciao"

It all went dark.

*

HISTORICAL NOTES
*

The Hungarian uprising was the most serious challenge to the Soviet version of the post WW 2 order. In many ways it also marked the end of western admiration for the Soviet Union. After the Soviet Union had been attacked by the Third Reich, the West had turned a blind eye to the enormous crimes of Stalin and his cronies. This was perhaps out of gratitude because they knew the Soviet Union had suffered tremedously from the Nazis, and had taken the heaviest losses fighting them. They also initially hoped they could make Stalin into a friend, not realizing Stalin did not need friends, he needed enemies.

The suppression of the Hungarian people opened the eyes of most people outside the Warsaw Pact to the real truth about the Soviet regime, a regime that did not believe in its own high rhetoric about freedom and brotherhood. Even many convinced socialists and communists turned away from the interpretation of socialism as offered by Moscow. In many ways it was the first small step towards the end of the Soviet Union, even if it took another 30 years before the empire collapsed. The Cold War became even colder after 1956, and several proxy fights developed over the next decade, mostly outside Europe. Inside Eastern Europe, malcontent among the oppressed peoples continued, and the next big step in the downward spiral of the Soviet Empire came in 1968, with the invasion of Czechoslovakia. It was not as bloody as the Hungarian operation, but the reasons for the revolt were similar, and the outcome was the same. The freedom of a small nation and its population was brutally crushed. After the invasion of Czechoslovakia the Soviets lost most of the few friends they still had in the West.

The Hungarian uprising cost thousand of civilian lives, and somewhere between 500 and 1,000 Soviet soldiers also lost their lives. Approximately 200,000 people left the country during, and immediately following, the conflict. The Hungarian leaders, headed by Imre Nagy as the prime minister, sought refuge in the Yugoslavian embassy when the insurgency failed. The Russians tricked Nagy into leaving, then arrested and executed him when he emerged from the safety of the compound. Another 340 Hungarians were executed in the aftermath of the rebellion, and thousands were sent to prison camps. After Hungary once again became an independent nation, Nagy's remains were reburied with full honor. October 23 is now a national holiday in Hungary. Recent developments in Hungary with regard to human rights is a bit of a mixed bag, and we can only hope that the country will emerge as a society fully devoted to freedom and democarcy. Anything less would be an insult to the sacrifices made in 1956.

The Suez crisis took place more or less at the same time as the revolt in Hungary, and allowed the Soviet regime to deflect some of the criticism as attention moved to the Middle East. The US forced the British and French to retreat from Egypt, and, in 1957, Israel had to withdraw from the Sinai. Despite having lost the actual war, the beneficial outcome insofar as Egypt was concerned, established Nasser as the undisputed leader of Egypt and the Arab world. It marked the end of French and British efforts to retain control over the Suez canal. In a way it made them understand their place in the new world order. They were medium sized powers in the age of super power rivalry. The rivalry, or the Cold Was as it is more commonly labled, was in full bloom and would last for another 40 years.

The T-54, and its improved version the T-55, remained the main tank for the Warsaw Pact forces, and many other Soviet client states, over the next 30 years. It was deployed for the first time in harms way during the Hungarian crisis, and the capture of several of these vehicles by the rebels, not least the one driven into the British embassy, gave NATO its first glimpse at what was for a long time their main adversary. It allowed NATO planners a head start insofar as finding countermeasures was concerned. In fact one great benefit from the information was the development of what would probably be the best tank gun in the post war period, the British L-7,

105mm gun. It would eventually equip most tanks in NATO, and in the Israeli army.

T-54/55's have been encountered in almost every armed conflict since 1956. Interestingly enough the Israeli Army pressed into service many T-54/T-55 tanks that they captured, and upgraded, in the six day war in 1967.

Even today, thousands of these 1950 era tanks are in service in various parts of the world. No longer on par with modern Western tanks, as was amply demonstrated in the two Gulf wars, its rugged construction makes it a favorite in less technologically demanding environments. It is without doubt the most manufactured tank in history, and as many as 100,000 may have left the assembly line. The exact number is unknown, but it is fairly certain its production record will never be beaten. The T-54/T-55 will be encountered in armed conflicts for many years to come, a tribute to its solid design.

*

REFERENCES
*

Several good books exist about the Hungarian uprising. For those looking for a reference type description of the events, I can recommend Osprey publishing. Their book called "The Hungarian Revolution 1956" by Erwin A Scmidl & Laszlo Ritter is no. 149 in their Elite series. It is in my view an excellent introduction to those world shattering events that took place in the heart of Europe 55 years ago

If you are looking for information about the tanks decribed here, and in my other WW II stories, Osprey publishing also has an excellent series on tanks and armored vehicles. Their New Vanguard series book No. 102 by Steven J Zalaga deals with the T-54 and its close sibling the T-55. Another resource on armored vehicles is "World Encyclopedia of the Tank" by Christopher Chant, available from PSL Publishing. An enjoyable book dealing with the operation of tanks is Hans Halberstadt's "Inside the Great Tanks"which has excellent detail pictures from the inside and ouside. In general it must be said that there is an enormous amount of books available about tanks and tank warfare.

Finally, Osprey Publishing has a good book about the Suez crisis. "The Suez Crisis 1956" by Derek Varble is available in their "Essential Histories" series.

For those wanting a short description of all the post WW II conflicts, I can recommend "World War, 1945 to the present day" published by The Daily Mail.

Some interesting biographies are available in English about the events of 1956, but, to my knowledge, very little from "the other side." This is unfortunate, but probably reflect the fact that very few people today consider the invasion of Hungary as anything but a blatant crime.

OTHER BOOKS BY JORGEN FLOOD

- To Live and Die in 1030
- The Twilight of the North

ACKNOWLEDGEMENTS

This book would not have been possible but for the generous contribution of several friends and family members. In particular I would like to mention the following persons:

My wife, Susan, who has patiently accepted my late night writings and survived my sudden dashes to the PC, day or night.

Our good friends Paula Pierce and Dick Lolla & June and Oliver Brooks have helped me tremendously with suggestions and editing

My Aunt Lita and her husband, Anders Ringnes, without whose support this book would not have happened.

To all of you, please accept my deepest appreciation for the work and time you have contributed to this book. It would not have happened without you.

Made in the USA
Charleston, SC
18 November 2013